WISH
UPON
A STAR

Also by Mary Sheldon

Reflection

Halfway Home

WISH UPON A STAR

MARY SHELDON

KENSINGTON BOOKS
KENSINGTON PUBLISHING CORP.
http://www.kensingtonbooks.com

KENSINGTON BOOKS are published by

Kensington Publishing Corp.
850 Third Avenue
New York, NY 10022

All Kensington titles, imprints and distributed lines are
available at special quantity discounts for bulk purchases for
sales promotion, premiums, fund-raising, educational or in-
stitutional use.

Special book excerpts or customized printings can also be
created to fit specific needs. For details, write or phone the
office of the Kensington Special Sales Manager: Kensington
Publishing Corp., 850 Third Avenue, New York, NY 10022.
Attn. Special Sales Department. Phone: 1-800-221-2647.

ISBN 0-7582-0312-8

First Hardcover Printing: April 2004
First Mass Market Paperback Printing: December 2005
10 9 8 7 6 5 4 3 2 1

Printed in the United States of America

For Greta Verdin,
who loved all things beautiful,
who was all things beautiful.
We will never forget you.

ACKNOWLEDGMENTS

I would like to express my gratitude to:

My family: magical Bob, huge-hearted Lamb, and precious pirate Snugs. Thank you for your overwhelming support, sweetness, and patience. I owe you everything, including this book.

And to those blessed souls whose encouragement and belief in this project kept me going: Sidney and Alexandra Sheldon, Rowana Trott, my friend and agent Dorris Halsey, Yvette Gellis and Willia Osby. And especially Abigail Bok, Judith Hutchinson Clark, and Christopher Stone, for their sensitive and constructive editing.

Also to those people who took the time to share their expertise with me: Bonnie Black, who gave me a feel for what it's like to be an agent; Abigail Bok, who came to my rescue on all the computer details; Jill Janger, who kept me informed on all things trendy in L.A.; Nancy Thurston, member of the Stuntwomen's Association of Motion Pictures, who introduced me to the fascinating world of stunts; the Honorable Richard Van Dusen, who guided me through the legal jungles; and especially Gary Zornes, whose thoughtful and thorough e-mails made the Palm Springs chapters possible.

Also to all the hardworking people at Kensington.

And to Bathsheba Everdene, without whom.

"Come," said Gabriel, freshening again; "think a minute or two. I'll wait a while, Miss Everdene. Will you marry me? Do, Bathsheba. I love you far more than common!" . . .

"I cannot," she said retreating.

"But why?" he persisted, standing still at last in despair of ever reaching her, and facing over the bush.

"Because I don't love you. . . . It wouldn't do, Mr. Oak."

—Thomas Hardy,
Far From the Madding Crowd

Prologue

It's colder today. I can't stop coughing. I'm asleep; it wakes me up; I think I'm something else, an animal being shot.

I was dreaming. Gene was alive; we were screwing in the office. Troy was there, watching, but that didn't seem strange. He came over, bent down, cupped a hand over my breast, grinning. That grin hurt me so, I woke up.

Wind going all night, newspapers blowing. *Variety*'s by the trash can, if I can get to it.

I'm too tired, I don't want to get up.

A girl going by, walking down the street. Blond, flirty; swishy little dress. Could have been her, the day she first pranced into the office.

The Pandora in the myth, the one who opened up the box and let all the troubles of the world fly out.

Gary

I was eleven years old the first time I saw her.
It was a beautiful morning in the Palm Springs
desert, full of birdsong and oleanders and September sunshine. But it was the first day of school,
the first day of sixth grade, and I wasn't in a mood
to appreciate any of it.

I bicycled down Tachevah Drive as slowly as I
could. All too soon, I reached the familiar redbrick
school building, and tied up my bike. Not a whole
lot had changed at Katherine Finchy since I'd said
good-bye to it in June.

My friends were already there in the play yard.
We did a little roughhousing, and started a game of
handball, but none of it really got off the ground.
We were bored with one another already. We had
spent every afternoon that summer going to each
other's houses, playing in each other's yards, cool-
ing off in each other's swimming pools.

One by one, we gave it up.

I noticed the new girl the moment she came
into the schoolyard. She was different from any
girl I'd ever seen before. For one thing, she was
very pale—her skin made me think of vanilla ice

cream and my mother's best china. And she was wearing a dress. No girl I knew did that, unless it was church or a birthday party, and even then it was just a skirt and blouse. This girl was wearing a real dress, white, with flowers all over it.

But the thing that struck me most was her hair. It was long, almost to her waist, and shining gold, just like Sleeping Beauty's in the movie.

She was carrying a big plaid book bag, and it kept bumping against her legs every time she moved. The closer she got to us, the slower she walked.

"You look just like a robot!" someone yelled.

The girl's face started to turn red. It was as if a glass of burgundy wine had been poured over her cheeks.

"What's your name?" someone else called out.

The girl shook her head. "I won't tell you."

She had a strange voice—I'd never heard one like it. It seemed to hit two notes at the same time.

I thought it was great that she wouldn't tell us her name.

The bell rang then, and Monster McClellan, with her blue hair and pointy eyeglasses, came out of the classroom. She told us to come along inside and choose our seats for the year.

Everyone rushed in, grabbing desks, and calling out to their friends to sit next to them. I had done the same thing, too, every other first day of school, but this year I waited. I wanted to see where the new girl was sitting.

She was the last one to come into the classroom. There were only two desks left—the worst ones, closest to the door. She took the first, and I sat down beside her at the second.

I could see my best friends, Bobby and Tom, staring at me in amazement.

"Welcome back, Falcons," Mrs. McClellan told us with a big smile. "I swear you've all grown a foot since I last saw you. I hope you had a restful summer and are ready to get to work." She waited for the expected groan from the class before continuing. "As you can see, we have a new student this year. She's just moved to Palm Springs from Barstow, and I know you'll all help her feel at home here." She pointed toward the desk by the door. "Class, this is Pandora Brown."

Everyone turned around and stared. *Pandora?*

I wondered what Pandora's parents had been thinking of, to give her such a crazy name. We'd all read the myth last year, and Rick Jameson next to me came up with the obvious joke.

"Pandora's Box!" he whispered, so that everyone except McClellan could hear.

We all knew that a *box* meant a girl's private parts, and everyone started to giggle. I looked over at Pandora. She was staring down at the desktop, her face bright red again.

I didn't pay much attention to school that day. I just kept looking at Pandora Brown—the way she sat, the way she held her pen, the way she fiddled with her silver chain bracelet.

I spent most of the morning figuring out a way to get into a conversation with her. I would go up at lunch and say, "Hi, I'm Gary Ortiz; I think Pandora's a great name. I know a place where you can catch catfish a foot long—if you like, I could take you there after school." And when the last class was over, Pandora would get on the handlebars of my bike and away we'd go.

* * *

When the bell rang for recess, everyone jumped up and started for the playground. Everyone except Pandora; she just stayed at her desk. A few of the kids, seeing she wasn't moving, stopped right outside the door and waited to see what would happen.

"Pandora," Mrs. McClellan said in a loud, slow voice, as if Pandora were stupid, "it's recess. It's time to go out and play."

Pandora finally stood up and walked to the door. The minute she was outside, the kids were swarming all around her.

"Pandora! Pandora! Pandora's box!"

They kept on teasing her—first about her name, then about wearing a dress, then about her book bag, and then about her hair. They weren't mean kids, not most of them, they were just trying to get a rise out of her. If she hadn't paid any attention, they would have stopped in a minute. But Pandora started breathing real fast, as if she were trapped in a cage with a leopard. Then she picked up her book bag and hit Matt Meltzer square in the face.

The kids scattered to the ball cart and the handball court. Pandora walked back into the classroom, and sat down at her desk again.

At lunchtime, we got our lunch boxes from our lockers and went out to the benches. Tom and Bobby had saved me a place, and I sat between them just like I'd done every day since nursery school. I looked around for Pandora, but she wasn't at any of the tables. I told my friends I'd be right back.

I finally found her, clear around the other side of the school building. She was sitting on the ground, in a patch of sun, and I could see her pale knees starting to turn red.

"You'll get sunstroke," I said.

She shook her head. "No, I'm fine."

I remember them clearly, the first words that odd, two-note voice ever spoke to me.

I saw she didn't have a lunch box. "Where's your lunch?"

She shrugged. "We had a cafeteria at my old school. My mother didn't think I'd need to bring any."

"Wait here a minute," I told her.

I went back to the bench and picked up my lunch box.

"Go on without me," I said to Tom and Bobby, and left before they had the chance to ask any questions.

I went back around the building to Pandora. I sat down next to her, opened my lunch box, and pulled out a chicken leg.

"Take this," I told her. "My mother always gives me way too much to eat."

"Thanks." She took a bite out of the drumstick and gave me a smile.

"It's really good."

I leaned back against the side of the hot building and watched her eat. I didn't say what I had planned to, the line about taking her fishing for catfish, but it didn't matter. I can't remember ever feeling better in my whole life. I guess the truth was, I loved her the minute I saw her.

Up until I met Pandora, every friend I'd ever had was pretty much a carbon copy of myself, with

pretty much the same life. We all lived in the
Mesquite area of town; we all had stucco houses
with tile roofs and swimming pools; we all bought
one another's birthday presents at Uncle Don's
toy store, and Ron at the mall gave us our monthly
haircuts. And our parents had the same kinds of
jobs. For the dads, it was storeowner, paint contrac-
tor, plumber; for the mothers, receptionist, nurse,
teacher. We spent all our time together, hanging
around town or at one another's houses, bicycling,
swimming, going to movies. There was soccer on
Saturday mornings, and Pac-Man at Shakey's after
the game. And whenever there was a special out-
ing, it was always something communal—one family would plan a trip to Disneyland or Raging Waters,
and the whole gang would caravan down for the
day.

But Pandora Brown's life was nothing like that.
For one thing, she lived in Dream Homes. Dream
Homes was a housing project built in the 1950s for
low-income families, and by the time I was born it
was a pretty dangerous community. It was okay during the day, but at night the area was known for bur-
glaries, break-ins, drug sales, even drive-by shootings.
All the kids I knew were forbidden, on pain of being
grounded, to go there.

About a week after school started, Pandora invited me over to her house. I asked her where she
lived, and when she said Chia Place, I couldn't believe it. I thought there must be two Chia Places,
or that she'd gotten the name wrong.

"What's the matter?" she kept asking me. But if
she didn't know, of course I couldn't tell her.

I almost said I couldn't come, but then I changed
my mind. I just made sure I didn't let my mother
know where I was going.

We bicycled over to Pandora's after school. I'd never seen a home like hers before. The rest of our families were maybe a little too house-proud; we tended to repaint before we really needed to, and our gardens never had a weed. But Pandora's house seemed very neglected. The roof had tiles missing, and weeds were growing up through the asphalt on the driveway. Pandora didn't say anything about it, though, so neither did I.

The inside was a little rundown, too, with dusty orange rugs and shabby furniture. But I thought Pandora's room was great. It was filled with books—not the Nancy Drew/Hardy Boys books the rest of us read, but grown-up books: poetry and biographies. And she had posters on her walls, like we all did, but they weren't of Madonna or Markie Mark. They were all posters from old movies.

"Undercurrent? The Third Man? Christmas in July? Who ever heard of those?" I teased her.

"Me," she said. "I've heard of them. My uncle Gene gets them for me."

Pandora's parents were out that afternoon—her dad had a doctor's appointment—so she and I had the house to ourselves. She thought up a wonderful scary game, a cross between Vampires and Hide and Seek, and we played it till nearly five o'clock, when I had to go home. As I bicycled back to my house that evening, I remember thinking that maybe Chia Place and Dream Homes weren't so bad after all.

That was the start of it. For the rest of sixth grade, at least twice during the school week, always on Saturdays, and sometimes on Sundays as well, I'd go over to Pandora's, bicycling up Sunrise to Ramon, down Ramon and over to the Palm Springs airport. I still trace that route in my mind.

It took me until October to get up the courage to tell my mother where I'd been going. She said she knew all about it—it's hard to keep secrets in a town like Palm Springs. And that as long as I was home by sunset, she guessed it was okay.

The first time I invited Pandora home with me, I was a little nervous about her seeing my house. It was so much bigger and better kept-up than hers, and I was afraid she'd mind. But she didn't seem to at all. She went slowly around every room, admiring all of Mom's knickknacks, and saying how beautiful everything was.

I was also afraid that, being a girl, she wouldn't be interested in any of the things I liked—computers and comics and model cars—but she enjoyed them all. What she liked best, though, was my basketball setup in the backyard. We played a game of one-on-one all afternoon. She wasn't very good, and I had a great time teasing her, twirling the ball up just high enough so she couldn't get at it.

The girl certainly hated to lose.

When it got to be dinnertime, Mom invited Pandora to stay and have supper with us. It was a fun evening, though I could cheerfully have killed my fourteen-year-old sister, Janine—all through the meal she kept making little remarks about "Gary and his girlfriend." I was relieved to see that Pandora paid no attention.

After dinner, Pandora said she'd bicycle home, but of course Mom wouldn't hear of that. We loaded Pandora's bike in our station wagon, and drove her back to Dream Homes.

When we pulled up in front of the house, Pandora hesitated.

"Would you like to come in?" she asked. She seemed a little embarrassed, and I could tell she didn't want Mom to see her house.

"Not tonight," I said quickly. "I still have that science project to finish."

She gave me a quick smile.

As we were driving home, I asked my mother, "So what did you think of her?"

"She definitely has character," Mom said. "I like that."

"And what drawer is she in?" That was the system my mother always used for labeling people.

It took her a while to answer.

"I can't decide if she's top or bottom."

That always stayed with me.

The following Friday I finally met Pandora's mother. Pandora had been absent from school that day, and after classes were over a few of the kids invited me to get a soda with them at Denny's.

When we got to the restaurant, I noticed that there was a new waitress. She looked like someone on a television show, with long red hair twisted up in a braid, and a face made up with orange lips and glittery blue eye shadow. She wore chains and bracelets, and long dangling earrings with bright gold balls on the ends.

"Hey, kids," she said. "What can I bring you?"

Julia Haight looked over at me, making sure I was getting the full picture.

"Well, first of all," she said in this phony little-girl voice, "we wanted to know how Pandora was doing. She wasn't at school today."

"Aren't you sweet to ask," the waitress said. "She's fine—it's just a little cold."

Julia shot me a triumphant smile, and I got the point that this odd-looking woman was Pandora's mother. I made my face as flat as I could, and didn't show any surprise or disappointment.

I liked Mrs. Brown when I got to know her, though. I even came around to thinking that it was great she was so different from all the other mothers. She didn't give a hoot about how her house looked, she didn't want to join any of our local women's clubs, and her cooking was a big joke— once she sent Pandora to school with a raw turnip in her lunch box. But she was good-natured and a lot of fun, and she made me feel welcome whenever I came over.

I liked Pandora's father, too, though he was also quite unusual. All the dads I knew worked outside the house at an office or store, but Mr. Brown never seemed to do much of anything. Every time I came over, I'd find him in his den, sitting in his recliner, watching TV or doing crossword puzzles.

"Doesn't your dad work?" I asked Pandora.

"Not anymore. He used to be a loader at Sears, but a few years ago a refrigerator fell on him, and since then he's been on disability."

I wasn't sure what disability was, but I thought it sounded ominous. Frank Brown wasn't ominous in the least, though; in fact, he seemed kind of sad to me, just sitting alone in his little den hour after hour. Pandora told me he enjoyed playing Parcheesi, so I made a point of challenging him to a game whenever I came over.

Sixth grade was a tough year for Pandora. As smart as she was, she didn't concentrate in class or always do her homework, so her grades weren't very good. She wasn't popular, either—she put no effort at all into getting along with the other kids. I knew it was just shyness, but it was a pity—it made everyone dislike her. The girls used to call her Jellyfish, because she was so pale and her hair was so long.

Pandora didn't care—she said girls were catty and dull. "Except for Steph, of course," she'd always add.

Steph Bradley was a girl Pandora knew back in Barstow, her best friend from the time she was a baby. I used to hear a lot about Steph, about all the things she and Pandora used to do together, and, to be honest, sometimes I got a little jealous.

Then one weekend, Steph came to visit, and Pandora invited me over to meet her. To my surprise, we got along just fine. Steph was a freckle-faced tomboy, very friendly and funny, and the three of us had a blast, riding skateboards all around the neighborhood. Pandora made up a phrase for the two of us: "Steph, my Glorious Girlfriend, and Gary, my Best Boy Buddy." I felt like I had passed some kind of major test.

As the year went on, I thought Pandora would start to make more friends in Palm Springs, but she never did. She continued to be the odd one out, the one who was whispered about. And because we were always together, that reputation started rubbing off on me, too. I had always had a lot of friends, but now things began to change. Two girls who had had crushes on me since kindergarten started ignoring me all of a sudden, and some of the guys—but never Bobby or Tom—quit asking me over to their houses. My mother worried that I was less popular than I used to be, but I didn't care. I was perfectly happy just being with Pandora Brown.

Those days with Pandora. Looking back, I can see that we really didn't do anything so very extraordinary. It was just that whatever we did, Pandora had the gift of making it fun.

She was interested in everything, and nearly every week she had some new craze going. For a while it was birdwatching, then it was diving, and then it was gymnastics. We spied on the neighbors, we collected rocks, we baked bread, we tried to write a play. Even my sister Janine helped with that one.

Pandora also loved going on hikes, so we spent a lot of afternoons up at Taquitz Canyon. The very first time she went, she made it all the way to the waterfall—I was very impressed.

But her biggest passion was old movies. Her uncle Gene was a talent agent in Hollywood, and he sent her all the classic films—we never had to go to the Wherehouse to rent anything. We'd make some popcorn and sit on her bed, and watch *Citizen Kane* and *The Philadelphia Story,* and everything in between.

Occasionally—I think these were my favorite times of all—Pandora and I would just hang around her backyard and talk. She loved to dream about the future, but her plans kept changing. Sometimes, she said she wanted to be an actress; other times, it was a painter, other times, a pediatrician. But her biggest goal was to end up very rich—she wanted to be able to take care of her parents someday.

Pandora and I would usually end our afternoons together by taking a walk across the street to the Palm Springs airport. We'd stand by the chain-link fence for an hour sometimes, just watching the planes taking off.

"I wish that were me," she would always sigh.

I didn't like it when she said that. I didn't like to think of her ever going away.

For Halloween that year, I was a pirate, and Pandora went as Audrey Hepburn from *Breakfast at Tiffany's*. She bicycled over to my house and we trick-or-treated all around the neighborhood. By the time we'd finished it was eight o'clock, and past dark. Pandora said she could bicycle home by herself, but I told her I would come with her. We sneaked out without my mother seeing.

I'd never been to Dream Homes after dark before, and it was definitely a little scary. Nothing was going on, exactly, but there was a distinct feeling that at any moment something bad could happen.

When we turned the corner of Pandora's street, we stopped. From a block away, we could see that her house had been completely trashed. Rolls of toilet paper were strung through the bushes, garbage was dumped all over the front porch, and the fence was spray-painted with graffiti.

Pandora stood staring at the mess. Under the streetlight, I could see that her face had faded to the color of cottage cheese.

"I hate this place," she whispered. Her voice sounded hard, like a grown-up's. "I want to get out of here."

I didn't know what to say to make her feel better. She started crying, and I put my arms around her until she stopped.

The next day was Saturday. I came over early in the morning and helped her and her mother clean up all the mess.

That November, I finally met Pandora's Uncle Gene, the agent from Hollywood who sent her all the posters and videos. He drove down from L.A. for Thanksgiving dinner, and Pandora invited me over for dessert.

I have to say, I didn't particularly care for Uncle Gene. He looked like an agent—he had a punk hairstyle and his shirt was open almost to the waist. All he talked about was show business, and the actors and actresses he handled. I'd never heard of any of them, so most of it went right over my head, but Pandora and her father didn't miss a word.

When I finally said I had to go, Uncle Gene shook my hand.

"Nice to have met you, Larry," he said. "If you ever want to break into the business, give me a call. You've got that Tom Sawyer look going. I might be able to do something for you."

I was embarrassed, but Pandora was thrilled.

The next morning, she called to say that Uncle Gene had invited her to come back to L.A. with him for the weekend. She was very excited about it, telling me all the places he was going to take her, all the things they were going to do together.

"But I thought the two of us were going hiking on Saturday," I reminded her.

There was a long pause. Then I quickly got hold of myself and told Pandora to go to L.A., and have a great time.

All weekend long I was scared I'd get a call

from her saying she was never coming back, that she'd decided to stay in L.A. forever. But Sunday afternoon Pandora returned, and I bicycled straight over to her house.

She couldn't stop talking about what a wonderful visit she'd had.

"We went to the Hollywood Wax Museum, and the Farmer's Market and the La Brea tar pits. I even got to see Uncle Gene's office, and I met this very famous agent who works upstairs."

I must have looked a little forlorn, because Pandora grinned at me.

"I almost forgot; I brought something back for you."

She handed over a small plastic Oscar, with a plaque on the base that said "World's Greatest Friend."

"It's not real—it's only made in China," she told me.

But I didn't care where it was made. It was the most wonderful gift I'd ever received.

December sixth was my father's birthday. Dad had died when I was eight, but Mom, Janine, and I still celebrated with a cake and presents for one another. One night out by the airport, I told Pandora about our tradition. I was afraid she'd think we were weird, but she said she thought it was a wonderful idea.

"What was he like?" she asked me.

I didn't talk about Dad much—I still missed him a lot. But I told Pandora a couple of things: how he used to love to hike, and what a beautiful singing voice he had.

Suddenly I couldn't go on. I was scared I was

going to burst out crying. Pandora put her hand in mine, and we didn't talk about him anymore. The day of Dad's birthday, though, she came up to me at recess and handed over a little wrapped gift.

"In honor of you-know-who."

The day school let out for Christmas vacation, the fifth and sixth grades had a special assembly. A professional artist, a children's book illustrator, came to speak. Instead of lecturing, though, he went around the room and handed each one of us a pencil and a sheet of paper clipped onto a board.

"I want you to do some drawing from life," he told us. "The only real way to learn about art is by practicing it."

He looked around the auditorium, at the rows of seated children, then pointed to Pandora.

"And I think we'll use you for our model."

He went down the steps, walked over, and took her arm as if she were a grown-up. Then he led her back up on the stage and settled her onto a chair. I could see from the other girls' faces just how envious they were feeling.

For the next twenty minutes, our assignment was to draw a portrait of Pandora. The girl on my left drew her as a cartoon figure with stick arms and legs; the girl on my right drew her as a buck-toothed monster, covered with scales.

I didn't draw anything. I just kept looking at her, sitting so still and beautiful on that chair, her face slightly raised, her hair tumbled over her shoulders, and I wrote her name all over my piece of paper, in every different handwriting I could think of. *Pandora Brown. Pandora Brown. Pandora Brown.*

When school was over that day, I waited for her

by the lockers. She finally showed up, holding a large piece of paper.

"What's that?" I asked.

"Nothing important."

But I grabbed it anyway. It was a sketch of Pandora. The artist had drawn it while the rest of us were doing our pictures in assembly. It was so beautiful that it made me feel shy.

"He's really famous," I said. "You could probably get a lot of money for that."

Pandora made a face. She put her other hand up to the paper and I could see she was about to tear it right down the middle.

"Don't do that," I told her.

She stopped and held the paper out to me.

"You want it?"

"Okay," I said with a shrug.

I had never wanted anything more.

I was what you'd call a normal twelve-year-old boy, and I certainly had my share of fantasies about Pandora. I'd dream about holding her hand and kissing her, but I never did anything about it. Pandora always made fun of the kids in the class who went steady, and I figured I'd better not try anything, in case she got offended. I decided it was more important that we remain friends; the rest could always come later. But that didn't stop me from being as jealous as Othello.

In April a new boy, Jason Moss, was transferred to our school. I could see he had a crush on Pandora, but I couldn't tell what Pandora thought of him. Whenever I'd bring his name up, she'd just laugh. But it was a teasing kind of laugh, so it could have meant anything. It drove me crazy.

One morning, Pandora told me she'd lost her favorite key ring, a lanyard her friend Steph had made her. Later that afternoon, I was passing by Jason's locker, and I saw the key ring on his shelf.

"What are you doing with that?" I demanded.

"None of your business."

I grabbed Jason, he grabbed me back, and the next thing I knew, we were into it, beating each other up out there by the lockers. The kids started flocking around, cheering one or the other of us on. Mrs. McClellan came out to see what the fuss was about, and went running for the principal. In a few minutes, Mr. Beebe had pulled Jason and me apart, and I was given detention for the first time in my life.

I was sitting in the office, an ice pack over my eye. I was going to have a whopper of a bruise, but I hadn't lost the fight—that was some comfort.

The door opened. I thought it was Mr. Beebe, coming to tell me I was expelled, but it was Pandora. She looked serious and scared. She marched up to me and put her hand on my arm.

"You didn't need to do that, Gary," she said. "I'm sorry I teased you."

In June we had our sixth-grade graduation, and afterward there was a party at Susan Chalmers's house. I wasn't sure if Pandora was going to show up, but she did, and we had a great time swimming and playing Ping-Pong all afternoon. Then, after dinner, Susan brought out a video of *Psycho* for us all to watch in her room. Pandora and I had just seen the movie, so we stayed in the den, and played with Susan's Ouija board. I'd never played before, and at first we couldn't get the board to work at all, but finally the pointer started to move. I asked a few questions, but it kept spelling out nonsense.

Then Pandora asked, "Who am I going to marry?"

The pointer started moving toward "J." Pandora had a big crush on Jonathan Taylor Thomas, and I was sure that was what the "J" was for. I didn't want her marrying Jonathan Taylor Thomas, so I started pushing the pointer toward "G" instead. After "G," I was about to move it onto "A" when it just wouldn't budge anymore, and I realized Pandora was pushing it from her side, trying to keep it from spelling out my name.

We both kept pushing in opposite directions. Finally the pointer ended up shooting off the board and flying halfway across the room. We laughed—and never mentioned it again.

Pandora and I spent most of that summer together, hiking, skateboarding, sitting in her room and watching movies; but all too soon it was September, and seventh grade began.

I went on to Raymond Cree, while Pandora started at Nellie Coffman. I told myself that being at separate schools wouldn't make a difference, and for the first few months it didn't; we saw each other almost as much as ever. I still bicycled over to her house every chance I got, and we watched videos and went on hikes, and walked over to the airport to see the planes take off.

But after a while I had to admit that things just weren't the same. Pandora and I had different activities now, different teachers, different in-jokes. When I made the swim team, sports practice started to take up more and more of my afternoons, and then Pandora got involved in an after-school drama class. At some point, there just wasn't much time to spend with each other anymore.

And then I started noticing that when we did get together, there was less and less to talk about. Pandora seemed shy with me suddenly, and I felt self-conscious. It made me sad, seeing our friendship fall apart like that, but I didn't know how to improve things. I still had dreams of kissing Pandora, but it would have been more awkward than ever now, and I never got up the courage.

Then in January, Andrea Cramer, the prettiest girl in my class, invited me to a movie, and I accepted. Andrea made it very clear that kisses would be welcome, and we spent the whole time making out in the back row of the movie theater.

After that, I stopped thinking so much about Pandora. Weeks began to go by without our seeing each other, and then it became months.

In ninth grade I started Palm Springs High School. Pandora went there, too, but by this time, we never saw each other at all—we were on completely different tracks now. I was an honor student, president of the computer club, and in case anyone might think I was a nerd, I was also the starting guard for the Indians. Pandora's grades weren't anything special, and she didn't seem to have much school spirit. Occasionally, we'd bump into each other in the hall, wave and say hi, but that was about it. It was strange to think that once we had been so close.

And then, in the fall of senior year, we had Homecoming Dance.

I guess that dance was pretty much like all the others, but knowing this was senior year, and our last Homecoming, made it feel different to me, melancholy. Everyone else seemed to be enjoying themselves—my date, Alicia Fern, was having a great time with her cheerleading friends—but all I could think about was how much everything was going to change for us in the next few years.

I went over to the refreshment table and found that someone had spiked the punch. I wasn't a drinker as a rule, but that night I had a few cups. Maybe more than a few.

When I looked up, I saw Pandora dancing with my friend Bill Higgins. I hadn't realized Bill even knew Pandora, or that he was bringing her to Homecoming. For some reason, it bothered me, seeing the two of them together.

When the dance ended, Bill went over to talk with some guys on the football team, and Pandora was standing alone.

I walked up to her. She looked like a mermaid, dressed in a dark green strapless gown with her hair down.

"I didn't know you were coming," I said.

"I wish I hadn't."

We walked outside to the terrace. The sky was very bright with stars.

"How are things going?" I asked her.

"All right."

"Have you made any plans for college?"

Pandora shrugged. "I applied for some scholarships back East, but I doubt if I'll get any—my grades aren't that wonderful. I'll probably end up at College of the Desert."

"It's a good school—I'm applying there, too," I told her. She didn't sound particularly enthusiastic to hear that.

I asked about her parents.

"They're fine," she said. "Mama's still working at Denny's."

I said I saw her there from time to time. "And is your dad still the master at Parcheesi?"

"Of course. And your family?"

I told her that Janine had gotten married and was living in Dallas now. "And Mom's working in a thrift store a few days a week. But it's costing her a fortune. She winds up giving all the customers discounts, and she has to make up the difference."

Pandora laughed.

And when she laughed, suddenly she looked like her old self again, that little eleven-year-old girl who had walked so slowly across the schoolyard the first day of sixth grade. And then, as I watched her laughing under the stars, wearing that green mermaid dress, all the old feelings came suddenly rushing back, and I knew what I needed to do. I took Pandora by the shoulders and kissed her and kissed her.

She pulled back after a while, looking puzzled.

"After all these years," she said.

I pretended it had been the punch.

I pretty much kept away from Pandora for the rest of the year. In April the college acceptances came out, and our school published the list of who was going where. Pandora had been right—like me, she was going on to COD. I felt bad for her, because I knew how much she'd always wanted to leave Palm Springs behind.

College was a busy time for me. I majored in business, specializing in computer technology, and afternoons, I helped out in the computer lab. Weekends, I worked at the local body shop, trying to save enough to buy myself a Yamaha.

My social life was very full, as well. I'd made a lot of new friends, and I was going with a girl I'd met in my poli sci class. I didn't take the relationship very seriously though. I was years away from anything like a commitment.

Occasionally, freshman year, I'd see Pandora walking to class or eating at the cafeteria, and we'd chat a little. She said she was majoring in journalism, and that she wanted to be a news anchor after she graduated. I thought it was a very good idea—I could imagine Pandora Brown excelling at something like that.

During my sophomore year though, I didn't see her around at all; then one day in April we ran into each other outside the 7-Eleven.

"I haven't seen you in ages," I said. "What's been going on?"

Pandora looked down. "Actually, I quit college," she told me. "My dad has bone cancer. It made sense for me to get a job."

I thought it was a shame she'd given up on her education, but it wasn't my place to say anything.

"I'm so sorry," I told her. "Please give him my best."

She promised she would.

Two years went by before I saw her again.

One Saturday morning, about a month before graduation, my friend Tom called, asking if I'd like to go off-roading with him. I jumped at the chance. I was eager to see how my latest baby, my Yamaha OT 250, would handle the Cut-out. We rode out by Highway 111, and I started up the dune. Halfway up I heard a squealing coming from my engine. Before I could do anything about it, the world started to slip out from under my wheels, and the next thing I knew, everything had flipped over into blackness.

I came to with Tom standing over me. I felt more stupid than anything else. There wasn't much blood other than where I had cut my cheek on the wheel of the bike, but my arms and chest were scraped raw, and the gray sand that had gotten under my skin made it look like I had morphed into a lizard.

By the time we got to the ER at Eisenhower, the pain had started kicking in. Everything seemed unreal, like a dream. Tom had his arm around me, though I kept insisting I could walk alone.

We got to the front desk, and the receptionist looked up. It was Pandora. She gasped when she saw me, her face going pale. Seeing her like that didn't surprise me at all—it just seemed to be part of the dream. I started to say something witty, but I guess I fainted before I got all the way through it.

The next day, Pandora called me at home, to see how I was feeling. She invited me to come by when I was better, and about a week later I went over to her house. It was like old times. Her mother made us brownies and told jokes, and her dad and I played Parcheesi. And Pandora fluttered about like a beautiful, golden-feathered bird.

After the game she and I went into her bedroom. We put on the latest video her uncle Gene had sent; but I couldn't stop watching Pandora. Halfway through the movie, I put my arm around her shoulders, and I began to kiss her.

I guess what happened then was kind of inevitable.

That first time with Pandora was very sweet. I remember thinking how natural it felt, making love to her at last. The coolness of her skin, the hair so gold it was almost green, the movements of her body under mine; somehow they were all familiar, as if they had been a part of me for a long, long time.

Afterward, I watched Pandora as she lay there on the bed. She was curled like a child under the covers, her hair breaking in waves over her shell-pale face. I thought the words *I've always loved you,* but I didn't say them out loud.

We were together for over a year after that. It was a wonderful time. I felt as if I'd gotten those happy days of my childhood back again. Pandora still had that gift of making everything special, and if I could have, I would have stayed in that place forever.

She wasn't always the easiest of girlfriends—she could be pretty moody sometimes—but I felt so incredibly lucky to have her. Sometimes, when we'd be walking, or watching a movie, I'd just stare at her, trying to get used to the fact that, after all those years, Pandora Brown was actually mine.

After graduating from COD I decided to start my own business, and I set up as a computer consultant, creating networks for small local companies. I was lucky enough to get some clients right away, and I looked forward to serving the whole Coachella Valley one day.

When her father's health eventually stabilized, I hoped that Pandora would change her mind about getting her degree, but she said she had outgrown college. She didn't seem happy working in the ER, though, so I wasn't sure the decision was wise.

We had both gotten our own apartments, but after we'd been together about ten months, Pandora gave hers up. Her dad's health had deteriorated again, and she decided to move back home for a while to help her mother look after him.

And it was about that time that things began to fall apart for the two of us.

Little by little, I could feel Pandora starting to pull away from me. I couldn't understand why. She just didn't seem to want to be with me anymore. She would break dates or make some excuse for not coming over. She was restless and distracted, and we started making love less and less.

Everything was so up in the air with her father's health that I didn't like to press her, but I was anxious about the future, and where our relationship was going. I was afraid to bring the subject up, though, afraid of what she might tell me.

I guess I loved her too much to want to hear.

Pandora

It's three o'clock in the morning—I've given up trying to sleep.

There were two reporters waiting outside the office today. They followed me to the car, calling out Troy's name, John Bradshaw's.

I keep pretending I have a magic escape button. I'm always going back. I guess I shouldn't; it all started there. It's not that I think I could change things if I had it to do all over again—I'm not as crazy as that—it just feels somehow safer.

I try to pinpoint the moment it started. I think it was that New Year's Day. Yes—I even had some sense of it at the time. I remember waking up and thinking, *This year, everything is going to be different.*

I lay in bed for a long time that morning. It was foggy outside, and that seemed strange and magical. Palm Springs is so rarely foggy; it felt like an omen.

I got out of bed, and went into the kitchen to make breakfast for Mama and Daddy. I cooked some French toast and brought it to them in bed.

"Happy New Year, Andy-Pandy." Daddy kissed

me on the cheek. His skin felt hot, like scorched parchment. "I want this to be your best year ever."

I echoed the same wish for him, but my heart felt squeezed. He was looking so fragile. He always did in the mornings, his hair white and wild.

I turned on the television and flipped to the Rose Parade. It was drizzling in L.A., and the announcers looked damp and uncomfortable.

"Maybe we'll see Gene," Daddy said. "He told me he might be going to watch the parade."

I doubted if we'd be seeing Uncle Gene amidst the hundreds of thousands of spectators, but it entertained Daddy for two hours, looking for him.

After the show was over, though, he started getting depressed. He kept patting my hand and sighing. "Another year, another year. It all goes so fast; it's over before you know where you are. I wish I'd been a better father to you, Andy-Pandy."

I didn't know what to say. I reminded him of all our special times together—the picnics, the Cootie game, the pueblo for my fourth-grade project. That made him smile, but then I started to get sad myself. All those memories were fifteen, twenty years old, and there was nothing new to replace them. I got this image in my mind of a moth, flat on the wall, slowly dying, getting dryer and dryer until it finally just dropped down and crumbled into dust.

All afternoon Daddy napped and I paced the house. The moment Mama came in from her shift, I took off.

To cheer myself up, I decided to go look at houses, the most beautiful houses I could find. I drove over to the Andreas Hills area, and saw that all the real estate signs were out. There was even a FOR SALE sign in front of the big Spanish house on

Stonehenge Drive, and I pulled up across the street from it and parked.

A broker from Maryann Hill was out in front. I was relieved to see that she wasn't one of the ones I knew. I was always careful to space out my visits to open houses so nobody would get suspicious.

The broker smiled as I walked up the front steps.

"Happy New Year," she said. "Are you in the market for a house?"

"Yes," I said. "But I'm getting discouraged—it's so hard finding just what I want."

"Well, maybe this will be the one."

She handed me a brochure and let me wander around.

I spent half an hour going through the house, and imagining all the things I would do with it if it were mine. When I finally came back downstairs, the broker was waiting for me.

"Any luck?"

"It certainly has potential," I told her airily. "I'll definitely come back and see it again. And then I might go ahead and show it to my fiancé and my business manager."

"I understand completely," she said with a smile.

There was something about that smile that made me wonder if maybe she'd been on to me the whole time.

I spent the rest of New Year's Day working on what I'd dubbed my Treasure Board. This was one of my resolutions—I'd read in a self-help book that the subconscious mind responds to images, and that collecting pictures of what you want from life will help you get it. So I went through a dozen magazines, cutting out pictures of everything that took my fancy—a BMW, an antique sapphire ring, a chalet in Switzerland—then I pasted them all onto a big piece of poster board.

When the Treasure Board was finished, I propped it against the bed. My eyes flitted over all the images—the elegant Colonial house, the sleeping baby, the ski resort in Whistler. It was almost too much, going from one beautiful dream to the next.

Around midnight I heard Mama come in. It made me so nervous, the way she always tiptoed around in case Daddy was asleep. She knew perfectly well he wasn't—he could never sleep for more than a few minutes at a time. But he never said anything to let her know he was awake. I could hear all the noises through the wall, her undressing, getting into bed, him turning over. But neither of them talking.

I thought of how when I was little I used to hear their voices all the time—it was the cheerful, splashing background to my days. It always made me think of a stream, the way the voices flowed along together. But after Daddy's accident the stream started to get less and less. And then when he got cancer it dried up completely.

January second I started back to work. As I drove toward the hospital, I tried hard to get motivated. I told myself that this was the year—my year—and that I was going to make some changes. I'd ask for a raise, maybe get a better job.

But as I turned down Bob Hope Drive and made a left into the parking lot, all that optimism drained away. I stopped the car and stared up at the gray square building. It looked like a suffocating wave about to crash down. I sat in the car, unable to move, barely able to breathe.

I felt like weeping. Who was I trying to kid? This new year was not going to make any difference. Nothing was ever going to change for me. None of the things I wanted was ever going to happen; none of the pictures on my Treasure Board was ever going to come true. I would live in this little town forever. Work in this emergency room. Probably die right here in this hospital.

It was just too late. I had made all the wrong choices a long time ago.

It was hard to get through that morning. Around eleven o'clock, an accident case was brought in: a fifteen-year-old boy.

"My son's number one in his class," his mother kept telling me. "He's going to go on to Harvard, be a doctor someday. He'll work in a hospital—maybe even this one."

I didn't know what to say. I could see that the boy wasn't going to make it, and he didn't. He died around noon.

I wasn't in the mood to sit in the cafeteria for lunch, so I brought my sandwich outside to eat on the lawn. It was sunny and cheerful, but every time I looked up, I could see the hospital. Even when I turned my back, I could still feel its shadow.

I stalled as long as I could, but finally it was time to get back to work. I always dreaded that moment, when I had to walk past the patients to my desk. I could see the envy on their faces, and I knew they were thinking, *Why me and not her?*

Gary called as I was leaving to go home. I waited until I was in the car to play back the message.

"Hi, Pandora, it's me. I was wondering if you were free Friday night, and if so, whether you'd like to have dinner at the Desert Turtle. Let me know."

He sounded so nervous. As I drove home his

anxious voice kept going through my head, making me feel guiltier with every block that passed. I wondered what sort of a bitch I must be if Gary needed to sound so apologetic when he invited me to the best restaurant in town.

I had been so cold to him lately. I knew that, but I couldn't seem to help myself. Something had changed; and I wasn't even sure what it was. I think one day I just realized that Gary loved me in a way I didn't deserve and had never deserved. A way that I could never love him back. At the beginning, I had thought I could. When we first got together, I even imagined we might get married one day. But as time went on that somehow had stopped being a possibility.

Mama and Steph couldn't understand—they thought I was crazy. Gary was completely wonderful: kind, reliable, loyal, never picky or petty. And on and on. He had every good quality in the world.

But that was part of the problem—I didn't want someone who had "qualities." I didn't want to be able to list the fifty reasons why I loved a man. I wanted it to be "just because."

And there was no "just because" with Gary. Maybe it was because we'd met so early and I knew him so well—there hadn't been any surprises since I was eleven years old. I used to wonder about that sometimes, about what would have happened if we'd met ten years later, at a local bar or the cafeteria at COD; would things have been different then? Would I have found him more exciting? Somehow I doubted it.

I hated myself for thinking that way about Gary, for being so disloyal and ungrateful. But I was so sick of my whole life—never having enough money, never doing anything interesting, being stuck in

this crummy town. Everything in me was screaming out for a change. And here was Gary, so pre-
dictable, so content with his little business and his
little interests, so completely happy to stay in the
old world.

It wasn't his fault that I had gotten restless, but I
knew I couldn't keep on hiding the way I felt.
Pulling into the driveway, I made up my mind that
I had put it off long enough, that I needed to end
this relationship once and for all.

I decided to do it that Friday night at the Desert
Turtle, but I didn't have the heart. Gary was so excited, talking on and on about some new client
he'd gotten, some startup firm who'd hired him to
do their programming; and seeing his proud, excited face, I lost my courage. I told myself that it
would be kinder to break things off gradually, one
step at a time. In a way, I guess I had begun to do
that already.

As we left the restaurant, Gary put his hand on
the small of my back.

"Would you like to go back to my apartment?"

It had been weeks since we'd made love.

"I'm sorry," I told him. "I'm too tired tonight."

"That's all right," he said quickly. "Is there anything else you'd like to do?"

"Yes, actually. If it's all right with you, I'd like to
go look at houses."

We drove out to Andreas Hills. As we passed the
Spanish house on Stonehenge Drive, I saw that the
FOR SALE sign was still there. The house was even
more wonderful at night, tantalizingly magical, with
purplish lights at the base of all the palm trees.

Gary stopped the car across the street from the
house. He put an arm around my shoulders, and
started fiddling with my hair.

"I can see the two of us living here someday," he murmured. "I'd be working on a program, you'd be watching some old movie. And when you looked up, there I'd be, and when I looked up, there you'd be."

I thought about how that would be, looking up and seeing Gary for the rest of my life. Involuntarily, I jerked away from him.

He drove me straight home. We didn't talk; I could see how hurt he was. I hated hurting him, hated him loving me when I could no longer love him back.

January went on—foggy weather, work, guilt, failing at all my New Year's resolutions.

One drizzly Friday night, I couldn't take it anymore. I put on my best dress, told Mama not to wait up, and headed off for Bananaz.

The moment I got to the nightclub, I regretted having come. It was loud and too hyper, and I knew I'd been foolish to expect any kind of rescue here.

I went up to the bar, sat down, and ordered a drink. I was on my second glass of wine when I caught the scent of Drakkar aftershave. I turned around. A man was standing behind me. He was in his early thirties, blond, wearing a faded denim shirt and jeans.

"You look nice," he said.

I told him I was nice only on alternate Sundays.

He said his name was Dale, and he bought me another drink.

We got into one of those stupid bar conversations—"I can tell what sort of woman you are" kind of thing. But I knew, right away, that I had him if I wanted him, and that I did want him. I didn't let myself think about Gary.

I kept looking at the skin on Dale's chest. It was like tan cheesecloth; I wanted to put my tongue to it, taste it to see if it was really as soft as it looked.

He asked what my job was. When I told him, he laughed.

"I thought you looked familiar."

He said he'd been brought into the ER a few months ago with a broken arm, and that the two of us had had a little chat. I didn't remember anything about it.

"You gave me this spiel," he said.

"It wasn't anything personal," I told him. "I give it to everyone."

"Give it to me now," he said. "I thought it was sexy."

He kept asking, and by this time I was on my third glass of wine.

I starting rattling the speech off. "After the insurance provider is billed, any balance payable by the patient will be billed them along with an EOB . . ."

Then I stopped. It wasn't something to be making fun of; it was an awful thing to joke about.

Dale leaned forward and kissed me.

"I told you it was sexy."

In two minutes, we were out of there. His Yamaha was parked by the curb. I felt strange, climbing onto it. I'd never ridden on anyone's motorcycle but Gary's before.

We got on the freeway to Vista Chino and drove toward Sunrise. I had the sudden awful feeling we were headed for the Desert Park Apartments, and we were.

Dale pulled into the lot, and we walked toward the complex. I tried not to look at the graffiti splattering the walls, or the broken toys and rusty barbecues lining the hallway.

His apartment was filthy; junk everywhere, crusted pots in the sink. I asked Dale to change the sheets on the bed, and then we got right down to it.

Afterward, he made me some coffee, slimy with Coffee-mate in a Styrofoam cup, but I put it down without tasting it. I could sleep with the man an hour after I'd met him, but I couldn't drink his terrible Nescafé. That struck me as funny. Dale asked me what I was laughing at, and I said, "Nothing." "Nothing" was a good answer; there was nothing I wanted to tell him, ever. I just wanted to get home.

I said I had to go, that I had work in the morning. Dale offered to take me back to Bananaz, where my car was, but I told him not to bother, that I'd call a taxi.

I waited outside the building. It was cold, and the stars were big and clear. I kept trying to push myself right up into the sky and then look down so I could see how small and unimportant all of this really was.

I felt sick the next morning, so ashamed. All morning long, I kept smelling ghastly warm puffs of Drakkar aftershave. I took two showers, but the scent still stayed in my skin and my hair. I kept staring at myself in the mirror. I hated the way my face looked, furtive and sly.

I called Steph that night. I hadn't planned to tell her what had happened, but I ended up blurting out everything. When I finished, there was a long silence.

"Well," she said finally, "I guess the big question is, was it worth it? On a scale from one to ten, how was he?"

"About a two." We both burst out laughing.

We talked about other things for a while, her new job at the bank, and how friends back in Barstow were doing, but I could tell that Steph was still thinking about what I'd said.

"Pandora, have you ever considered going back to school?" she asked me.

"No. You know that's never been for me."

"Well, you've got to do something." She sounded suddenly very serious. "You've got to make some kind of change. If you got a degree, at least you could get a better job. But this business of picking guys up at bars just because you're bored—to tell you the truth, it scares me."

It scared me, too.

The next day, after work, I found myself making the turn off Highway 111 and pulling into the driveway for the College of the Desert. I stayed in the car for a few minutes, watching the kids flying along the paths; everyone looked so energetic and determined and young.

I got out of the car finally and walked onto the campus. It felt very strange to be there again. I wandered into the Continuing Ed office, and the woman behind the desk asked if I was interested in some brochures. I said I hadn't made up my mind, but she pressed a handful on me, anyway.

When I got back to the car, I took a look through them. Some of the courses—psychology, anthropology, French, and my old major, journalism—sounded kind of fun, and it struck me that if I really wanted to, I could start over from scratch, begin a whole new career.

But I decided to opt for the most practical route. The only sensible thing to do was to stay in the field I was already in. The school offered both emergency medical tech and nursing as night classes, and if I signed up for those, I could earn an associate degree in two years. With any luck, I could eventually end up working in a doctor's office, maybe even as a pediatric nurse.

That night, I called Steph.

"I think I'm going back to school," I told her.

She didn't even have the decency to sound surprised.

The following evening, I met Gary for coffee and told him what I'd decided to do. He was thrilled, as I knew he would be—he had always wanted me to get my degree. He hugged me and tried to kiss me, but I pulled away and took a deep breath.

"But, Gary," I said, "now that I'm doing this, there are going to have to be some other changes in my life as well."

He was still smiling; I hurried on, not able to look at him.

"Classes will be taking up a lot of my time from now on, and I won't be able to see much of you for a while."

The words were out; they had been said.

Gary was silent. The smile went away. At last he nodded.

"I see."

I felt very guilty, yet wildly relieved. I had finally

done it, gotten it over with. I had taken the first step.

Classes started at the beginning of February. I dressed for the first one in jeans and a T-shirt and felt like a fake, like someone trying to impersonate a kid. When I got to COD and walked toward the classroom I hoped to feel some new sensation, some new thrill, but all there was was the same warmed-over fatigue I'd always had at school.

Listening to the professor drone on during class, it occured to me that going back to school might not be such an easy answer after all. Around me, men and women were busily taking notes, earnestly asking questions. And all I could do was stare at the clock and wish it were over.

Valentine's Day was coming up. I worried about finding just the right card to send Gary, something that was funny and warm, without being sentimental. I finally found one I liked, and put it in the mail. The next night, I came home to find a dozen roses waiting on my doorstep.

I called Gary to thank him, and he asked if he could take me out to dinner that night.

"It's been a long time since I've seen you," he added wistfully.

I told him I was sorry, but that I had a paper to write for class.

March second was my parents' thirtieth wedding anniversary. At breakfast Daddy announced that he was taking Mama out to lunch at the California Pizza Kitchen.

"Just like old times," he said, smiling at her.

I remembered how, when I was little, the two of them used to go out on their "dates." Mama would wear her newest dress, and Daddy would put on a jacket and tie, fastened with a clip shaped like a tiny ship's wheel.

I helped Daddy dress for the Pizza Kitchen; he even went so far as to put on a tie, but in the end, he didn't feel up to going. I don't think Mama really expected he would.

I spent the afternoon cooking a special anniversary dinner: veal piccata, roast peppers, and chocolate cake. Uncle Gene was driving up from L.A. to be with us, and it was all that Daddy could think about.

"Have we got that wine Gene likes?" he asked anxiously, wandering into the dining room while I was setting the table.

"Yes—I stopped by the liquor store this afternoon."

"It'll be good to see him," he said. "Though I'm sorry Marilynn couldn't come."

I didn't bother to answer this. None of us had been sorry, or very surprised, when Aunt Marilynn declined our invitation.

"Gene said something on the phone about getting a new client," Daddy went on eagerly. "I'm sure he'll tell us all about it tonight."

I settled him on his chair and left him watching out the window for Uncle Gene's arrival. I felt very happy myself, and excited about the evening.

But it turned out to be awful. Uncle Gene was in a strange, tense mood, and from the moment he arrived at our house he started drinking. By the time the meal was served he could barely walk to the table.

In the middle of dinner, he started yelling at Daddy. "You've wasted your whole life, Frank. You know that, don't you? Even before the accident, you were never any use to anyone. I'm saying this for your own good—you need to grow a backbone, do something, get hold of yourself."

Daddy laughed it off, acting like it was all a joke, but I could see it was killing him.

After dinner, I took Uncle Gene aside.

"How could you do that?"

He shook his head. "I'm sorry, Pandora. It's just . . . when we were kids, I admired Frank more than anyone in the world. And seeing him now, sitting in that fucking chair, not doing anything, not even trying to do anything—it gets me crazy."

I understood how he felt. Sometimes, though I would never admit it to Uncle Gene, or anyone else, I had those same sorts of thoughts myself.

We ended up taking a walk together. We went over to the airport and stood by the fence. We watched one plane come in and then another.

"What are you doing these days?" Uncle Gene asked me.

I started to tell him about the medical tech class I was taking, but he cut me off in the middle.

"You should come to L.A.," he said.

The words went through me like arrows.

"I'd love to do that someday."

"Why not now?"

I shrugged. "Daddy, for one thing. And I'm not sure L.A.'s really the place for me."

Uncle Gene laughed, then he threw out his

arms. The gesture managed to include our house, our street, all of Palm Springs, my job, even the guy Dale from Bananaz.

"And this *is?*"

I didn't know what to answer.

He sighed and dropped his hand.

"I love you, Pandora," he said.

When we got back to the house, he behaved well. He kissed Mama's hand and apologized for being such a bastard. Then he shook Daddy's shoulder and said, "Frank, you drive me crazy, but you know I love you better than anyone."

The two of them shook hands. Uncle Gene's hand was tanned and strong; Daddy's was blue-white and looked like it had been modeled out of Play-Doh.

After Uncle Gene left, I sat down on the front porch and stared up at the stars.

Lori

Oh, I'm good. I'm so good it scares me.

In the middle of dinner, he calls. I hear the phone; I know it's him. I told him not to call me at my mother's; he never listens. I get up, I go to the phone in the kitchen.

He's horny. "Baby, baby. I need to see you right away."

My mother's yelling, "Lori, who is it?"

"It's a friend," I tell her. "She's calling from the four-oh-five. She's been in an accident—I have to get down there right away."

You'd think she'd have a little pity, but no, not her, not my mother.

"Tell your friend she's very inconsiderate. Tell her you're in the middle of dinner."

I say, "I'll meet you at the office in an hour."

I go to my room, pick out some clothes. Blue jersey dress—easy to get out of in a hurry—the new heels. Can't wear them here, she'd get suspicious, I put them in my tote.

But she catches me. "Lori, why are you taking a bag?"

"My friend might have to go to the hospital; I thought I'd bring her some things."

She buys it.

Drive down Santa Monica; guy hookers out in force, a few good-looking ones. Some tricks chase my car down Highland. Cut up Crescent Heights to Sunset.

Big line at the Comedy Club. I'd like to go there, I've told Gene that a hundred times; he ought to take me. It kills me the way he never takes me out; it wouldn't hurt him to do that once in a while. But no—it's always just screwing in the office.

Park in the back lot, change clothes in the car. Unlock the door, go inside the building. I hate being there at night, it gives me the heebie-jeebies. The posters on the walls, the old movie stars, their eyes follow you.

Gene's waiting in the office, his shirt unbuttoned. His hand starts pulling up my dress before I'm all the way in the door.

I say, "What about a hello first?"

"I'll give you a hello. The best hello you ever had."

I ask him how his wife is. That should shut him up. I don't like being grabbed without being talked to first.

It works; he lets go for a second, then he's back onto me.

The dress is around my ankles. I can't believe how stupid Marilynn is, how she trusts the bastard.

He asks me is anything wrong.

No, nothing's wrong. What's Marilynn to me? She's got everything she wants. The house in the Hollywood Hills, the Volvo. Gene is all over my boobs now. What do I have? Nothing, that's what I have.

He's on me now, pushing and grunting.

I shudder, moan the way he likes.

It's over soon enough.

We're lying on the rug. You can tell he's proud of himself. You can see he thinks he's the big stud.

I get up and go over to the bookshelf. Take a look at Marilynn's picture. With her perfect little hairdo and the big fat pearls. He's such a hypocrite. Fucking me every chance he gets, but he still keeps her picture up. I make a mark with my finger on the silver frame. I always do that, my little tradition. The frame's getting tarnished—it's starting to look like a vampire's been at it.

He's making strange noises, like he can't breathe. I look over, his face is bright red.

I don't want him getting a stroke, I don't want to have to call the cops.

"Are you okay?"

He turns on the big macho smile. "Sure." He squeezes my hand. "I'll be fine. Thanks for caring."

Like I care.

He gets back down on the rug. He wants to hold me some more. I let him. I like looking down at my body; it's just about perfect. I don't look at his. I think of old whales, covered with barnacles.

"Have you thought any more about what we discussed?"

I don't have to say anything else, he knows what I'm talking about.

I think I'm being very reasonable. I don't expect him to leave his wife. I don't expect him to put me in some fancy apartment. I don't even want a car. And what I do want, it's only something I deserve.

"Sure," he says. "September—let's say September. I'll make the announcement then."

I want to jump up and holler. It's the first time I've gotten a date out of him.

I'll be a partner by September. The Gene Brown and Lori Max Agency. The Max and Brown Agency.

I turn him on his back, give him some strokes for good behavior. He groans but can't get it going again. That's fine by me.

Just wait till Troy hears the news.

Driving home. September, my life will change in September. I've been waiting for this so long, now it's almost here.

Try it on for size: "I'm a partner with the Gene Brown Agency."

Now my mother can brag about "my daughter the partner." We're finally through with her telling me, "You'll never amount to anything; you'll end up on the streets someday."

Or who knows, maybe not. Nothing I ever did was fucking good enough for her, why should *this* be? I spent my whole life hearing, "What's the matter with you? Why can't you try harder? Why aren't you more popular? Why can't you get better grades? Why don't you go to college, get married, give me grandchildren?" Yakety-yakety-yak.

And finally it's going to be "My daughter the partner." But guess what, I don't think I'll tell her; she doesn't deserve to know.

Get home around one. She's still up, yakety-yakking all the way to my room. "What took you so long? I needed my bath; I needed my medicine. You're so inconsiderate."

I tell her, "Leave me alone. My friend just died in the hospital."

That shut her up for once.

All she does is complain, "My arm hurts, the cast itches." It's driving me crazy. You'd think no one ever broke their elbow before. I wonder, did she do it on purpose? Slip on the step, just to get attention? I wouldn't put it past her.

Can't wait to get out of here, back to my own place.

"You promised me you'd stay until the cast is off."

I called the doctor today, begged him to take the cast off. He says he has to wait another week.

Our anniversary, three years to the day I met Troy. Gets me happy even thinking about it. It gives me chills. How I went to Chips alone that night. Had a drink, looked up, and saw this guy come in the door. Black eyes, black hair. I knew, the second I laid eyes on him how it would be.

He didn't come over right away; he made me wait. Then finally he walked up and asked for my phone number. I thought he'd take his time, but he couldn't wait either; he called the next day.

Our first date we were supposed to go to The Pier, but we never made it out the door. We just stayed home and screwed our brains out.

Looking forward to tonight. Went to Frederick's of Hollywood, Troy likes me in their underwear. Got a red silk cutout teddy. Stopped by The Paper Place, got a tropical origami kit. Folded some figures of Troy and me by the beach, lying naked in a hammock between two palm trees.

We're meeting at eight. He's taking me to dinner at Pastis. My mother's driving me crazy. "You're so inconsiderate. What about my medicine? You can't leave me like this."

Decided to wear the black Chloe with the gold belt. Came out of my room. Mother nearly peeing all over herself. "Where are you going, who are you going with, when will you be back?"

Get to Pastis a few minutes early; I like it, everything's done in yellow and blue. It's supposed to look like the South of France, not that I've ever been. Maybe I'll go next summer once I'm partner, take Troy with me.

The captain shows me to a table, I sit there alone. Lots of guys staring. That used to be great; now I don't even care.

Troy finally comes in. Every girl's mouth falls open, every girl's mouth starts to water. I go crazy, watching him walk.

He sees me, comes over, kisses me. God, I could do it right there on the table. I can see, so could he.

"Let's not stay too long." He's touching my leg. "Whose idea was it to come here anyway?"

"It's our anniversary, remember?"

I give him his present, the Burberry shirt. He opens the card I made. He laughs at the origami figures underneath the palm trees.

"I guess I owe you a present," he says. "I came up a little short this month."

I tell him, "Don't worry, I wasn't expecting anything."

I wait till we get our drinks, I say, "I've got news.

I finally got a date out of Gene. September. He's going to make me partner in September."

But I can tell Troy isn't listening. I look over; there's a girl staring at him, making little signs. He's not answering, but he isn't not looking, either. Damn him, why does he always have to do this?

Reach over and turn his face to me. I tell him again.

"He's going to make you partner?"

"That's what he said."

"Do you have it in writing?"

It's funny about Troy, he doesn't seem like a practical person at all, but sometimes he'll say things like that.

"No."

I start smiling, thinking of Gene naked like a whale with his dick lying on the rag rug. And me handing him a contract. *Would you mind signing this?*

"I'll get it in writing next time," I say. "This time we were just a little too busy."

Troy's sure all focused on me now. The big, bad, dark light in his eyes.

"Too busy? Too busy doing what?"

I start telling him. I can see the sweat start by his hairline. He touches my forehead where my scar is, strokes it with his thumb. I go on telling him. I wish just once he would be jealous, but he never is; he loves hearing all this. He hooks his legs over mine and starts squeezing, out and in, out and in. The waiter comes up to take our order.

Troy tells him with a beautiful smile, "We've changed our minds about dinner, just bring us a check for the drinks."

Don't make it to Troy's apartment. Pull over on Fuller and do it in the backseat. Lovely, gorgeous, the best.

Trying to get some sleep. My mother starts beating on the door. "Time to go to church." I say, "No way I'm going." But I still have to haul my ass out of bed, get her ready.

All the time, it's yakety-yak. "I wish you'd come with me, you never go to church anymore; when I think of all the money I spent sending you to Sacred Heart. You're headed straight for hell, you know."

Finally got her downstairs. Waited with her on the sidewalk until her friend picked her up; Jesus Christ, only five more days until the cast comes off.

Go back to bed. I get nuts just being back in this house. It freaks me out how fast I've gotten used to it again.

Get out of bed, go into my father's den, stupid thing to do. Stand by the door, look around. The plaid couch where it used to happen.

Come in, Lori, come look at my stamps. Aren't they pretty? Which one is your favorite?

I don't have a favorite, Daddy, I've seen them before.

My back hurts. Daddy must be getting old. Rub it for me, Lori, right there, where you always rub it. Now down, down, keep rubbing. You don't look comfortable, Lori, sitting like that. Relax, relax. Here, let me get you relaxed.

I'm relaxed, Daddy. You don't have to do that.

I know what's best for you, Lori. This won't hurt, this will make Daddy so happy.

It did hurt, Daddy. It hurt a lot.

And, remember, we mustn't tell Mommy—this is our secret, our special secret.

But I told her once. We were in the car, I said, "When you're away, Daddy makes me lie down on the sofa and he does things."

She took her hands off the steering wheel, she put them over her ears. I was screaming. I thought the car was going to crash. She pulled over to the side of the road. She slapped me. She said, "Never, never tell lies like that again."

I like to think about the night he was killed. I was in bed. The walls of my room got red—it was the light of the police car. Two cops came up the walk, stiff like dolls. I left my room, came out to the banister.

"Mrs. Max, we have some very bad news. I'm afraid there's been an accident."

I start screaming, I'm sobbing; they all look up at me. My mother rushes up and hugs me, I can't stop crying. How funny, they all think it's because I'm sad.

Go out onto the porch, it's better there, a little air. It makes me think of Grandma; she always liked going out on the porch.

Those were the best days, when Grandma came. Waking up early. *Grandma's coming.* I'd put on a dress; she liked me in dresses. I'd go pick flowers for her. Waiting on the sidewalk, watching for her old green Buick. I had to be the first one to see her before my mother did. *Grandma, Grandma!*

Lori, my good little girl. Her hug always being right, always smelling right. Opening her bag. *Here's a little something for my Lori.*

Sitting with her on the porch, holding her hand, watching her drink her tea. My head in her lap; she'd stroke my hair.

My mother hated it. *Why are you such a baby with Grandma? Act your age!*

She was jealous, jealous that I loved Grandma best, that Grandma loved me.

I'd close my eyes and let Grandma stroke my hair as long as she liked. *Lori, my good little girl.*

Got to get out of this house. Take a walk down Laurel to Santa Monica Boulevard. All these old chicken-leg ladies with their magenta hair staring at me, shaking their heads—*Look at that little tramp*, cluck, cluck. Fuck them.

Mother comes back, all shiny from church, God's good little girl. She says, "I want you to drive me over to see Grandma."

She never wants to visit Grandma; church just makes her feel guilty. I don't mind going, but I don't tell her that.

It's blistering hot in the Valley. Down Van Nuys Boulevard—pawnbrokers and bail bonds. Get to the old folks' home. A flock of them, smiling at us, surrounding us in their wheelchairs and their walkers. Skinny little arms in plaid shirts, everyone white as a slug. Get me out of here.

Go up to Grandma's floor, tap on the door. She calls "Hello" like a little bird. She's glad to see us. She smells like biscuits baking, the same as usual, and I keep next to her, like always.

It's not one of her good days, I can tell she isn't listening. Mother's whining, how much her arm hurts, how I don't take care of her the way I should. Grandma's off somewhere else. I want to tell her my news—being made partner in September— but I don't. I don't want my mother to know.

Then Grandma turns to me with a big smile.

"Ann?"

I feel sick, I am so angry that she mixed me up with my mother. I get up, say I need some air. The room next to Grandma, the door is open. A crazy old lady is stark naked, running around the room. I watch her for a while.

I never want to get old.

Need a little kick today. Call my friend Suzanne, she sounds down. She told me she just heard from her sister Ellen, the cancer's spread.

"I might have to move to Seattle to take care of her."

Hate Suzanne going to Seattle. Hate Ellen being so sick.

"Let's take your mind off it," I tell her. "Let's go spend some money."

She says that's a great idea.

We meet at Re-Threads. God, I love that store, everything about it. I love the way they display the clothes, show them off, let them breathe. And they've got a whole batch of new stuff in, evening dresses; the woman said they were from the Whoopi Goldberg premiere last week.

One silk Escada, it's covered with beading; it can stand up without a hanger. It's gorgeous; if I had that dress, I'd be happy. I'd keep it in my closet, look at it every day.

Suzanne found a blouse. She's sniffing it, like there's still sweat left over from the previous owner.

I tell her don't worry—it was rich and famous sweat; maybe if she's lucky, some of it will rub off on her.

Suzanne doesn't like thinking who the clothes belonged to. For me it's the best part. What rich bitch had it, where she wore it, why she sold it. I wonder how many of the husbands know what their wives are up to? Buy a dress, six thousand a pop, sell it to Re-Threads, keep the change.

And then little Lori gets her chance at it.

Ended up with a lime green Prada shirt and some pinstriped Stella McCartney pants. But what I want is that beaded Escada. One day—September— when I'm partner—I'll get it then.

Love buying stuff. *Ca-chink! Ca-chink!* Leaving stores with big bags, it's a rush.

Bad night, weird dreams—there was an earthquake; I couldn't get out of my apartment.

Monday morning. Take off the weekend skin, put on the work clothes. Tried out the Estée Lauder perfume sample—not bad. I'll get Troy to buy me a bottle; he still owes me for our anniversary. One day I'll be so rich I'll take a bath in it.

Mother still sleeping. Be thankful for small mercies. Ate breakfast in peace. Left early. Nothing better than the sight of Laurel Street shrinking in the rearview mirror.

Drove down Santa Monica. Nothing open yet. Turned the radio up loud, K-ROCK oldies; opened all the windows. No one up but me and the homeless.

Stopped at Crescent Square, had some coffee and a doughnut. All the bums hanging out there.

The coffee smelled like piss. Got an extra doughnut for Jessa, I haven't seen her in a while. Drove
down Sunset. She was there, sitting at her corner.
She has a new cart, some new bags. Gave her the
doughnut; she didn't even look up.

Suzanne thinks I'm crazy. *Why don't you give to a
decent charity? Why do you waste your time with
someone like her?* But there are too many fucking
charities, and I like Jessa. She isn't grateful, she
doesn't give a damn, she doesn't ever complain. If
I were on the streets, that's the way I'd want to be,
like Jessa. The thought comes to me sometimes—
one day I could be.

Get to the office, drive past the sign in the lot:
PARKING FOR TENANTS ONLY. It's only eight months
till September; then I'll park there every day. For
now, it's park on the fucking street.

Let myself into the lobby. John Bradshaw himself getting into the elevator. Not often we catch a
glimpse of His Holiness. He's wearing a great suit,
gray twill, blue silk Gucci tie, Troy would look
good in it.

Bradshaw just stared past me as usual. Snob.

Emmett comes running downstairs. He's going
so fast he almost falls on his ass. We've got the
same job. He's an assistant, and I'm an assistant,
but he's really Bradshaw's slave.

"Got to get His Majesty some cigarettes. Want to
come along, gorgeous?"

I come along. I like Emmett. He's bitchy gay; he
tells me Bradshaw's in an assy mood today.

"And what about Sir Gene?"

I say I don't know, I haven't seen him yet.

Emmett doesn't have a clue about Gene and me, I keep that under wraps; I don't trust Emmett that far.

Gene comes in at ten. "Good morning, Lori."

He's stern, all business, it's always the same on Monday morning; he must go to church on Sunday, too. But five minutes later he's looking down my blouse.

I've gone through the calendar, he's got a one o'clock lunch with Shirley Hudson. The big try to win her back to the agency. I ask him if I can come along.

"No, Lori, I'm afraid not; who would look after the office?"

Don't condescend to me, buster; I know what you look like on this shag rug. "Oh, come on, Gene. I can leave the office for an hour. And if you're going to make me partner in September, don't you think I should start getting to know the clients?"

Don't need to say anything else. I never use threats; I just give him the smile.

The Mandarin is top-drawer; I could eat here every day. The ceiling thatched like a pagoda, everything hushed and rich.

Watch all the people coming in for their power lunches. The men in Armani suits, Hermes ties—even the ugly ones look good. I'll bring Troy here one day, in a suit like that.

The women all look like shit. Wrong clothes, bad makeup. If I had their money, I could do a whole lot better. I don't see any stars today.

Shirley Hudson comes in half an hour late—"Oh, I do apologize, the traffic was awful."

Gene's nervous; he jumps up, pulls out her chair.

It's his fault she left the agency. I have a sense about these things—who's going to be a star, who it's a waste of time handling. Shirley hadn't booked anything in a while, Gene wanted to get rid of her. "She's dead weight." I said, "You're wrong. Hang on to her," but of course he knew best. Then comes *Mango Tree* and *Sunset in Orange County* with featured roles, and now it's this big panic.

Can see Shirley's enjoying this lunch. Can't say I blame her. She knows Gene's here to squirm. Can't tell if she's going to come back to the agency or not.

We don't talk any business during the meal. Shirley's got some great stories about Tom Cruise. I like Shirley; she looks at me, not just Gene. She even talks in my direction occasionally. She orders the Napa Reserve Merlot, I can see Gene turning into a calculator: how much is this lunch going to cost him? I want to laugh.

The waiter brings the fortune cookies. Gene takes his and gives a big nervous laugh.

"Well, Shirley, what's my fortune? Are you coming back to us?"

Shirley leans forward in the chair, gives Gene a big smile.

"Well, we're certainly going to be seeing a lot of each other again."

Gene's all smiles now, too.

"Yes, I'll be in and out of your building all the time—I've decided to sign with the John Bradshaw Agency."

Good for you, old girl.

Gene's pissy for the rest of the day.

Three o'clock, the big new client comes in,

Enrico Morales. Handsome enough, but Troy leaves him in the dust.

I can hear Gene through the wall. He's pulling out all the stops.

Sitting at my desk, steaming; it's so goddam frustrating. Gene's charming this guy, and Troy's scrounging for work. But there's nothing I can do. Troy gets so angry about it—*you never do a fucking thing to help me,* but he doesn't understand, I can't. I told Gene about Troy, showed him his picture. When Gene and I got together, I said we'd broken up. I had to.

What does Troy think I'm screwing Gene for— his fat old ass? It's all for him, and once I'm part-ner we're home free.

Troy had a stunt near La Brea this morning. He had to crash into a truck. I put my hands over my face and couldn't look till it was over.

"That made me sick."

Troy shrugged. "All things considered, I was lucky to get it."

"All things considered" is something we don't talk about. It's that Troy can't fall, he never learned how. It sounds like a joke, a stuntman who can't fall, but it's not funny. It means he can't be choosy— he has to take whatever work he can get.

Afterward we have lunch at Marie Callender's. I like that place; it feels safe—the big booths, the old-fashioned ceiling fans—but Troy can't wait to get out of there.

"Come on, let's go to the tar pits now."

I can't stand the tar pits, all those animals who died, sucked down in the tar. We went up to the observation tower so Troy could get a better view.

He picked me up. "Look out, I'm going to throw you in!" I hit him; it wasn't funny.

Walking back, we saw this Psychic Cat. You give the guy a dollar, this little Siamese cat pushes a button, and a rolled-up fortune comes out of the machine. Troy blew thirteen dollars on it, till he got a fortune he liked.

My mother's cast is finally off, hallelujah; not that she isn't still complaining.

"The doctor set the bone wrong; it hurts worse than ever."

For now anyway I can tune her out; I can just go home.

Packed up my stuff in ten minutes. She followed me all the way to my car. Yakety-yak. "I thought you were going to stay another week. A good daughter would stay. The doctor says I shouldn't be left alone at my age."

Back at my place, home sweet home. Stand in the front hall, look around. It's all such crap; it's like an old lady's apartment. Even when I get away from my mother, I can't get away.

When I was little, I thought I would live in a castle someday. Everything in my room was going to be pink.

In September, when I'm partner, I'll do this whole place over, get new furniture, new everything, maybe even something pink.

Gene calls; he's horny, wants to see me. Asks if he can come over. I tell him no. He was here only once. He looked around, and I could see it on his face—he pitied me. He said it wasn't that; it was just my place reminded him of his brother's house in Palm Springs. Not a compliment; I know all about the loser brother.

Took him straight into the bedroom, made him forget all about where I live, but I'm never bringing him here again.

He's begging me now. "Come to the office. I'll tell Marilynn I have a meeting." I say I'm too tired. I'm not his slave; he doesn't own me.

Take a drive around the neighborhood. Go by Jessa's corner, give her a few groceries. She doesn't say thank you or even look up. What else is new.

Come home, clean up a little. My two best things: the pink silk Hermes scarf with the camellias Gene got me for Christmas, and the Sony TV he got me for my birthday.

Go over to the closet. Take out the scarf, drape it over the TV. Arrange them till they're perfect, like a little still-life painting.

Go to bed early. The minute the light's off, the couple upstairs start in. This time he's doing the yelling; she's just whimpering. Then, right on schedule, the hitting starts up. It used to bother me; it doesn't anymore. In five minutes, of course, I hear the creaking of the bed; they're at it for hours tonight.

I'm thinking it sounds kind of like a lullaby.

Pandora

I drove up Coldwater Canyon today; all the signs for open houses were out. For a moment I thought about stopping and going to see some, pretending I was back in the old days. But what would have been the point? All that ended more than two years ago—it's a past life now.

And yet I often find myself thinking about those days—maybe because they were so hopeful. It's very soothing to pretend I'm back in Palm Springs on that Sunday in May when it all started. It was a sort of quiet parenthesis, a last respite before everything began to go crazy.

The day hadn't started out very promisingly, I remember. I woke up, feeling depressed. It had been a bad week at work, and I had a paper due for class the following evening.

I thought I'd cheer myself up by going to see some open houses before I started on the assignment. I hadn't done that in a while. I looked in the paper for the new listings, and after breakfast I headed over to Las Palmas.

Half a block away from the house, I saw Fran Selwin, the broker from the condo on Stevens, standing out in front. I almost turned the car around—I didn't want her recognizing me. But she looked up, saw me, and waved.

I parked the car and walked toward the house. I thought I was finally in for it, the lecture about how I was wasting everyone's time, looking at houses I had no intention of ever buying.

But Fran was smiling.

"I'm glad you came today," she said. "It would have been hard getting in touch with you otherwise—you've given us so many different names and telephone numbers."

I stared down at the front steps, my face turning red.

"I don't know if you've heard," she went on, "but our office is about to open a new branch in Palm Desert. We're going to be needing a lot of new brokers, new recruits—and you were one of the first people who came to mind. You seem to have such an affinity for property. I don't know what your current job situation is, but have you ever considered a career in real estate?"

A career in real estate.

I shook my head. "No. I haven't."

"Well, think about the possibility."

She handed me a business card and smiled. "Although I know you have several of these already."

As I drove home, I kept saying the phrase over and over to myself. *A career in real estate. A career in real estate.* It was as if there had been a click in my mind—as if a switch I wasn't even aware of had been suddenly flipped to "on."

The moment I got home, I rushed over to the computer and logged on to the Internet. I found out what getting a real estate license would entail.

It wasn't all that daunting—in fact, it was far less so than the night courses I was already taking. All I'd need to do was sign up for a Real Estate Principles course, then take the California Salesperson test. If I passed that, I'd get a provisional license for eighteen months.

I started doing some excited calculations. If I got started on it right away, by August I could actually be a broker.

I sat back in my chair. It was wonderful, incredible to think of. In only a few months, I might be a real estate broker with Maryann Hill, with a permanent license and a business card of my own.

I got up from the chair and went into the den. Mama was sitting at the table, doing a jigsaw puzzle.

"Mama," I said, "this may sound crazy, but I think I'm going into real estate."

She carefully fit a piece of the sky into the puzzle; I wasn't sure she had even heard me.

"But you're training to be a pediatric nurse," she said at last.

I felt myself flushing. "I know. But I'm not sure I'd really be happy doing that. I'm pretty burned out with the whole medical field. I think I could do with a change, try something completely new."

"But why real estate?" Mama asked, puzzled. "You don't know anything about real estate."

It was embarrassing to confess that for the past few years, I had spent most of my Sunday afternoons visiting open houses.

"I see," she said. It never took Mama long to get over a surprise. "Well, in that case," she added, as if it was now the most obvious thing in the world, "you'd be an idiot not to do this."

Daddy's reaction was even better. When I told

him the news, he got out of bed and actually started pacing around the room, he was so excited.

"Did you know, Andy-Pandy, that before I started working at Sears, I went for a real estate license myself?"

I couldn't believe he'd never mentioned that before.

"It must be something in the genes," I told him. "Why didn't you become a broker?"

"My mother got sick, and it was something I just put off doing."

I felt the parallel between us, but I don't think Daddy saw it.

It ended in us all staying up till nearly midnight, trying to find Daddy's real estate license. It was like a party, or a scavenger hunt. We got some flashlights and started going through all the boxes in the garage. We never found the license, but we came upon a lot of other things—some of my old Halloween costumes, Daddy's letters to Mama when he was in Vietnam, the daisy afghan my grandmother crocheted, full of moth holes now.

The next day I called Fran Selvin.

"I've decided to try for my license," I told her.

"Wonderful," she said. "Keep us posted on how you're doing; we look forward to receiving your application."

"I just have one more question," I told her before we hung up. "You mentioned that the new office was in Palm Desert. Would the brokers need to live there?"

"I'm not sure what the policy on that would be," she said. "We haven't discussed it yet. It would certainly be more convenient, but I don't believe it's necessary."

I hung up the phone, wishing she hadn't given me that answer. A yes or no would have taken the responsibility away from me. But now the choice was mine. My own apartment in Palm Desert; there was nothing I would have loved more. But abandoning Mama and Daddy in order to get it—I didn't think I could do that.

Mama was in the kitchen, washing vegetables for dinner.

I said, "There's a good chance that if I take the real estate job, I'd have to move to Palm Desert."

She nodded. "Yes, that would certainly make sense."

I watched her hands, competent and wrinkled, scrubbing away at the carrots.

"But I couldn't do that to you and Daddy."

Mama put the carrot down and dried her hands deliberately.

"Of course you could, Pandora."

I felt tears, ridiculously, come to my eyes. I left the kitchen before she could see.

A few minutes later, she came into my room.

"I just had an idea. If you go to Palm Desert, that means Millie could come live here."

"Millie Sanders?" I asked in surprise.

"Yes. She called again this morning—poor thing, she's at such a loose end. Her children don't want her, and I think it would do her a lot of good to get out of Barstow. She could come here, stay in your room, help take care of Frank. It would be perfect."

She was smiling as if the matter was completely settled. I looked at her, so touched I didn't know what to say. I was sure the last thing in the world

Mama wanted was an old school chum moving in with her and Daddy and I knew that she was doing this all for my sake.

I got up and hugged her. "Thank you, Mama."

She went in to talk to Daddy, and put in a call to Millie. Within an hour, everything was fixed up.

The next day, I quit my classes at COD, and signed up to take the Real Estate Principles course. I found myself absolutely loving it—I could even understand the math. The California Salesperson test was still weeks away, but I had already begun studying. There would be a hundred and fifty questions, multiple choice, and I could get up to forty-five wrong and still pass—but I had no intention of getting anything less than a hundred percent right. I had never felt so motivated in my life.

Every weekend I drove out to Palm Desert, looking for a place to rent. I found some wonderful possibilities, and each evening, I'd go through decorating magazines, imagining how I was going to furnish my new apartment.

It was such a hopeful time, such a happy time. And then, in one day, everything in the world changed.

The morning of July nineteen, Mama, Daddy, and I were sitting in the kitchen, having breakfast. The phone rang.

"It's probably Millie," Mama said, as she got up to take the call.

We could tell instantly, from Mama's voice, from the way she was standing, that something terrible had happened. We watched her, frozen, waiting for some clue to what it was. Finally she said, "Thank you for letting us know, Marilynn," and Daddy gave a groan, as if a fatal arrow had found its spot in him.

Mama hung up the phone. "Gene's had a heart attack."

I left for L.A. that afternoon. I drove directly to the hospital, and they let me into Intensive Care. Uncle Gene was hooked up to all the monitors and machines, the ones I knew so well from the ER. It was awful to see them on him.

I spoke to the doctor. He said the tests were inconclusive. That at this point he couldn't tell whether Uncle Gene would pull through or not.

I sat with Aunt Marilynn in the waiting room all morning. I knew she didn't want me there, but I needed to stay.

"He's going to die," she kept saying. "I know he's going to die."

The nurse finally suggested she go home. I drove her back to the house. I asked if there was anything I could do, make any calls, get groceries, but she cut me off.

"How long do you plan on staying?"

I told her that if she wanted, I could move into a hotel.

"Of course not," she said. "You're my husband's niece—you can stay in the house; just don't expect me to cook for you or do any of your laundry."

Later that afternoon, before going back to the hospital, I drove to the Beverly Center and walked around the mall. I thought about old times, how Uncle Gene used to bring me there when I was a little girl. We'd always have lunch at the food court first, then he'd take me over to K-B Toys. I could see him then—laughing, eating pizza, being Uncle

Santa Claus—and superimposed over that the way he was now, lying gray in the hospital across the street, hooked up to machines.

The next morning, we waited outside the ICU for an hour; finally the doctor came out, smiling.

"Good news," he said. "The latest test shows a big improvement. I think we're officially in the clear now."

I ran out into the hall. I started to cry and couldn't stop. There was a pay phone on the floor, and I put in a call to Daddy. When I told him the news, he started crying, too.

Uncle Gene was moved out of Intensive Care that afternoon and into a room of his own. I sat down on the bed and held on to his hands. They felt substantial and warm. I gave them a squeeze, and he squeezed back.

"I love you, Andy-Pandy," he whispered.

That afternoon I stopped by the Warner Brothers store and bought a toy Tweety Bird. I thought it would be the perfect mascot for Uncle Gene until he came home.

The next morning, we went over to the hospital after breakfast. When we got to Uncle Gene's room, there was a nurse waiting for us outside the door.

"I'm so sorry," she said. "We tried calling you, but you'd already left."

She told us Uncle Gene had died that morning.

* * *

I drove Aunt Marilynn back to the house. I put her to bed, then I went into Uncle Gene's den and sat in his chair. I stayed there for an hour, staring at Tweety Bird and waiting for Uncle Gene to come in, so that I could give it to him.

Finally I called Daddy. The phone rang four times before he answered. He wasn't worried anymore, he had stopped expecting bad news. But when he heard my voice, he knew. He kept saying, "Little Eugene, little Eugene."

Mama got on the phone. She sounded brisk and cheerful.

"I'll take care of Daddy," she said. "We're proud of you for holding the fort."

I told her I wasn't holding anything. We didn't even have a chance.

I stayed with Aunt Marilynn for the rest of the day. I did what I could to help, calling people, making arrangements.

By the end of the afternoon, Aunt Marilynn had recovered enough to take over. Her relatives were there now, and she was holding court in the living room.

I kept going back into Uncle Gene's den. As long as I was there, I could pretend he was, too—that he had just gone into the kitchen to get himself a beer.

I could even hear his voice, if I listened very hard.

"So give me some news, Andy-Pandy; tell me what's been going on."

What's been going on? You died this morning, Uncle Gene, and I miss you more than I can believe.

I looked around at all the videos in the bookcases, the framed posters on the walls. I'd never really thought about it before, how similar our rooms were.

I went over to the bookcase and took down the signed still from *The Wizard of Oz*. When I was a little girl, it was my favorite thing in the world. I'd trace those signatures: Judy Garland, Ray Bolger, Bert Lahr, over and over with my finger. And I'd tease Uncle Gene—"When you die, can I have this picture? Promise, promise?"

But I never thought he would ever die.

I was packed, ready to go home, when Aunt Marilynn came into the room.

"I just spoke to the lawyer," she said. "He's coming over, and he wants to talk to you. I've no idea why."

I didn't know, either, but I didn't see why it couldn't be handled by phone. Irritated, I put my suitcase in the car and waited for the lawyer.

He turned out to be a young man, overeager and too full of sympathy. I tuned all his words of condolence right out—he had never even known Uncle Gene.

The three of us sat down at the dining room table, and he started to read the will. I tuned this out as well and stared out the window.

Suddenly I heard Aunt Marilynn gasp. She was staring at me; her lips were white.

"What?"

I stared back. I didn't know—I hadn't heard.

The lawyer had to repeat it three times before I understood.

"Your Uncle Gene left you his talent agency."

Aunt Marilynn rose from her chair. I thought she was going to hit me.

The lawyer looked a lot less sure of himself now; he started backpedaling, trying to calm her down. He might have overstated things . . . the agency wasn't strictly mine . . . I would only have access to the income; Aunt Marilynn would get eighty percent of the principal . . . no major decisions could be made without her consent. . . .

"But Mr. Brown did make it clear that he wanted his niece to run the business after his death. Unless she declines, and agrees to be bought out."

Aunt Marilynn looked down at me and spat the words. "Of course she'll decline."

I left the house. I went across the street, to the little park on Highland. *He left me the agency, left me the agency.* But the words made less and less sense with every repetition, like an audiotape running off its spool.

I sat down at a bench under an oak tree. I thought of the last time Uncle Gene had come to Palm Springs—the time we'd walked to the airport and he told me I should move to L.A. I wondered if that was when he had gotten the idea. Or had it been long before—all those years I was growing up, when he gave me the posters and videos, was he planning on giving me the agency as well?

The whole thing was completely ridiculous, insane. I guessed it was meant as a backhanded way to help Daddy and our family, but we didn't need any deus ex machina. We didn't need any agency, and we didn't need Uncle Gene judging us, saying we weren't good enough as we were.

But I knew I wasn't being fair. He had given it to me because he loved me. Because we were so alike.

And he probably knew it would kill Aunt Marilynn. I pictured the expression on her face, when the lawyer read the will—I began to get dizzy. I slid off the bench and lay back on the damp grass, staring up at the trees.

I got back to Palm Springs very late that night. Mama and Daddy were already asleep, and I didn't see them until the next morning.

Daddy seemed to have turned overnight into a very old man. He made me sit down on the bed and tell him everything about Uncle Gene; we went over those last days over and over again.

I put off saying anything about the agency, but at breakfast the subject of the will came up. Mama told me the lawyer had called, saying that Uncle Gene had left Daddy a cash legacy. She already had it earmarked for new treatments for Daddy and a salary for Millie. But I could see there was no joy in any of it. I know she was thinking the money had come too late. And Daddy couldn't bear to talk about it at all.

I waited until the meal was over.

"He left me something, too," I told them. "The agency."

I shouldn't have put it so bluntly. Daddy went white. I reminded myself of the lawyer, talking quickly, explaining that it wasn't left to me outright, that a big percentage of the money would still be Aunt Marilynn's, but that Uncle Gene had wanted me to take over the business.

"And what did you say?" Mama asked finally.

"That I'd think about it. But of course I'm going to say no. What do I know about running an agency?"

* * *

I felt too tired to do much that morning. After breakfast I went into my room and put *Singin' in the Rain* into the VCR; that was "our" movie, Uncle Gene's and mine. But I pulled it out after a few minutes—watching it made me too sad.

I went in to see Daddy. He was sitting up in bed, looking at one of the old scrapbooks we'd found in the garage. The glue had dried, and the photos kept fluttering out like dead leaves.

He smiled at me when I came in.

"Did I ever tell you how your mother and I met?"

Of course he had—a million times—but I sat on the edge of the bed and let him tell it again.

"Gene was with me that night. He thought Meg was absolutely terrific."

He looked so frail sitting there, tears leaking out of his eyes.

"We all looked up to Gene, even though he was the youngest. He had this way about him—we all knew he would do something, make something of himself. And he did. That agency of his—it's a big deal. Something he built from scratch. Something to be proud of."

I got up from the bed and walked over to the window.

"Do you want me to run it, Daddy?"

He sighed. "It's not my business, what you do. You do whatever you want to, Andy-Pandy."

I went into the kitchen and made myself some coffee. Daddy's words kept coming back—how the agency was something to be proud of, something Uncle Gene had loved and built from scratch.

Of course, I had no business running it; I had no credentials, no credibility. But Uncle Gene knew that, and he'd left it to me anyway. Surely he wouldn't have done that if he hadn't believed I could do the job. Maybe I was just being cowardly, turning the offer down so fast. Maybe it wouldn't be so difficult after all. Maybe I could learn to be an agent.

I pictured what would happen if I let the agency go. Aunt Marilynn would sell it in a minute, I knew that. There would be new owners—maybe it would become another talent agency or, more likely, a one-hour photo shop or skin-care salon. The first thing the new owners would do would be to change the name; and there wouldn't be a Gene Brown Agency anymore.

I went back in to Daddy.

"I've decided to give it a try," I said.

I could see from his face how happy I'd made him.

Later that morning I put in a call to Fran Selvin. I told her what had happened and explained that my plans for working in real estate needed to be postponed for a while. She told me she was sorry, but that she certainly understood, and wished me luck.

That night, I went over to Gary's apartment and told him the news. He was silent for a long time. "But I don't understand," he said at last. "If you sold your share in the agency, you'd have enough to buy a house—maybe even one in Palm Desert. And you'd be able to take care of your parents. I thought that was what you always wanted."

"It still is," I told him. "But my share in the agency

wouldn't come to nearly that much. This way, I'll be making more money—I'll be getting a salary and commissions."

"But do you really have to move to Los Angeles?" The expression on his face broke my heart.

"Gary, I need to do this—for so many reasons."

"And I'm obviously one of them," he said bitterly. "I guess you've made that clear enough."

I started toward him, but he backed off.

"I think you're being completely irresponsible," he said. "You just don't want to face your problems—you're running away from reality."

I finally left.

Mama was still up when I got home.

"Do you think I'm being irresponsible and selfish?" I asked her. "Do you think I'm running away from reality? If you do, just tell me, and I'll forget the whole thing. I'll sell my share and stay in Palm Springs."

Mama put her arms around me.

"Go, go, go," she whispered.

The next morning, I put in my first call to the agency. A woman answered the phone. I wasn't sure who she was, so I was careful not to say too much. I just told her I was Gene Brown's niece and that I was going to be overseeing things for a while.

There was a pause.

"Yes," she said. "The lawyer's explained everything to me. I'm Lori Max—I was your uncle's assistant."

She sounded pleasant enough.

"Do you have any idea when you'll be starting?"

"How about August first?"

"That'll be fine. But in the meantime there are

some checks here that need your signature. Why don't I FedEx them to you?"

She took down my address. "They'll be there by tomorrow."

I put down the phone, visualizing the FedEx truck on its way to me, with checks needing my signature.

There was no backing out now.

I went in to the den where Daddy was and sat down on the arm of his recliner.

"I'm twenty-four years old," I told him. "Nobody's going to take me seriously."

"Gene was only twenty-eight when he started the agency," Daddy reminded me. "Besides, remember where you'll be. Isn't twenty-four already over the hill in Hollywood?"

I laughed and told him he had a point.

Uncle Gene's memorial service was the following Tuesday. Daddy wasn't well enough to go, so I drove to L.A. alone.

The service was held at Forest Lawn, near Pasadena. I was gratified to see that the chapel was filled, although apart from Aunt Marilynn I didn't know anybody there. I looked around at the unfamiliar faces, wondering which of these people had been Uncle Gene's clients—my clients now.

I went up to Aunt Marilynn and touched her arm. She turned, but when she saw me standing there, she walked quickly away. I didn't go near her again.

I missed Uncle Gene so much—I kept wishing he were sitting in the seat beside me. He would have loved the funny stories people were telling about him; he would have been the best audience of all.

* * *

The day before I left for L.A. Millie arrived at
the house. I had always liked Millie—she used to
come over all the time when we lived in Barstow;
but I never thought she'd be moving into my room
one day.

That evening, Mama and Daddy gave me a
farewell party, a buffet dinner in the backyard. All
the neighbors came, and my friends from the ER.
Everyone said how happy they were for me, but
they said it like I was going off to war, or prison.

Toward the end of the party, Gary showed up. I
hadn't been sure if he would come or not. He
kissed me on the cheek. "I know you'll be a great
success," he said.

I felt tears coming. "Thank you."

I hugged him for a long time. I didn't say anything about when we would be seeing each other
again, and neither did he.

I arrived in Los Angeles late the following afternoon. It felt strange not to be taking the Highland
turnoff and heading straight over the mountain to
Uncle Gene's house.

I went into Hollywood and found a little hotel
there. The man at the desk told me it was just
down the street from where Janis Joplin died.

Outside my window was a view of Hollywood
Boulevard. I watched a homeless man come up
and urinate on the corner of the building. I didn't
remember Hollywood looking like this before.
When Uncle Gene showed me around it had always seemed so very glamorous.

* * *

I didn't get much sleep. I woke at six, had a bath, and ate breakfast at a little coffee shop across from the hotel. I watched two morning news shows, then gave up and just waited until it was time to leave for the agency.

At nine o'clock I set off down Sunset. When I reached West Hollywood, I drove around for a few minutes, getting a feel for the area. I liked it. It was elegant, but in a casual way, with older brick buildings and trendy shops and restaurants.

I found the agency and circled the building, not sure where to park. There was a lot in back, but the sign said it was for tenants only. I was just about to pull away when it hit me—I was a tenant now.

I drove in and parked the car. Then I sat there for ten minutes, too nervous to get out.

Finally I made myself walk up to the building. I tried the front door, but it was locked. I found the button for the Gene Brown Agency and pushed it. There was a loud buzz, and someone let me in.

I pulled open the heavy door and went into the hallway. It looked different than I remembered. There were big framed posters on the walls, of all the old movie stars. Those massive faces crowded together made the place seem a little haunted.

Lori Max was waiting for me. She didn't look at all the way I'd imagined from her voice on the phone. She was absolutely beautiful, arresting, with green eyes and long black hair, and she couldn't have been more than twenty-two or -three.

I told her how happy I was to meet her and thanked her for everything she had done in these last weeks.

"As you probably already guessed, I don't know anything about running an agency," I said. "I hope you're planning on staying."

She smiled. "I wouldn't dream of leaving."

She took me into the office. It also seemed different from what I remembered, but I told myself that I was seeing everything from a new perspective today. When I'd visited before, the agency had been Uncle Gene's; now it was mine.

The place seemed rather dark and cramped. There was a square entrance lobby, completely taken up with a reception desk, and behind it was my office. Lori worked out of a smaller office on the left, and on the right were two tiny rooms, more like closets. One was set up for a secretary, and the other was for filing and storage.

"Who else works in the building?" I asked.

Lori rattled off a list: there was a literary agency, a real estate office, and a few production companies.

"And of course, upstairs there's the John Bradshaw Agency. He's got the whole floor."

I remembered meeting John Bradshaw once. I must have been about eleven years old. A tall, elegant gray-haired man had come out of the elevator, and Uncle Gene introduced us.

"You've just met a legend," he told me afterward.

I went back to my office. It was still filled with all of Uncle Gene's belongings, his books, his scripts, his framed photographs. I sat down at the desk, imagining I felt his presence there.

"Well, let's get started," I told Lori. "Tell me all about the agency—what goes on here every day."

"Right," she said brightly, and began.

". . . We've got fifty clients, broad-spectrum, motion picture and TV; leading men, ingénues, comedians, stand-up, improv, commercial, stuntmen, kids. Nine-thirty in the evening, we start work; pull

down breakdowns from the Internet. Eight- thirty
A.M., get to the office. Pull clients' pictures from
files. Get on the phones. Call casting directors.
Wire pix to courier services. Set up auditions. Call
clients. Arrange bookings. Negotiate clients' fees.
Set up meetings with casting directors. Interview
new clients. Meet with studio representatives. Do
bookkeeping. Order supplies. We leave at six-thirty,
and start checking the Internet again for the next
day's breakdowns. . . ."

She smiled at me. "Did you get all that?"

I swallowed. "How on earth do you manage?"

"Oh, you get used to it."

All the time Lori had been talking, the phones
kept ringing, the answering machine kept picking
up, papers kept spurting out of the fax machine. I
thought of my life up until that day, slow-paced
and undemanding: playing Scrabble with Mama
and Daddy in the evenings, working in the garden,
asking ER patients for their insurance information. And now it had changed to this. Arrange
bookings. Negotiate clients' fees. Meet with studio
representatives.

"So," I said. "What do I do first?"

By the time I left the office at seven, I was completely exhausted, but buzzing with all that had
happened that day. I was far too jazzed to go back
to the hotel, so I drove around L.A. for a while, trying to get the layout of the city. Eventually I took a
wrong turn down Beverly Boulevard and ended up
by Cedars-Sinai Hospital, where Uncle Gene had
died.

I didn't feel like going on after that, so I drove
back to the hotel. On the way, I passed Gardner

Street. Lori had mentioned that she lived there. It was a pleasant area, if a little rundown, and I drove down the street for a few blocks, trying to guess which building might be hers.

Meeting Lori had certainly been one of the highlights of the day. I loved her energy and competence, and it was a tremendous relief to know she'd be staying on as my assistant.

I thought it was odd that Uncle Gene had never mentioned her.

Lori

I was all over the intercom the second she buzzed. The last thing I want is Emmett there first, getting his hands on her.

Got a look through the door. Tall, pukey-pale, long yellow hair. Little Miss Alice in Wonderland.

Couldn't believe it, couldn't fucking believe it. She's an imbecile; she's a moron. Showed her around the office. She doesn't know the first frigging thing.

It kills me. It's insane. How could Gene have done it, given the agency to her? Was he fucking her, his own niece? It's the only thing I can think of.

Don't blow it, don't let it show. Make myself charming, keep up the big smile. She says how relieved she is I'm staying on.

Like there's a chance in hell she could get rid of me.

"I'm surprised Uncle Gene never mentioned you," she tells me.

I only ran the fucking agency, and the bastard never mentioned my name.

"Tell me all about the agency. What goes on here every day?"

Let her have it with both barrels, the list goes on and on, she's taking notes, the phones keep ringing, the fax is going crazy. Think she's going to cry. Poor baby, my heart just bleeds.

Go back to Gene's office, only I guess it's the bitch's now. Pandora the Bitch Brown. Miss Pandora. Miss Pandora's Box. Miss Box.

On the shelf behind Gene's desk, the Oscar Mack Sennett gave him, a million years ago. Miss Box didn't even notice it was there. She doesn't deserve to have it; she's gotten everything else. Can't think why I haven't taken it before.

Poor little Miss Box needs a box to live in. She comes in this morning all shook up. She's staying at some crap hotel in Hollywood; last night there was a raid.

"Oh, Lori, it was awful—they were shooting."

I hope to God Troy had nothing to do with it.

Miss Box can't take it, she won't stay there another minute, she needs to find a place of her own.

Bingo. My first chance to get in with her, you better believe I jump at it.

"I might be able to do something, help you find a place."

She's all over me. "Oh, Lori, how wonderful. You're a lifesaver."

Ask what area she's thinking of—Santa Monica, Centinela, Culver City, West Hollywood? She says maybe West Hollywood, it's closest to the office.

"And I know that's where you live. In fact, I

drove down Gardner last night; I tried to guess which was your building."

She's smiling. She likes me. This is very, very good.

I tell her I've got a few friends with places to sublet.

"Would you mind talking to them about me?"

Say that I'll do her that favor.

Got to think this one out. There are a few oddballs I'd rather Miss Box didn't meet; she might hold it against me. Then I remember Suzanne. That could work out. Suzanne's pretty low-key; her place is okay. And we went to Sacred Heart together. How innocent; how sweet. All nice and cozy for Miss Box.

Call Suzanne. She says we can come over. Tell Miss Box I think I've found a place for her.

"Oh, Lori, you're wonderful."

We check out the apartment after work. Ask Miss Box if she wants to take separate cars. She says no, she'd rather go with me. We walk to my car, way down the street.

She's panting, I'm making her walk so fast.

"Shouldn't you be in the lot behind the building?"

I say it's for tenants only.

"But that's not fair. You work so hard—do you want me to give you my spot?"

"Oh no, I couldn't possibly take it."

I'm not wasting my favors on small potatoes like that.

My car's full of office work, cartons of files and breakdowns. "Sorry about the mess," I tell her.

She gets the point. She bites her lip, ashamed her own car's so clean.

"I guess mine will be looking like that in a few weeks."

Don't bother to say anything.

We drive to Suzanne's. All the way, it's yakety-yak, Miss Box asking questions. "What is Suzanne like? What is the apartment like? Why is she subletting?" I tell her Suzanne's moving to Seattle—her sister Ellen has the big C; the doctor gives her six months. Then think maybe Miss Box might want a year's lease, and change it to "or a year."

She starts in. "Oh, how awful. What kind of cancer? What treatment is she getting?" The phony little bitch, she's never even met them.

We get to Suzanne's, it's more of the same: "Lori told me about your sister. I'm so sorry. I used to work in an ER. If I can help in any way . . ."

Then comes the big surprise. The moment we stop talking about Ellen and get on to the apartment, Miss Box completely changes gears. No more sweetness and light. Suddenly she's all business.

"There are just a few things I was wondering about . . ." And she's on Suzanne's back for the next half hour. "What was the date of the last termite inspection? How long has it been since the elevator cables were checked? Has the fire marshal okayed the smoke detectors?"

She's crawling under the sink, she's looking for mold, she's running the taps in the shower, she's checking the water pressure.

Our mouths are hanging open.

Suzanne asks, "Are you in real estate or something?"

Miss Box nods. "Sort of. I was just about to get my license when Uncle Gene died and left me the agency. Real estate's what I really love," she tells us with a sigh. "I hated to give it up."

Feel like my face is on fire. Go into the bathroom. Grab on to the goddam towel bar, squeeze it till I can barely move my hand. Fuck him, fuck the slimy bastard. He gave her the agency and she didn't even want it.

She's dicking around for an hour. She looks at every drawer and dishtowel. Finally she ends up taking the apartment.

She flits around. "My first place in L.A.; I'm so excited! I feel like celebrating. Why don't we all go out to dinner—my treat."

Suzanne doesn't want to be with Little Miss Sunshine; she says she already has plans.

So it's just Miss Box and me.

You'd think she'd show her appreciation, take me somewhere nice, but, no, we end up at El Coyote.

God, I hate the place; it depresses the hell out of me. Christmas decorations from 1902, fat old waitresses in costume, food lying in grease.

"I love this restaurant," Miss Box says. "When I was a little girl, every time I came to visit L.A., this was where Uncle Gene used to bring me."

It kills me. The bastard never took me out anywhere in his life, not even on my birthday. Not to El fucking Coyote or anywhere else.

The server's hot. His name's Grant. Good body, but not as good as Troy's.

Miss Box busy being the perfect little hostess. All during dinner, I'm getting the talk-show act. Where did I grow up? What was my childhood like? Did I always want to be in the agency business? Did I have a boyfriend?

Her nerve burns me up.

Talked a lot of shit; didn't tell her anything. I may work for her, but it's nobody's business, nobody's, about my childhood or about Troy.

Then she starts in telling me her life story, whether I like it or not. Heard all about the sick dad, the house on the wrong side of the tracks. God, no wonder Gene couldn't stand to visit.

She pays for dinner. We get into the car. She turns to me.

"Lori, I'd like to give you a finder's fee for getting me that apartment."

I pour it on thick. "No, no, don't even think about it; it was a pleasure."

She leans over, kisses me on the cheek. "Oh, Lori, I was so afraid that with Uncle Gene gone, I wouldn't be happy in L.A. But you've been so friendly and helpful—and I know everything's going to be fine."

I drive her back to her place. This finder's fee business. I'll get it on the other end, from Suzanne.

Miss Box reminds me of Gene. There's that hole, always needing to be filled—sex for him, love for her.

"What are your plans this weekend?" she asks me.

That was the same thing he asked, the day it all got started between us. "What are your plans this weekend?"

"Nothing much," I told him.

"Me, neither." He gave a little laugh, a little laugh

like what he was saying wasn't really being said, it could all be taken as a joke. "My wife . . . is away."

And here's Miss Box, coming at me with those exact words. "What are your plans this weekend?"

No sex this time, at least. The trick here is to dig in, make myself indispensable, be the one she can't do without.

Help her move in to Suzanne's apartment. Her stuff is shit—flowered Palm Springs dreck. No decent jewelry, mainly turquoise junk. Most of the boxes are full of movie videos. She's unpacking them like they're gold bricks.

Seems that dear old Uncle Gene gave them to her. Got to hear all about it, how he taught her so much, how he was the big influence in her life, yakety-yak.

"Every time he came to visit, he'd choose a video that was special to him, and we'd watch it together."

Unbelievable crap.

Still, it gets me. If he loved movies so fucking much, why didn't he ever, ever once take me to see one?

Got home late. A smell like something died coming from behind the cabinet. Called the landlord—the fat ass says it's not his responsibility. I hate this place.

Took the Hermes scarf and arranged it over the TV again. Gene gave me presents, too, Miss Box; better things than videos. The scarf's got a moth hole, damn.

* * *

"Lori, we need a break; we've been working too hard. Let's go out for lunch—my treat."

We run into Lord Bradshaw himself coming down the stairs. Miss Box treats him to the big cheerleader smile; he gives her a snooty nod, walks away.

"That was John Bradshaw, wasn't it?"

"Yes."

"I met him once when I was a little girl—Uncle Gene introduced us. He's not very friendly, is he?"

"He doesn't have to be. He's Hollywood royalty."

"Still. We work in the same building—he could at least have said hello."

"He's like that," I tell her. "He keeps to himself."

"But I don't understand . . . Uncle Gene always said . . . I thought they were good friends."

I almost laugh.

"Not really," I say.

Miss Box looks miffed that someone would not want to be friends with precious Uncle Gene. She's quiet for a while. I can't tell what's on her mind.

"He's handsome for an older man, though, don't you think?"

Tell her I hadn't really thought about it.

"But I can't believe the way he snubbed us—there's absolutely no excuse."

So Miss Box has a little thing for John Bradshaw, does she?

Go over to Troy's. Haven't seen him in a few days; he's been on location in New Mexico. Very happy reunion. He brought me back a turquoise necklace. It's crap, but he thought of me. I'll wear it.

His movie, *Caravan Man,* is out. Went to Westwood to see the late show. The movie was shit, but
Troy looked hot. He played an Arab.

Two shots of him in the battle scene; then
there's a close-up of him getting whacked, slashed
right through the chest. He tricked me, he promised he didn't get whacked in this movie. I said
he was a bastard for not telling me. He just
laughed. "If I had told you, you never would have
gone to see it."

He's got a tough stunt this week: he burns up in a
car. I didn't want to hear about it, covered my ears.
He laughed, pulled my hands down, kept on talking.

I know he has to do it, it's his job—but I keep
thinking one day I'm going to get this call.

Came back to my place. He spent the night.
Another happy reunion. Hope the couple upstairs
heard it loud and clear.

Later, we're in bed, I'm nearly asleep, and suddenly he says, "So what does the new boss lady look
like?"

That woke me right up. He doesn't usually go
for blondes, but why take chances. Tell him Miss
Box is nothing special, not his type.

"You shouldn't keep calling her Miss Box. It
might slip out one day when you're talking to her."

I've had enough of this. Tell Troy I can call her
any fucking thing I want. Then I reach out my
hand, grab him, take Miss Box right off his mind.

She's got some instinct for the work, I have to
give her that. It's a good thing; I don't want the
agency run into the ground. Tricky balance here. I

keep myself indispensable, but teach her enough
not to fall on her ass, fuck up the business. So far
she's invited me everywhere, to all the meetings,
the lunches. She doesn't know any better.

I just want to make sure it stays that way, keep
her thinking "partner," not "assistant."

She's okay with the clients, too. Better than Gene.
She's bringing them in, introducing herself. She
wants me at all the meetings. "You know Lori Max,
don't you? I couldn't keep this agency running without her."

So true, Miss Box.

Negotiating the fees for Enrico Morales's Cool
Whip contract.

"Oh, Lori, I've got to call the ad agency; I've
never done anything like this before. Would you
stay in the room, make sure I don't screw it up?"

She does okay. Maybe it's all that real estate
training. Enrico gets the pay hike; she hangs up.

"Did I do all right? Would Uncle Gene have ap-
proved?"

Don't want her to get too sure of herself; don't
want her to forget she can't do it without me.

"You did great—just great." Say it with just
enough hesitation to keep her guessing.

Friday, as usual, "What are you doing tonight,
Lori?"

I had plans with Troy, he canceled on me. I'm
on my own. Tell Miss Box I'll probably go to a new
club that opened on Melrose, I can see she's dying
to come. Say I'll take her along if she wants.

"I'd love it! We'll have such a good time!"

* * *

Pick her up at her place at seven. She's changed the apartment around, moved some of Suzanne's furniture. It looks better, I have to say. She's gotten all dressed up—short black skirt, curly hair.

We take her Buick. Crap car, but it's spotless; she must clean it every morning. There's even one of those air-freshener trees.

And of course she's the perfect little driver, creeping down Melrose, stopping at all the yellows.

The club's pretty high-juice. Shakes your skin off the bone. Guys coming up all night. We do a lot of dancing. Some asshole says, "You two look like Thunder and Lightning." I'm thunder, get it? Because I'm dark. She's lightning, with her blond hair. Stupid line, but Miss Box keeps harping on it.

"Oh, Lori, he's got it just right—thunder and lightning, that's us. A killer team."

Or so you think, Miss Box.

She dances with a lot of guys. One asks for her phone number. She makes up something and gives it to him.

"My favorite method," she tells me after he goes.

"You didn't think he was cute?"

"He was okay. I'm just not in the market."

She's never mentioned a boyfriend. Shit. This could complicate things.

"You're involved with someone?"

"No, no, nothing like that. I just need to put all my energies into the agency for now." She gives a little laugh. "But of course if someone fantastic were to come along . . ."

Could she be thinking about John Bradshaw, I wonder.

All of a sudden she gives me a look.

"Lori, is it okay if I ask you something?"

I don't say anything; she asks anyway.

"I've been wondering. Emmett, from upstairs, said something the other day. It made me think that maybe you and Uncle Gene . . ."

Draw myself up like ice. She backs down in a second.

"I'm so sorry. It was stupid of me. It must be all the wine."

I don't say anything, she keeps on groveling.

I'll kill that bitch, Emmett.

Two o'clock, I'm getting tired, I say we should leave.

"This was so much fun, Lori—I'd love to do it again."

Tell her there's another club just opened up in Santa Monica, but it's hard to get into.

"Couldn't we try to go? Maybe next Friday night?"

Tell her I'll see. We go back to her place, she's still Miss Perfect Driver, even with all the shots. I get out of the car last, steal the air-freshener tree.

AIDS walk today. Met up at Gower, in front of the studio. The parking lot reeking from all the do-gooders.

Saw Giles from CBS there, down to about ninety pounds. Waved at him, but didn't go over.

Started walking down Beverly. Thought about Scott and Arthur, and how we used to do this every year. God, I miss them—the best friends ever. Hard

to believe Scott's been dead four years, Arthur nearly six. They never even got to meet Troy. Arthur
would have gone bananas over him, *I'm so jealous
of you, bitch,* but Scott, I don't know. I'm not sure if
he would have liked Troy or not. And Miss Box—
what would they have said about Miss Box?

We would have laughed a lot, that's for sure.

Got to Fairfax and decided to stop walking.
Didn't feel like going on anymore. It's not like anyone is sponsoring me, anyway.

We're filing in the front office. The buzzer rings.
"It's Marilynn Brown."

Miss Box jumps back with a gasp. This ought to
be interesting.

The door opens. Marilynn comes in; at last I get
to see what she looks like.

No wonder Gene screwed me every chance he
got. She looks like a praying mantis.

I think she's going to send me away, say she
wants to be alone with Miss Box, but I'm invisible
to the fucking bitch.

"This ridiculous will . . . if you mismanage this
agency . . . if you sabotage my security . . . I'm thinking of hiring an attorney." Yakety-yakety-yak.

Miss Box fluttering around. "Aunt Marilynn, I
understand how you feel, but I'm not sabotaging
anything. I'm doing everything I can to build this
agency. We haven't lost a single client. In fact, I've
been renegotiating some contracts. . . ."

Marilynn's mouth is a flatliner. "Well, we'll see
what happens." She looks around. "You've certainly managed to turn this place into a pigsty in
record time, haven't you?"

She leaves. Miss Box's face is bright pink.

"Sorry, Lori."

"Don't worry about it, we all have weird relatives."

She's pacing around.

"It's just . . . well, Uncle Gene always made such a fuss over me . . . And then leaving me the agency . . ."

Say I understand completely.

She bites her lip. "You don't think I'm mismanaging everything, do you? Tell me honestly—am I doing okay?"

Think fast here. The last thing I want is Marilynn getting her hands on the agency, selling it; I'd be out on my ass. My best chance, it's still with Miss Box. Give her the big smile.

"You're doing great. Honestly, you couldn't be doing better."

Thanksgiving next week. My mother's all over me. "Lori, what time are you coming for dinner? I need you to make the yams and the string beans, and don't burn them like you did last year."

Don't think I can handle it.

Could go to Grandma's instead—old people dribbling giblet gravy down their chins. I don't think so.

Troy's going away. He's visiting some friends in Denver. I didn't get asked to come with him. That pisses me off, the way he never thinks to invite me.

Miss Box all excited, she's going home for Thanksgiving. "Oh, Lori, I can't wait!" Asks me what I'm doing. I tell her I don't know yet. She gets this look in her eyes; she comes back a few minutes later.

"It's all set, Lori; you're coming down to Palm Springs with me."

Oh no I'm not, I couldn't take Miss Box for four straight days. Tell her thanks, but it would be too much of an imposition.

"Don't be silly," she says. "You've been so incredibly sweet; it's the least I can do. And my parents are dying to meet you."

Give it some more thought. It could be interesting. Meeting the loser brother and the crazy-ass wife. God, wouldn't Gene hate that. Yes, I definitely think I'll go. Better than my other options, anyway.

Miss Box asks if I've ever been to Palm Springs. I tell her, "No, but I've always wanted to go." *No, I've managed to keep away,* would be the truth.

Close down the office early Wednesday, stop by Sweet Lady Jane's, get a pumpkin pie. I don't know what crap they'll be feeding me; at least I'll have that.

Freaked out by the drive. Past San Bernardino there's nothing but dead little towns. Miss Box chattering away. "Don't you feel the peace? Don't you feel all your problems just dropping away?"

She smiles over at me. "I'm so glad you came. We're going to have so much fun."

We get to the desert. It's unbelievably creepy. We pass a diner; there are life-size dinosaur statues in back, and all the mountains are covered with windmills. We pass some designer outlet stores, I think maybe there's some hope. But, "Oh, no," says Miss Box. "We can do that sort of thing in L.A."

Get to Palm Springs. Ticky-tacky little town—

looks like a thrown-out Christmas card. We pull up to her house. It's trailer trash. Gene left his agency to trailer trash.

An old guy comes shuffling out. "Lori, this is my daddy!"

Watch Miss Box turn back into a two-year-old. She pops out of the car. Big hugs for daddy. Poor old guy's on his last legs—you can smell it on him.

The house is decorated for Thanksgiving, it looks like a five-and-dime: paper turkeys and pilgrims. I meet the mother, dressed like shit, made up like a clown. And Millie, this old woman who lives with them.

Miss Box takes me to my room, Day-Glo orange bedspread, shag rug, I'm in a seventies time warp. She's embarrassed. "My mother's always liked bright colors."

Looks like Miss Box and I will be shacking up there together—Millie's taken her old room.

Tried calling Troy, but no answer. He's probably left for Denver already. Don't know how I'm going to get through this weekend.

I'm the big topic of conversation at dinner. Mrs. Box wants to hear about the agency. Mr. Box wants to hear about Gene.

"My brother was a wonderful man," he tells me.

What he was, was a cheater and a worm. But I keep the old guy happy. "Oh, yes, he was incredible; it was a real privilege to have worked for him."

Catch an odd look from the mother. Get the feeling she wasn't so hypnotized; she knew what was what with dear old Gene.

After dinner it's speech time. The dad starts in.

"Pandora's told us how wonderful you've been to her, Lori. I just want to say how much we appreciate it."

It's Mrs. Box's turn. "Frank's right, dear. She could never run the agency without you."

I say, "Oh, no, your daughter's a natural; she would have done just fine in the business on her own."

They both start nodding like it's true; idiots.

Can't get to sleep in that crap room. Keep thinking about Troy, what he's doing in Denver.

Get up to pee. Pass this wicker cabinet in the hallway, there's a plastic figurine on the shelf, a woman wearing a blue dress.

I'm staring at it, I've seen it before. I can't remember where, though. It's driving me crazy. Then I think *Disneyland.*

It was my first time. I was five. My father took me on the Snow White ride. All the while he's got his hand on my thigh; he's patting me. *Don't worry, baby, I'll keep you safe. I won't let the witch hurt you.*

Later we go in the gift shop. *You can have a present, Lori. You can have a present for being such a good girl.*

I find what I want right away. It's this figurine, this woman with long hair and a blue dress. I just started Sacred Heart, I think it's a statue of Our Lady. In school she looks like a bitch, but here she's got a nice face, I wouldn't mind praying to her.

I tell my father, *I want this statue of Our Lady.*

He laughs at me. *That's not Our Lady, that's the Blue Fairy, Our Lady isn't at Disneyland.*

I tell him Our Lady is everywhere, of course it's her, look at the blue dress. People hear us. They're laughing. My father starts getting angry. *That's enough, Lori. Say it's the Blue Fairy, or I won't buy it for you.*

I won't say it's the Blue Fairy. He doesn't buy it.

The figurine's a piece of crap, not worth stealing, but I take it anyway.

The weekend goes on forever, Miss Box won't let me alone for a second. It's, "Oh, Lori, let me show you this"; "Oh, Lori, now it's time to do that." She drags me bird-watching; I get shown the Indian reservation; I have to climb up to the fucking waterfall.

"Now we're going to go down Palm Canyon Drive—I know you'll love it." Unbelievably crappy street. She drags me into every gift shop. End up buying some postcards for Grandma—she used to like coming to Palm Springs. Miss Box so happy I got the postcards; it means I'm having a great time.

Saturday we go on the aerial tram to the top of the mountain. That I actually like. It's snowing up there, quiet. Walk down a path into this park with pine trees, no one else around.

But the minute we're back down in Palm Springs, she's off and running again.

Sunday morning, we're going into Starbucks, I see a guy crossing the street. Good body, great ass. He's staring at Miss Box. I can see something's up.

He follows us into Starbucks. He's not bad-

looking. Dark hair, gray eyes, Indian blood maybe.
Hard to tell how old he is, twenty-five maybe. A
baby face, but smart eyes.

He says, "Hi."

Miss Box jumps a foot.

"Oh, hi, Gary." She hugs the guy. "It's good to
see you. I'm sorry we haven't had a chance to drop
by—it's been a crazy weekend." She turns to me.
"This is my assistant, Lori Max. Lori, this is Gary
Ortiz."

We all stare at each other in silence. Wonder
what's going on here.

Finally it's Sunday afternoon, the weekend's
over; just get me home. We leave at two, big hugs
for Mr. and Mrs. Box. Hold my breath when I hug
the dad. I don't want that stink of death in my
nose all day.

Miss Box quiet on the drive back to L.A.
Something's on her mind.

"Lori," she says, "I've been wanting to ask you;
Uncle Gene, he never promised you anything, did
he? I mean, about the agency?"

I think real hard about what to answer. I wonder
what that bitch, Emmett, might have said. I never
told him anything, but people guess.

This is a trick question here. If I say yes, she
might do something about it, she's so crazy about
me. But she also might get scared, start backing
off.

Finally decide it's too early to make any move.
Give her the big smile. "Oh, no, he never promised
me anything; I don't know what you mean."

Bingo. Guessed right. I can see her shoulders go

down. "Oh, I'm so glad," she says. "I would hate to
think that he had misled you in any way."

No, you're glad, Miss Box, because you think
you don't have to fight me for the agency.

Get home, go over to my mother's. She asks
about Palm Springs; I tell her it was crap. She asks
if I bought anything; I say there was nothing to
buy, I only got a couple of postcards for Grandma.
She says, "Why didn't you buy any for me? Grandma's not the only one who likes postcards."

She told me I went to Palm Springs when I was a
little girl, I say I don't remember it. "Of course you
remember. The motel we stayed at had a swing set
in back; you wouldn't leave it. Your father spent all
day swinging you—how could you not remember?"

I don't remember.

Can't stand the thought, my father's hands
pushing me on the swings, under the palm trees.

Go down Sunset to see how Jessa's doing. She
isn't at her corner. Some of the others are there,
strung out or sleeping. Ask around, where's Jessa?
Someone says they saw an ambulance going down
Sunset, but it was farther east.

Keep on walking. A few blocks down, I see Jessa
pushing her cart. Run up to her. Give her hell for
not being on her corner. She says she can move if
she wants to, same as anybody. Then she starts
laughing, like it's all some big joke on me.

I don't think it's so funny. I don't like it when
people move around.

Pull out a ten, give it to her. She says she doesn't

want it, it's too much, she wouldn't know what to do with it. Give her a five; she takes that. Tell her I have a new shopping bag for her—it's from some store in Palm Springs, purple with green letters. She says she doesn't want that, either, she has enough bags for now. She doesn't want my money, she doesn't want my shopping bag. Shit.

And Troy's back from Denver, but he hasn't called. Big surprise.

Gary

After Pandora left for Los Angeles, it was as if a hole had been torn from the center of my life. Even though we hadn't really been together for months now, it was unreal and depressing having her actually gone. I'd go on little pilgrimages, visiting the places that reminded me of her: Katherine Finchy Middle School, Eisenhower Hospital, the waterfall up at Taquitz. I kept imagining that I'd look up and there she would be, sitting in the park or hiking down by the canyon. Sometimes I'd go out to Dream Homes and ride my motorcycle up and down her street. It was easiest to imagine her there, standing by the chain-link fence, watching the planes take off.

From time to time, I'd drop by her house to see how her parents were getting along. Mrs. Brown was fine, as flamboyant as ever. An old friend of hers, a woman named Millie, was living with them now, and she seemed to be thriving on the company. I was concerned about Mr. Brown, though— he had lost a lot of weight and was having trouble getting from room to room.

But whenever I came over, he still managed to beat the pants off me at Parcheesi.

Our big topic of conversation was always Pandora. Her parents said she was working hard, trying to learn the agency business. There was a girl in the office, some sort of assistant, who had been very helpful; she had found Pandora an apartment and was showing her around town.

I was glad to hear that—I didn't like the idea of Pandora being lonely. But at the same time, I would have liked to have been involved myself, helping her move into the office and the new apartment.

But Pandora didn't seem to want me in her life at the moment, not even as a friend. I hadn't heard anything at all from her since she'd moved to L.A. I knew from her parents that she'd visited Palm Springs on several weekends, but she never called me then, either. In a way, it didn't come as a surprise, but it still hurt.

The last time I'd seen her was the night of her farewell party. I had kissed her on the cheek and wished her luck. After she left for L.A. I tried to imagine what magic phrase I could have used, what combination of words would have brought us back together again. But I was beginning to understand that maybe there was no such phrase, no such words.

My only choice now seemed to be to give her space. I didn't call or e-mail; I didn't try to see her when she visited Palm Springs. And as the weeks went by with no contact between us, I found that she had begun to live in a sort of limbo in my mind. I no longer pictured her in Palm Springs, but I had nothing to replace those images with.

Strange as it may sound, I'd never been to L.A. A lot of people in the desert haven't. We get the general idea of the place from movies and TV shows, and we're just not tempted to visit in person. So every time I tried to visualize Pandora there, I drew a blank. She had become a person in the abstract, leading a life I couldn't even imagine, in a city I didn't know.

But one day, about six weeks after she left, I found myself going there.

It started off as a completely normal Sunday. I got up early, read the paper, and took my bike out to the Cut-out. For once, though, the dune didn't do anything for me. I felt as if I were watching myself down the wrong end of a telescope, riding up the mountain on my foolish, noisy little machine, whole years of my life evaporated into sand.

I gave up on the dunes and started down Highway 111. When I reached Idyllwild, I figured I might as well visit my friend Bobby, so I drove to his apartment, but he wasn't home. And then, instead of turning back to Palm Springs, I just kept heading west. When the turnoff for the 10 freeway came up, I found myself taking it—I'm not sure even then that I let myself guess where I was headed.

I passed Beaumont and Banning, San Bernardino. At noon I stopped at Montclair for gas and some lunch. Then the 101 freeway came up, and I began seeing signs for downtown Los Angeles.

My first impression of L.A. was that it was way too big. Since I didn't have any idea where I was going, I just kept riding around, thinking I'd eventually get the feel of the place. But that turned out to be impossible—every block I went down, the whole atmosphere changed. One minute it was old residential buildings, the next minute burned-out lots, the next, modern high-rises.

Mrs. Brown had mentioned the name of the street Pandora lived on—something like Sweet or Goodland; I couldn't remember exactly. It was somewhere in Hollywood, that was all I knew.

I stopped and asked a taxi driver where Hollywood was. He rolled his eyes as he gave me directions—he must have thought I was out looking for movie stars.

When I got to Hollywood, I couldn't believe that this was the place people from all over the world came to see. It was the sleaziest neighborhood I'd ever been in: piles of garbage, boarded-up buildings, homeless people, XXX-rated stores on every block. We wouldn't have allowed any of that in Palm Springs.

I ended up at Mann's Chinese Theatre, where all the old movie stars put their footprints in the cement. I figured I might as well stop there for a few minutes and look around. None of the names meant much to me until I came to the cement block with Marilyn Monroe's little high-heeled footprints in it. She was always a favorite of mine.

As I got back on my bike, I remembered: Sweetser, that was it, the name of Pandora's street. I pulled into a gas station, and they let me borrow their *Thomas* guide, but I couldn't find the listing. I asked the attendant if he'd heard of the street, and he looked at me like I was the hick of all time. It turned out that it was in West Hollywood, not Hollywood, and that it was Sweetzer, spelled with a z.

I started toward it. I told myself I wouldn't actually visit Pandora—I would just ride over to Sweetzer and see what it was like.

I found the street and drove up and down, block after block. It was a pleasant older area, with buildings of brick and whitewash. A little past their prime, some of the houses, but friendly and decent—you could actually imagine people living there. But I didn't see Pandora.

And suddenly I needed to. I missed her so acutely that I began to ache. All my pride drained right away. I couldn't be this close without visiting her.

I called Mrs. Brown on my cell phone and asked for Pandora's address. I didn't say where I was calling from. She gave me the address, and I set off. But the closer I got to Pandora's block the slower I started driving.

When we were kids, I'd often done this kind of thing, riding by her house, hoping to bump into her "by accident." If she caught me, it was okay—I could always say I was there to see the planes taking off. But now I didn't have any excuse. I couldn't pretend to be in L.A. for any reason other than the truth.

I found the building and parked my bike by the curb. I waited a few minutes, hoping Pandora would come out and that our meeting could seem a little more casual. But no one left the building, and I had no choice but to go up to the front door.

The panel was filled with names and buzzers. One little tag said #3—P. BROWN and I stared at it. I had seen "P. Brown" so many times in my life—on the top of sixth-grade spelling papers, on the return address labels of Christmas cards, printed in indelible ink on the necks of high school gym tunics. Seeing that familiar name now, in these unfamiliar circumstances, made me want to cry.

I stood there for a long time, but I couldn't get

myself to press the button. What if Pandora was there? What would I say, what excuse could I give for showing up like this?

I ended up walking away. I promised myself I'd come back again soon, only next time I'd do it properly. I'd call Pandora in advance, saying I needed to be in L.A. to buy some software, and I'd invite her out to lunch or a movie. With that resolve in my mind, I was able to get back on my bike and head back to Palm Springs. By the time I reached San Bernardino, though, the whole idea seemed pointless, and I knew I would never come to L.A. again.

After that day, I finally accepted the fact that Pandora had really gone away and wasn't coming back. I started concentrating on my own life again, making some changes, and moving ahead. I even went out on a few dates, mainly with girls Bobby or Tom set me up with, but nothing really took. I also busied myself with my work, believing that there, at least, was one area of my life where I had some control.

Sometimes, though, in spite of everything, I'd find myself thinking about Pandora. I kept having a dream that I was in a mall, going down an escalator; next to me, on the escalator going up, I'd catch sight of her. I'd wave and call out, but she never heard me. I didn't need a psychologist to explain that dream—nor all the ones where Pandora and I were together by the creek, making love.

Her birthday was October twenty-five. I wanted to acknowledge it in some way, without going overboard. I ended up buying her a little beavertail cactus; I boxed it up and sent it along with a note that said, "In case you get homesick." Pandora wrote back, saying how much she enjoyed the gift. She didn't mention if she was homesick or not.

Occasionally I still went over to her house and visited with her parents. Every time I came there was a new story about a client Pandora had gotten or a deal she had made. Her parents said she loved the agency and loved L.A. I kept telling myself I was happy for her.

I knew Pandora would be coming home for Thanksgiving weekend, and I decided to go see her then. I figured I could drop by casually in the afternoon and visit the whole family; that way it wouldn't be too awkward.

Janine and my two-year-old nephew were visiting from Dallas, so I spent the morning with them, enjoying being a proud uncle as I wheeled Eli through the neighborhood in his stroller. Then, as soon as Thanksgiving dinner was over, I went over to Chia Place.

Mrs. Brown told me I had just missed Pandora.

"She went out about fifteen minutes ago, with her friend from the office. I'm sure they'll be back soon. Why don't you stay and have a piece of pumpkin pie?"

But I said no. I'd waited so long to see Pandora again, and this wasn't the way I'd envisioned the scene.

"That's all right," I said. "Just tell her I dropped by."

I stayed at home that evening, hoping there would be a call, but there wasn't.

* * *

I did end up seeing Pandora later that weekend, however. Sunday morning I was walking down Palm Canyon Drive to get a newspaper and there she was, crossing the street in front of Starbucks.

She had changed a lot since she'd been gone. She had cut her hair almost up to her shoulders and put in darker highlights. It was striking, but it didn't look like Pandora's hair anymore. And I didn't recognize any of the clothes she was wearing—she must have done a lot of shopping in L.A. She looked almost like a tourist now, a rich tourist slumming in our little town.

Her friend from the office was there as well. I guess most people would have called her beautiful, but I didn't care for her looks. There was nothing natural about them; the makeup, the hairstyle, the way she walked all seemed completely thought out, done for effect. And she was a shade too sure of herself for my taste. Every guy's eye was on her, and she knew it.

I followed the two of them into Starbucks. Pandora didn't see me, but I could feel the friend sizing me up.

I said, "Hi."

Pandora jumped when she heard my voice.

"Oh, hi, Gary," she said, and gave me a quick little hug. "It's good to see you." She sounded flustered.

She introduced her friend, and then no one seemed to know quite what to say.

I finally started talking about her parents, telling Pandora that I dropped by occasionally, to keep an eye on them.

"I know." She smiled at me. "They're always so pleased when you come over."

She suddenly sounded like her old self again.

The counterman called out an order number.

"That's ours," Pandora said. There was another embarrassed silence. "Won't you join us?" she asked finally. "I'll split my cappuccino with you."

"No, thanks," I told her.

"Well . . ." she said.

I kissed her on the cheek and left. Then I went home, sat down on the sofa, and just stared at the floor for a while.

Around three o'clock, the phone rang. It was my friend Tom, inviting me to dinner that night. His new girlfriend, Helene, was also coming over, and he wanted me to meet her. I told him I'd be there.

I hung up the phone with a feeling of relief. I had something to look forward to now, something to take my mind off Pandora Brown.

The evening started off well. I liked Helene a lot. She was soft-spoken and shy, with the kind of low-key prettiness that grows on you. And I got a huge kick out of the way she kept looking at Tom. No mortal man, especially my old pal Tommy, deserves that much adoration.

When dinner was over, Tom turned to me with a grin.

"We've got some news. Helene and I are getting married on New Year's Day. And we want you to be best man."

He went on with the details, but I was so stunned that I had a hard time taking them in. It didn't seem possible that my old nursery-school buddy was actually getting married. I managed to sound as pleased for Tom as I could, but then he said something about moving to Albuquerque in April.

"Albuquerque!" I yelped.

"Helene's from there, and she'd like to be closer to her family."

I nodded, but I hated the whole idea. It seemed to be becoming a regular trend in my life these days—all the people who meant the most to me moving on.

As I drove back home after dinner, I started to feel sorrier for myself with every block that passed. Thinking over the evening, remembering the way Tom and Helene had behaved together, laughing and kissing, I got more and more depressed. Why was it, I wondered, that my friend was getting to marry the woman he loved, and I was so estranged from Pandora that she didn't even bother to tell me when she was coming into town?

When I passed by the Alko-Bar liquor store, a few streets from my house, I found myself getting off my bike and going in.

I wasn't a big drinker as a rule, but that night drinking seemed like the best idea in the world. I came home, sat down on the couch, and broke out the bottle of tequila. There was a backlog of work waiting for me, but I kept putting it off. I had a shot of tequila first, and then another. Drinking was easier than focusing on the programming I was supposed to be doing, and a whole lot more pleasant than thinking about Pandora Brown.

By eleven o'clock I was ready to give up and go to bed, but I told myself I should at least try to get a little work done. This was my first assignment for a new client, and I figured I was still sober enough to do some preliminary calculations. I turned on the computer and sat down at my desk.

The next thing I knew, I was dreaming about a

fire. In the dream, I was surrounded by smoke and flames, but I was trapped and couldn't get away. Finally I managed to get my eyes open, and I saw that I wasn't dreaming.

The air was heavy with smoke, and flames were gushing from the computer. The monitor lit up like a jack-o-lantern, and I watched as it exploded. Fire was everywhere: in the carpet, the files, the curtains. I tried to stand up, but it was as if my feet were stuck in tar.

From far away I heard banging, but my throat was so dry I couldn't call out. Then the door of the apartment burst open, and I saw my neighbor, Mac, standing there. After that I don't remember anything.

I came to, out in the hallway. Mac was kneeling beside me. There was less smoke here, and I could breathe again. I tried to get back into the apartment, but Mac hung on to me and wouldn't let me go. Then the fire department came, and within half an hour the whole thing was over.

One of the firefighters yellow-taped the front door of the apartment, telling me not to go back in under any circumstances. But after everyone was gone, I cut through the tape and waded back into what used to be my living room. It was completely covered in a black sea of water and ash and soot— nothing was left.

I fell on my knees and started bawling like a two-year-old.

I don't remember very much about the next few days. It was as though the tequila fumes never left my head. I wasn't able to concentrate on anything, or maybe I just didn't want to.

I had all the insurance to deal with, the adjustors to see, the forms to fill out. The preliminary talk was that something had gone wrong with the fan on my computer, which had caused the processor to super-heat. They were saying it was a factory error, so it didn't look like I'd be put in jail for arson, but I felt as guilty as though I *had* set the fire. I knew that if I hadn't drunk so much tequila, I could have done something—prevented the overheating, or at least contained some of the damage—something, so that I wouldn't be standing here now, with my whole life gone into soot and ash.

Those were lost days. I couldn't do much of anything. I didn't even have the heart to ride my bike—I didn't think I deserved that relief, even though it only lasted a few moments.

I moved in, temporarily, with my mother. It was strange to be home again, a refugee. I spent most of my time shopping, trying to replace my possessions which had gone in the fire. Clothes and office supplies were easy enough to come by, but every day I'd remember something else, something irreplaceable, that had been lost—my high school yearbooks, my model planes, the artist's portrait of Pandora.

Mom kept a positive outlook through it all, looking forward to the insurance being settled, and my being able to make a fresh start. But I couldn't think that far ahead; I could barely manage to keep track of the things that needed to be done immediately. I'd go over the list again and again in my mind, until it melted away into gibberish.

As soon as I was able I tried to do some reconstruction work for those clients whose files had been lost on my computer. I wasn't very successful, but at least it helped the days go by a little more quickly. The nights were very bad, though. I was like a little kid, afraid of bedtime, afraid I'd dream I was back in the fire again. I'd watch old reruns, and drink cup after cup of coffee, trying to stay awake. With luck, I could hold out until the sun came up, then I'd lie down on the sofa and doze for a few hours. I felt about a hundred years old.

One morning, my mother came into the bedroom and said, "There's a phone call for you."

I guessed who it was even before I picked up the receiver.

"Gary, it's Pandora. I just heard what happened. I can't believe it. Are you okay?"

"I'm doing great."

"No burns or anything?"

"Nothing like that. The apartment's gone, though."

"I'm sorry," she said. "It was a wonderful apartment."

"Yes, it was."

I couldn't help thinking of all the hours Pandora and I had once spent together there—sitting on the couch, watching videos, lying in bed, our arms around each other.

"What are your plans now?" she asked me.

"Starting again, I guess."

"It seems so unfair."

"Don't worry; I'll be fine."

"I hope so," she said. "And if there's anything at all I can do, let me know."

I hung up the phone, feeling surprised and touched. Then, a few minutes later, she called back.

"Listen, Gary," she told me. "I've just had an

idea. I think there *is* something I can do for you.
These insurance things can take forever; it could
be months before everything's settled. Now, this
may sound crazy, but I think you should come to
L.A."

I laughed. "That's pretty crazy, all right."

"Just listen to me. It makes all the sense in the
world. You're having to start fresh anyway, so why
not come to a place where there are real opportunities? There's a hundred times the amount of business here—I personally know a dozen people who
could use you—and your company could really take
off." She paused. "And here's where I can help.
We've got a little back room in our office; we've
been using it for storage, but it wouldn't take me
long to clear it out. If you wanted, you could work
out of there. You'd save on rent, and you could stay
as long as you needed to."

I couldn't believe what I was hearing. "You're
inviting me to stay in your office?"

"Yes," she said, a little impatiently.

I still couldn't get my mind around it. "Sorry if
I'm being thick," I told Pandora. "It's very gener-
ous of you, and I really appreciate the offer. But, to
be honest, I'm a little confused. I mean, you've
made it clear lately that you don't exactly want me
around anymore."

Pandora was quiet for a moment. "Mama said
you almost died in that fire, Gary. I can't tell you
how I felt when I heard that. I know I haven't
been such a good friend lately, but you'll always
be my Best Boy Buddy. Let's just say I owe you
this."

Of course I told her she didn't owe me anything.

"Just think about it," she said.

So I thought about it; and in the end I found myself calling Pandora back.

"Can a guy change his mind?" I asked her.

She said that a guy could change his mind.

Mom thought I was crazy.

"Why do you need to go to L.A.? Just stay at home until the insurance is settled and, by spring you'll be back to where you were before."

But I told her I wasn't so sure that that was what I wanted anymore.

"Maybe that fire was telling me something. Maybe it's time I branched out, made a change."

Mom shook her head, sighing. But in the end she agreed, or at least pretended to agree, that going to L.A. was a good idea. And my friends were all excited; they said to remember them when I made my first million.

I suspect Mom guessed the real reason I was going and that it had nothing to do with business opportunities or making a million dollars. But it was something we never discussed.

I didn't sleep much the night before I left Palm Springs. It hit me suddenly how much I'd be leaving: the places I loved, the friends, the velvet quiet of a desert night. I'd be back, of course—but it would all be different.

The next morning, Janine called from Dallas to wish me luck. I could hear Eli's voice in the background, chanting, "Uncle Gary, Uncle Gary," and my throat started to close up.

"Bring him to L.A.," I told Janine, "and I'll take you both to a Dodgers game."

I finished packing up my Jeep and was ready to go. Mom hugged me for a long, long time, and I set off.

During the drive to L.A. I kept my mind busy going over the plans. When I reached town my first order of business would be to buy some new computer equipment. I figured I had enough in my account to get a standard PC, with an Oracle database, Windows NT office programs, C++, and Visual Basics. When the insurance was settled I'd be able to upgrade.

Step two was to set up a local consultancy business similar to the one I'd had in Palm Springs. I'd take out some ads, have some business cards made, and see where that led. If work was initially slow I could always hire myself out for tech support. It wasn't what I was best at, but in a pinch I could do it.

Thanks to Pandora, my work space was taken care of, and as far as finding a place to live, I wondered if at least for a few weeks I could crash in her back office. That would save a lot of money, a priority of mine at the moment. Hopefully, the room would be big enough for a couch; if it wasn't, I had brought my sleeping bag.

By ten-thirty, I'd reached the outskirts of Los Angeles. I followed the directions Pandora had given me and took the 10 freeway to Robertson, heading north.

This time around, L.A. seemed a shade less intimidating. Maybe it was because I was in my Jeep instead of on my motorcycle, or maybe because I had a better idea of what to expect. The agency was off the Sunset Plaza, and I liked the look of the area—it was well-kept but not glitzy.

I found the building without a problem, but I

wasn't sure where to park. There was a lot in the back for "tenants only," and I doubted that I qualified. I finally found street parking several blocks away and walked back along Sunset to the building. Then, not knowing what to expect next, I pressed the button for the Gene Brown Agency.

I was buzzed into the hallway. It was narrow and dark, the walls covered with huge posters of old movie stars.

A door on the left opened, and Pandora came flying out.

"Gary!" she cried, and threw her arms around me.

It was as if I were once again the eleven-year-old friend she'd loved, and everything that happened afterward didn't matter. And in that moment, I was so glad to be there with her, nothing else mattered for me, either.

She took me into the office. To be honest, it looked a little different than I'd always imagined. I'd heard about the Gene Brown Agency for so many years, and the reality turned out to be rather a disappointment. It was smaller than I had expected, shabbier, crammed with furniture and filing cabinets.

In front was a waiting room; Lori Max was there, organizing eight-by-ten photos into piles. When I walked in, she looked up and gave me a tight little smile. I shook her hand, saying that I hoped my being there wouldn't be too much of an imposition.

"Oh, no," she told me, "we're thrilled to have you."

I wondered if she'd been paid to say that.

Pandora gave me the rest of the grand tour. I was struck by how much commotion there was—

files were piled everywhere, phones were ringing, faxes were spewing out of the machine.

"And now for your room," she said finally. "I warned you—it's not much."

But it was just fine. I could see how much trouble she'd taken to get it ready for me. She had cleared everything out and put in a desk, a bookcase, and an overstuffed chair. There was even a small refrigerator fitted into one corner, and a hot plate on top of the filing cabinet. And next to the blotter was a tiny barrel cactus in a ceramic pot.

Pandora gave me a little smile. "That's so *you* won't get homesick."

Pandora

I was very shaken when Mama called and said that Gary had nearly been killed in a fire. I kept imagining myself sitting at his memorial service, listening to some minister talk about how wonderful my Best Boy Buddy had been.

Since I'd moved to L.A. I hadn't kept in contact with Gary at all. That had been on purpose. I thought it would be easiest, kindest, if I simply cut that tie. But now I felt horribly guilty. All that Gary had ever meant to me began to rush through my mind.

I called him to see how he was doing. He said he was fine, but underneath he sounded lost and forlorn.

I'm not sure what prompted my big idea. Guilt, certainly, and affection, and the memory of all Gary had been to me throughout my life. Whatever the reason was, I found myself calling him back and inviting him to come to L.A. and work out of my office for as long as he needed to.

The moment the words were out, I was horrified by what I had done. "I must be completely

crazy!" I wailed to my friend Steph on the phone
that night.

"Gary's one of the reasons I wanted to leave
Palm Springs, and now I'm bringing him to L.A.! I
mean, what's wrong with this picture?!"

"Nothing's wrong with it," Steph said. "It's a
matter of unfinished business between you two."

I wondered, a little uneasily, what she meant by
that.

Gary arrived a week later, looking shy and uncomfortable away from the desert. It was strange to
see him in L.A., standing in the hallway of the
agency.

I showed him around, and he seemed pleased
with the way I'd fixed his little office up.

"It's not much," I told him, "but hopefully it'll
be all right for you to work in."

"Actually," he said, "I was going to ask you if I
could stay here full time for a while—just until I
get things going with my business."

That took me by surprise. "But it isn't really set
up for living in. There's not even a shower."

"I'll figure something out," he said. "I'm not
fussy. And I'd like to start off by saving all the
money I can."

I told him, of course, that he could stay.

At first it was strange having Gary in the office. It
made me feel awkward and self-conscious, and I
wasn't quite sure how to treat him. As an ex-
boyfriend? A friend? A roommate? But right from
the beginning, Gary defined his own role. He behaved like a tenant—nothing more, nothing less—
a wonderful tenant who installed computer pro-

grams and fixed broken shelves and even delivered headshots when we needed it done.

Since I was responsible for bringing him to L.A., I wanted to make sure he was happy there. I offered to take him to lunch, show him around, and introduce him to potential clients. He took me up on the last offer, but turned down the rest.

"Relax, Pandora," he told me. "Don't worry; I can manage by myself."

I wasn't so sure about that, but I knew what Gary's pride was like, so I didn't press him.

Frankly, I was a little relieved that he was so independent. I kept remembering what Steph had said about there being unfinished business between me and Gary, and I was happy to keep things at arm's length as much as possible.

I was sitting at my desk early one Monday morning when I felt a rumbling start under my feet. Lori wasn't in yet, and I yelled out to Gary to get under a doorway.

"Don't worry," I added. "L.A. earthquakes never last long!" But this one didn't stop. The rumbling turned into shaking, and soon it became like a 747 landing on the roof of the building. When I looked up, I saw the walls of the office beginning to separate from the ceiling, and I started to scream.

Gary casually crossed the room, took me by the arm, and shoved me under the desk. When the shaking finally stopped, I crawled out, too embarrassed to thank him.

We went into the hallway to check on the other tenants. No one had been hurt; everyone was congregating by the stairs, exchanging horror stories.

It was comforting, in a way—I felt like I was in a neighborhood for the first time since I'd been in L.A. I looked for John Bradshaw, but Emmett said he hadn't come in yet.

Gary and I went back to the office to check on the damage. Everything was a shambles, with smashed glass and books and fallen furniture everywhere. I tried to call Palm Springs, to let Mama and Daddy know I was all right, but the phone lines were jammed. I dialed again and again but couldn't get through. I started getting hysterical, thinking about Daddy waking up to the news on the radio and not being able to get hold of me. Gary walked over finally, took the phone out of my hand, and hung up the receiver.

"You're just making yourself crazy," he said. "Try again later. For now, why don't we start cleaning up the office."

Half an hour later I finally got through to Palm Springs, but the phone just rang and rang. I couldn't understand it. There was always someone at the house; if Mama was away, Millie was sure to be there.

"It's Daddy," I said. "I know it. Something's wrong with Daddy."

Gary laughed. "You're such an alarmist."

Just then Lori came in. We exchanged our earthquake horror stories and then Gary picked up his jacket.

"Since Lori's here now, I think I'll take off for a while."

At ten o'clock I finally managed to get hold of Mama. All my worry turned out to be for nothing—she didn't even know there had been an earthquake. It was such a lovely morning in Palm Springs that she and Daddy and Millie had taken

WISH UPON A STAR   137

their breakfast out into the garden. They hadn't listened to the news or even heard the phone ring. I felt a little silly.

A few hours later, Mama called me back.

"You'll never believe who just left here."

"Who?"

"Gary. It was the sweetest thing—he came by to make sure we weren't worried about you."

When Gary returned to the office later that afternoon, I didn't know quite what to say.

"That was incredibly thoughtful, your going to see my parents," I told him. "But I was able to get in touch with Mama right after you left."

"I figured you would," he said. "I talked to my mother, too. But I thought our families would appreciate being told in person that everything was all right."

Christmas was coming up. It was my first holiday season in L.A., and I wanted to make the most of it. I listened to costumed carolers sing on Beverly Drive, I visited the DWP festival of lights over by the zoo, I drove out to Candy Cane Lane in Woodland Hills to see all the decorated houses. And I spent long Saturday afternoons shopping for presents.

I was passing by a Crate and Barrel a few days before Christmas when I saw a cobalt blue teakettle the exact color of Aunt Marilynn's kitchen. I hadn't been intending to buy her a gift, but it was Christmas, after all, and this seemed like a good way to mend a few fences.

I drove over to her house that evening to deliver the present. I hadn't been there since the night the lawyer read the will.

Aunt Marilynn opened the front door and stared at me.

"Yes?"

"I just wanted to wish you a Merry Christmas," I said and held out the package. "And to give you this."

Her mouth flattened out.

"I certainly hope that made you feel better."

She took the package and slammed the door.

I closed the office for a week's vacation and left for Palm Springs on Christmas Eve. It was glorious to be back home again, not having to worry about résumés or contracts, not having anything to do but watch videos and eat shortbread.

The house looked very festive. Mama and Millie had decorated every surface imaginable. There were Santa Clauses and holly and elves throughout the house, and the tree was up, resplendant with all the ornaments I'd loved since childhood.

"But of course we saved the doves for you," Mama assured me.

I took them out of their special box, those fragile papier-mâché ornaments Mama and Daddy had gotten on their honeymoon. I climbed up the stepladder and carefully put them in their spot at the very top of the tree. It was truly Christmas now.

At the end of a wonderful week, I left to go back to L.A.

"Are you sure you can't stay over New Year's?" Daddy asked. "It'll be the first time we haven't seen the Rose Parade together."

I hated to hear the wistfulness in his voice, and

part of me would have loved to stay; but at the same time, I was impatient to get back to town.

The following night was New Year's Eve. Several clients had invited me to parties, but I decided I would rather spend a quiet evening at home. When midnight came, I opened a bottle of champagne, put on an old Randy Newman CD, and lay down on the sofa.

I thought back over the year, back to last New Year's Day, when I had felt so miserable and trapped, when I had made that Treasure Board, fearing that I would never achieve any of the images on it. And now my life was barely recognizable. I had moved to a wonderful new city; I was working at a marvelous new job—I was living out my dreams.

Picking up my glass of champagne, I toasted Uncle Gene.

The first morning of the new year I took a long drive. I went through Brentwood, Westwood, and Beverly Hills, up and down the wide streets, in and out of the pattern of shadows cast by the palm trees.

Then I drove along Coldwater Canyon and ended up at the loveliest little park. It was full of couples and families sitting on blankets, playing catch, kicking soccer balls, wading in the stream. Off to one side, a little girl was having a birthday party—the old-fashioned kind, with a paper tablecloth blowing in the breeze, and Sleeping Beauty party hats, and a piñata tied to the tree.

Watching it all, I began to get a little wistful. I felt as if everyone else at the park—those couples, those families—were like a solid band together, making a thick, secure braid. And that next to them, my own life seemed completely fragile and insubstantial.

Then into my mind came the image of a gold necklace from Tiffany's. That was thin and fragile, too, but how beautiful. So what if my life was like that for now? I wasn't ready for a family of my own yet—I didn't really even have room for a boyfriend at the moment. All my energy needed to be concentrated on the agency. I told myself there would be plenty of time for Sleeping Beauty birthday parties later.

The next day, Lori and Gary returned to the office. I ordered in sushi as a little celebration and made a speech, saying how glad I was to be starting a new year at the agency and how pleased I was that they were both there with me. Gary made me a little bow, but Lori kept her eyes on her food. I wondered if anything was wrong; then she looked up and gave me the brightest of smiles.

The next morning she called in sick. She sounded tense and upset, but not ill, and I found myself wondering what the problem really was. I suspected it had something to do with her boyfriend. I'd never met the guy—Lori was always very secretive about her private life—but I somehow got the impression that he gave her a lot of grief.

"Don't worry about it," I told her. "Stay home and rest, and I'll see you tomorrow."

Without Lori in the office, my morning was twice as hectic, as usual; when lunchtime finally came I decided to treat myself to something unhealthy at Mel's Diner. I thought about inviting

Gary along, but he was out on a job, so I ended up going alone.

I had the world's cutest server, bubbly and petite, with wild yellow hair. Even her name, Ginette MacDougal, was pure Busby Berkeley. I noticed that she spoke with a slight accent, and I asked where she was from.

"Denver," she said. "I just moved out here a few months ago."

"Why L.A?"

"I want to be an actress."

"Really?" I said. "Have you had any luck so far?"

She sighed. "Nothing yet. Before you can get anywhere here, you need to have an agent, and that's just about impossible."

Right on cue, I pulled out a business card from my wallet and handed it to her.

"Call me when you have a monologue prepared."

Her face was absolutely something to see.

It stayed with me all day; I felt so happy and proud whenever I thought about it. I was building the business; I was out there spotting talent—I was doing what Uncle Gene did.

Ginette called the following day.

"I'm ready with the monologue."

I hadn't expected her to be so quick about it, and I wasn't quite sure of the protocol. All my other clients had been in place when I took over the agency.

Trying to sound confident, I told Ginette to come by the office, and she said she'd be there in half an hour. She arrived looking very sophisticated in a suit I recognized from the last Macy's sale.

"I've prepared Lucinda Matlock's speech from *Spoon River Anthology*—is that all right?"

I pretended I'd heard of *Spoon River Anthology* and said it would be fine.

"Would you mind waiting here a moment?" I asked her. "I'd like my assistant to hear you, too."

I went into Lori's office. She had been in a strange, silent mood all morning. I told her about Ginette and asked if she would mind coming in and hearing her monologue. Lori gave me an odd look but didn't say anything as she got up from her chair and followed me into my office.

Ginette began to recite the speech; I found it very moving. When she finished, I looked over for Lori's reaction, but her face was a complete blank. This was obviously going to be my call.

"I think you have a lot of potential," I told Ginette. "And I'd like to take you on as a client."

All the sophistication went away, and a squealing little girl came flying across the room to hug me. I hugged her back. It was a very happy moment. I imagined Uncle Gene there, smiling at us from the leather chair.

"We'll get a contract prepared as soon as possible," I told her, "and then we can send out your headshots."

Ginette looked distressed. "Actually, I don't have any. I've been saving up to get some, but I can't afford them yet. Maybe by March."

Once again, I wasn't sure of the protocol, but it seemed ridiculous that Ginette should have to wait that long.

"Get some made now, and tell the photographer to send the bill here," I told her. "You'll pay me back when you get your first job."

There was another shriek, another hug.

When Ginette left the office, I watched her from the window. I had heard the expression "dancing down the street," but this was the first time I had ever seen anyone actually do it.

Lori was still in the room. I could suddenly tell that something was very wrong.

"What's the matter?" I asked.

"Nothing," she said, but her voice was icy.

"Come on, Lori—what is it?"

"All right," she burst out. "This isn't the way agents work. They scout little theaters. They interview clients on recommendation. They don't pick up waitresses at Mel's Diner."

She made it sound as if I were a pimp.

"But didn't you think she had talent?" I stammered.

"Frankly, no."

She started to leave the room. At the door she turned around again.

"And real agents never pay for headshots."

I sat at my desk, chagrined, feeling like a complete imbecile. Real agents, she had said—real agents. And I wasn't one of them. I had embarrassed myself. There were rules, traditions in this business; and in my eagerness to be Uncle Gene, to play the fairy godmother, I had completely overstepped the line.

A few minutes later, Lori came back into the room.

"I'm sorry for what I said," she told me stiffly. "You're the boss, and I have no business criticizing."

"Of course, you do," I said. "You know I couldn't run this place without you. Besides," I added, trying to get her to smile, "it's all your fault. If you hadn't been sick, I wouldn't have to eat lunch by myself, and I never would have met Ginette in the first place."

Lori did give me a slight smile. "Incidentally," she said, "your protégé just called. She wanted to know the best place to get headshots made. I told her Ray Cumberland or Tom Soames. I pushed Ray, though—he's the cheapest."

"Thanks."

Lori left the room again, but a few minutes later she came back in.

"Have *you* ever had any headshots done?" she asked me.

I laughed. "Heavens, no. The last performance I gave was in second grade. I threw up on the prompter."

"I didn't mean for acting. A lot of agents have glossies made; they use them for business cards or ads."

"I hate being photographed," I told her. "I always come out looking like a blond version of Olive Oyl."

She smiled. "I doubt that. All the same, Ray's pretty good. You should think about it."

I thought about it. The suggestion made sense, though I didn't like the idea of seeing my face on any ads. Mainly, I was so relieved to have Lori being friendly again that I wanted to keep the momentum going.

I went into her office.

"I've decided to take your advice on the headshots," I said. "And why don't you have some made too, while we're at it? We'll call it a business expense."

I could see how pleased she was.

* * *

I had been at the agency for over five months now and had become friendly with most of the tenants in the building. They were a lovely group of people, pleasant and helpful—with one exception. That was John Bradshaw. At first I'd been thrilled at the idea of having this Hollywood legend as an upstairs neighbor, but as time went on, I realized that he was the most aloof, unsociable man I had ever seen in my life. I passed him almost daily, either in the lobby or walking along Sunset Boulevard, and he still never so much as acknowledged my presence. He simply walked past, unsmiling.

As the months went on, I found his rudeness more and more unacceptable. We were cohorts, fellow agents working out of the same building, and I didn't think he had any right to such a superior attitude. I made up my mind that the next time I saw him, I was going to make him speak to me.

Toward the end of January, I was in the Hugo Boss boutique on Sunset Plaza looking for a birthday present for Daddy. John Bradshaw came into the store. He caught sight of me, and, as usual, turned away.

Determinedly, I walked up to him, holding two sweaters.

"Sorry to bother you," I said, "but I need a man's opinion. My father's birthday is coming up, and I can't decide between these sweaters. Which one do you like?"

Bradshaw stiffened. He looked down at me if I were a slug that had just crawled out of his salad.

"I'm afraid I really couldn't say." He turned and left the store.

Mortified, I ended up buying both sweaters.

For the rest of the day I couldn't stop thinking about what had happened. I went over and over it and still couldn't understand the man's rudeness. I hadn't been *that* pushy—certainly not enough to warrant such behavior. I wondered if I had insulted him by saying the gift was for my father. Did he think I was implying he was an old man?

The look he had given me—I couldn't get it out of my mind.

The following day I had lunch with Alyce Ryhs, from Lizbo Productions. Bradshaw's name came up in the conversation, and I told Alyce about what had happened at Hugo Boss. She rolled her eyes.

"Typical Bradshaw behavior." She laughed. "Did you ever see that article in *Variety*? 'The Ten Scariest People in Hollywood'? I think it came out sometime last summer."

I said I hadn't seen it.

"Well, you should look it up. John Bradshaw's name was top of the list."

When I got back from lunch, I logged immediately on to the Internet. I couldn't find the article Alyce had mentioned, but I did come across some others, hype pieces mainly, about the big deals Bradshaw had put together and the stars he'd created.

I also found out that he'd been married, but his wife died in 1993.

"I'm not surprised," I called out to Lori. "She probably just couldn't take living with him anymore."

And I learned he had a daughter, Amanda. There was a picture of the two of them at some charity event. She was only fourteen at the time, but she already looked like she'd inherited her father's superiority complex.

Most of the articles had been written quite a while ago, and the more recent ones were far less flattering. They made it sound as if in the past ten years John Bradshaw had become almost a recluse, going out as rarely as possible and then only with a client. I was starting to feel sorry for him, but then I remembered that voice—and the look he'd given me.

The day Lori and I were to have our headshots taken, we had lunch at Il Sole, and managed to finish a bottle of wine between us. We got back to the office in a very, very good mood—I could see that Gary was a little scandalized.

We shut up shop early, and drove to Ray Cumberland's studio on Vine Street. The walls of his lobby were filled with blown-up photos, and, seeing them, I felt encouraged—he made everyone look absolutely gorgeous.

Ray came out of the office and introduced himself. He was an older man, with long silver Salvador Dali hair and moustache.

"So—which one of you wants to go first?"

"Lori does," I said.

"Would you like to come in and watch?"

I glanced at Lori. "If she'll let me."

She shrugged. "Why not?"

The session went wonderfully. Lori was a natural model. She knew exactly how to pose, and the vitality just leaped off her. She was wearing a tailored suit and silk blouse, nothing risqué at all, yet

she somehow managed to look incredibly sexy. Ray
had a lot of fun with her; toward the end, he was
taking some pretty provocative shots.

And then it was my turn.

I did my best, but it was hopeless. Ray was very patient—he kept arranging me in different poses, trying to make me look less prissy, but I could tell from
his face—it was Olive Oyl as usual.

Finally Lori burst out laughing. "Oh, come on,
Ray," she said. "This is ridiculous. We need one
shot—just one—that she can be ashamed of."

The two of them descended on me. Ray roughed
up my hair, and Lori started tugging on my dress.
They sat me sideways on the stool, hiked my hem-
line to my thighs, and arranged my hair so that I
looked like an Italian actress in a bad fifties' movie.

"Now blow a kiss to the camera," Ray crooned.

"I'm suing you both," I said. "Isn't this defama-
tion of character or something?" But Ray snapped
away.

Lori said she would frame the picture.

I had such a good time that afternoon, I didn't
want it to end. I asked Lori if she were free for dinner, but she said she already had plans. Her face
took on its "No Admittance" look, and I guessed
she was seeing her boyfriend.

When I went home that night, my place seemed
very lonely. I thought about calling Gary and inviting him to a movie, but I decided it was probably
better not to.

I made myself some dinner and sat down at the
computer. I logged on to the Internet and, for the
third time that week, went to Google.com and
typed in John Bradshaw's name.

I spent the next half hour reading over more
old articles about him. Then, just as I was about to

turn the computer off, I came upon a photo I hadn't seen before. Bradshaw was sitting at his desk, holding a book, his face in profile. The picture seemed familiar—it reminded me of someone else, but I couldn't think who. Finally I remembered: it was Mr. Crumm, my high school chemistry teacher. Mr. Crumm had actually been very like John Bradshaw, around the same age, with similar features and the identical air of superiority. Most of the girls in the class, myself included, had had a huge crush on him. Maybe because it was so hard to get, his approval was what we all most wanted.

But, unlike John Bradshaw, Mr. Crumm hadn't been a total bastard.

The following Friday was my father's sixty-sixth birthday, and I went down to Palm Springs to celebrate with him and Mama.

Daddy didn't seem well, but I told myself that maybe he just looked worse to me because I hadn't visited in a few weeks. I brought down both Hugo Boss sweaters to let Mama choose which one should be for his birthday and which should be for Father's Day—but I ended up giving him both. The maroon was his favorite, and he put it on right away. It made his skin look like gray parchment. I wished I hadn't bought it.

After dinner, Millie turned off the lights, Mama brought in the cake, and we all sang "Happy Birthday." Daddy said the cake was our best ever, but he ate only a bite or two. I thought about that other birthday party I had seen—the one at the park on Coldwater, with the piñata, the Sleeping Beauty hats, and all the little kids racing around—and I felt so sad.

Lori

Woke up thinking about Gene. I could hear his voice saying my name. Sometimes, it's crazy, I miss him. He used to look at me like I look at Troy, like I was the best thing he ever saw in his life.

If he hadn't died, I'd be partner five months now. The Max and Brown Agency. You can go crazy thinking like that.

Troy says I scare him, I'm like a steamroller. "You'd do anything to get what you want, wouldn't you?"

Of course I would.

And so would he. He's at it again, nagging me about Miss Box.

"Why don't you introduce us? It might help; I might finally get an agent."

I tell him it's too soon. "I've got my own ass to think about, I don't want to cash in on too many favors yet."

He gets mad. "It wouldn't be a favor; I'm a god-dam good stuntman."

But you can't fall, I think. *Who wants a stuntman who can't fall?*

I tell him, "Stop harping on it. I'll talk to Miss Box about you. Just give me time."

He's not happy, but he lets it go for now. I wish he'd forget the whole idea, stop nagging. I just don't want him and Miss Box to meet; I get this bad, bad feeling about it. And she's curious, too; she's always wanting to know about Troy. But I don't tell her anything, I change the subject, never even mention his name. Maybe I'm crazy, paranoid. Maybe it wouldn't be such a big deal. Maybe I should do it, get it over with and introduce them. But I just don't want to.

Suzanne called from Seattle; Ellen died yesterday.

Thinking about her all morning, it got me blue. Ellen was the best pal, always up for anything. Smoking behind the gym lockers, hiding out from the nuns. She always treated me like I was something special. *You're going to leave the rest of us in the dust, Lori; I don't know what you're going to do, but you're going to be famous, remember me then, okay?*

The last time I saw her, it was just after she got knocked up. They sent her off to boarding school; she was crying. "I'll never forget you, Lori. Take care of Suzanne." She kissed me on the mouth.

Suzanne said she was in a lot of pain toward the end; it was a good thing she died. And she was bald from the chemo.

Can't even imagine that.

Asked Suzanne if she was coming back to L.A. now that Ellen's gone. She says no, she's staying in Seattle for a while.

"Your friend can take over the lease on the apartment if she wants."

Call Miss Box, tell her Suzanne's sister died, she can have the apartment.

"Oh, Lori, that's just awful. I'm so sorry. I'd like to send some flowers."

What a phony, she's not sorry. She never even met Ellen. She's just glad to get her hands on the apartment.

Suzanne for Miss Box, what a trade-down. Shit.

Feel so blue, keep thinking I see Ellen walking down the street, her long hair swinging the way it always did. I hate this life; it's shit. I need something good to happen for once, not all this crap.

Miss Box called. Her car's broken down; she can't get to the office. She needs some contracts copied right away and would I ask Gary to do it? I say don't bother him—I'll take them down myself.

Feels great to get out of the office. Drive to Crescent Square, give in the contracts, tell them I'll wait. Go to the beauty supply place, buy some eyeliner. Go next door for a doughnut. I feel a tap on my back, probably a bum. Turn around, I can't believe it, it's Troy. It's never happened before like that, running into him out of the blue.

He's kissing my neck.

"What are you doing here?"

"I had a meeting; it fell through. Now I'm free for most of the day." His hand moving to my ass.

Tell him I'm free, too. Call Miss Box, make my voice shake.

"I feel so awful, I feel so sick. I went down to the Xerox place, and I got so dizzy I couldn't stand up."

Troy squeezing my ass. Miss Box squeaking, "Oh, Lori, that's terrible. Don't worry about the contracts. I'll get a taxi and pick them up myself. You've got to go home right now and rest. Are you okay to drive? Do you want me to send Gary to pick you up?"

Troy's tongue in my ear.

"No, no, I'll be fine. I'll see you tomorrow."

Get the hell out of there before she comes. Take Troy back to my place. Love doing it during the day. It's like time stolen—the best.

Afterward we get dressed, and Troy says, "Why don't we do something fun—let's go to Ripley's Believe It or Not Museum."

Not my idea of fun, but okay.

Troy's wild about the place. He's running around, dragging me to all the exhibits. He's like a little kid. I'm not into it so much. Freaks make me sick. But I like this one thing, this little Japanese shoe. It's only about three inches long, some woman slit her soles and cut off her toes so she could wear it. Crazy, but I keep coming back to it, it's so beautiful.

We go in the gift shop next to the museum, they have a copy of the little shoe. Troy buys it for me. That makes me happy; he's not usually big on presents.

Get some sushi and head on back to my place. Troy's got an audition at three. He says he has to leave soon. I kiss him for luck; it ends up he almost misses the audition. Then he really does have to go.

Feel a little blue now he's gone. Today was the best. I wish it could always be like that between us.

Maybe it's my fault it isn't. I forget what a kid he is. I take him too seriously; I get him nervous. I should lighten up, stop nagging, stop trying to change him, just let him be.

Goddam him to hell.

What's the fucking point? I'm just kidding myself; he's never going to change; it's never going to stop. We're at Flings. We're having a drink; everything's under control. Then this girl comes in—over-the-top sleazy, big floppy boobs. She goes right up to Troy like I'm not even there. "Remember me?" She says she was the script girl on his shoot in Santa Fe. Who gives a shit? She goes on and on, yakety-yakety-yak. I wait for Troy to say something, tell her he's busy, get rid of her, but he doesn't do it.

Don't let him see how upset I am—he hates that. The bitch finally leaves. I try to go back to the way we were before. He's acting jumpy. I'm wondering if he's still thinking about the girl. He says he needs to take a leak, but there's something in his voice. I make sure he heads toward the can.

I stay at the bar. Some guys come up to me.

"Hey, beautiful, how about a dance?"

I don't do it, but it gets me in a better mood. I'll be ready for Troy when he comes back. But he doesn't come back.

Finally I see him; I can tell he's been using. I can tell by the way he's walking, Mr. Macho, bragging with his steps. There's a guy next to him—he cuts off fast. I've seen that guy around, I know who he is.

I go up to Troy. I grab him. "What the hell were you doing, were you dealing?"

He says no, real sharp.

"You're lying, you bastard, I know you are."

He doesn't say anything, he won't look at me.

I slap him in the face. I get up and leave. Take a taxi home.

God damn, it kills me; I thought we were through with all that. I can put up with a lot, but not that. Not anymore.

I hate this place. There's no air in this stinking hole. It smells like shit.

Pick up the Japanese shoe Troy bought me, throw it against the wall. It doesn't break. Find a hammer and smash it to pieces. I only wish it were Troy's goddam face. He promised me so many times, "I'm through with that, I'm through with all that."

He's nothing but a lying bastard. I'm wasting my time with him; I've wasted three years. Who am I kidding, there's never going to be any nice life, any peace. It'll always be me working my ass off, and him taking all the money. And cheating on me. And dealing. And ending up getting shot by some junkie.

Get my wallet, take out all the pictures of him. Start to rip them up—but when I look at them, he's so beautiful, I can't.

My whole life, it's been crap. All the things I didn't get, all the things I didn't get to do. But Troy, the way he looks, the way I feel when I look at him, it's the one thing that's not crap.

Sit down with the pictures. Try to imagine the way he'll look when he's old—he'll be wrinkled and gray. But I can't do it. I can't think of Troy as ever being old.

Drive to his place, knock on the door. He opens it right away; he's been waiting for me. Get into those arms. They're like a vise around my shoulders. I know I'm home. It may be shit, but it is home. He's crying, he's saying he's sorry. He never wants to lose me. In a minute we're on the floor, he's on top of me. I'm not ready, but it's all right. The pain feels almost good, it's like the little shoe.

Can't sleep. I keep looking at him lying beside me. So what happens now? We're back where we started from. Who am I fooling, I'm never leaving. I've just got to find a way to make it work, that's all.

He just needs a break. If only he could get a break. If he made some money, got something solid, maybe he'd settle down.

He keeps saying agent, he needs an agent. But he's had agents; it hasn't worked. No one wants a stuntman who can't fall.

He says it would be different with Miss Box. Maybe it would. If Troy was with the agency, I'd work my ass off for him, getting him work. But I don't want to do it; I don't want to ask her. I don't want her mixing in my personal life. I don't want her being Lady Bountiful. And I don't want her meeting Troy.

Sometimes I think about going to John Bradshaw—that might work. I could do it through Emmett: introduce Troy to him first, say he needs representation. Emmett would fall for him, too, but that's okay—Troy could lead him on long enough to meet Bradshaw, sign a contract.

Have to find out if he handles stuntmen.

* * *

Miss Box brought Bradshaw up again today; it had to be the tenth time this week. "I saw him going into the elevator at lunch—as usual he completely ignored me. Lori, what's with him? He's simply the rudest man I've ever met."

It's turning into an obsession with her. So obvious what's going on—it's a father thing. Can't say I'm surprised; with that pathetic dad of hers, no wonder she's still looking. And Bradshaw has to be fifty, but he's still got it. Handsome for an old guy, rich and plenty of clout.

My take on it is that he's attracted to her, just not showing it. I've seen him look at her sometimes; there's definitely something there.

That could be interesting, if the two of them ever got together. Quite a thought. And if they merge the agencies, that could pan out just fine for me: Bradshaw, Brown and Max.

Wonder what the best way to work this is. First I should find out how deep it goes with her. It's hard to tell. It's always yakety-yakety-yak with Miss Box, but not usually about guys. She clams right up when it comes to that.

I'll take her to lunch, give her something to drink; that should do the trick.

We go out to Il Sole. I order some wine.

I say, "Look at the bartender—isn't he a hottie?" And that gets us right on to the subject.

"How are things with your boyfriend, Lori?" she starts out by asking.

No, thanks, Miss Box, this little talk is about you, not me, I'll ask the questions. You don't need to know anything about Troy.

I tell her, "If you don't mind, I'd rather not talk about it."

The eyes get wide. "Oh, Lori, I'm so sorry. I didn't mean to pry."

She's groveling now, she feels bad, I can ask her anything I want.

"But how about you? You've been in town six months—haven't you met anyone?"

"I haven't been looking, the agency's kept me so busy. But I'll admit, lately I've started to think maybe I could handle a relationship, too."

"Sure you can, it would be good for you." Ask it casually: "What kind of guys do you go for, anyway?"

"Well, what I really want—I hope this doesn't sound too shallow—is to be with someone substantial; someone I can look up to."

That's good news. Bradshaw might have a chance. He fits that picture. I say, "I'm sure you can find someone like that. Maybe he's even closer than you think."

She's blushing. "Oh, I don't know. Even if I met the perfect man, I'd probably do something to ruin it—I'm not very good with guys."

Pile on the bullshit. "You've got to be kidding—you must have had so many admirers." Nearly gag on the words, but I can see Miss Box likes it—it fits right into her princess image.

She shakes her head. "No, honestly—I've never been popular at all."

Lay it on even thicker. "I don't believe a word of it. I've seen you at clubs. Come on, there has to have been someone."

She clears her throat. "Well, actually, there was—one man. I was even thinking about marrying him, but I knew it wouldn't work out." The eyes get big;

the hands are fluttering. "He's a wonderful person; he's got all the best qualities, but . . . I don't know. I just didn't . . . don't . . . love him." She looks down quickly, like she's about to give away some big secret.

Oh, give me a break. Like I can't guess it's Gary. I've known that little tidbit from the first time we saw him at Starbucks. But I don't let on I know. If Miss Box wants to keep her big high school crush a secret, let her.

From the way she's looking down, though, I'm wondering. She's so dim, maybe she does still have a thing for him, and she doesn't even know it.

Miss Box and Gary—what would that do for me? Absolutely nothing is what it would do. Gary can't stand me. He and Miss Box get together, I'm history. *Lori's not a friend—I don't think she's a good influence. I'm not even sure she should be working at the agency.* No, thank you, I'm not promoting that little romance. But I don't think it's ever going to happen, Miss Box treats him like shit.

Still, probably better to bury it. I tell her, "I'm sure you did the right thing. There's nothing more boring than someone with all the best qualities."

Miss Box looks up, her eyes widen, her face lightens. I can see she's a little shocked, a little guilty, then she laughs.

Wonder about it from Gary's end, how deep it still goes. She hasn't given him any encouragement, but you never know. Maybe a truce between him and me might be good, just in case.

Stay late that afternoon, wait for Miss Box to leave, then wander into Gary's room. He's sitting at his computer, doesn't look up.

"Hey," I tell him, "I just wanted to see how you were doing."

Say it nice, like I want us to be friends. I go over to his desk, ask him what he's working on.

"Something for a client."

I move in closer. "Is everything okay for you in the office? Is there anything I can do?"

For a second, he looks up. He's going to say something, I can see it, but he doesn't, he stops himself.

I move in even closer. Stand next to him, give him the big smile. "You're such a good friend to Pandora."

"Yes," he says. "I get the feeling she needs one."

The way he says it, the way he's looking at me, the bastard.

Start to shake, I could kill him. *How dare you, Mr. Holier-Than-Thou prick? What the hell do you know about anything? Who the fuck are you to judge me?*

Asked Troy to stay over tonight; he said he couldn't. Says he can't stay over every time, I shouldn't expect it. The bastard.

Feel wasted today. Could have slept in, it's Saturday morning, forgot the fucking alarm was set. Couldn't get back to sleep.

Went into the bathroom. Scared myself when I looked in the mirror. Nothing I can point to exactly, no wrinkles or crow's feet. It's more like shadows—it's like I can start to see how my face is going to look someday.

Got the hell out of there, it's like a ghost chasing me. Need a day at the spa.

Drive to the office. Gary might be there. I'll

have to come up with a good excuse if he asks what I'm doing. But the place is empty.

Go into Gene's office—excuse me, Miss Box's—and lock the door. Get under the desk, feel around for the panel, pull out the cash box. One day Gene got morbid, *I want to show you where this is, in case anything ever happens to me.*

Don't really think Miss Box needs to know about it.

Open the box—eight hundred dollars left. Take three—never know when I might need the other five. Maybe Christmas, for Troy's present. Hear Gary coming into the front office. Get the box back just in time. Step out of the room, give him a big hi, say, "I'm just picking up a few files." Can see the little wheels turning; he's trying to figure out what I'm up to, but he can't quite work it out.

Drive to Hollywood, to the Sunset Spa. Put myself down for the works: massage, wrap, facial. I love it here—it's damp and warm and steamy; it's like a little jungle pool. But then it gets spoiled, all the fat elephants come lumbering in. I hate them, those rich bitches, their whiny voices, their assy conversation. I wish there was an earthquake—I'd like to see them running out onto the street, a herd of elephants with their paper slippers and mudpacks.

The woman comes to give me my massage. Her name is Tonya; she's from Romania. She's got a little boy, he's sick at home, she wants to make sure he's okay, but she can't make any personal calls, the spa would fire her ass. Loan her my cell.

Feel better now, much better. Look like a quality piece of meat again, face pink like a pearl, no more shadows. The ghosts all gone.

What I need now is something good to wear.

Can't stand these old clothes over this gorgeous new skin. Need something silky, something clingy.

Head on back to the office. Gary isn't there. Go back to the cash box, take out the other five hundred. Screw Troy's Christmas present. Put the cash box back empty. Think of Gene showing it to me, his secret stash, bragging, *I never let this get empty.* And now it's empty for good.

No, not for good. When I'm running the office, I'll fill it again, keep it filled.

Head straight for Anna Sui. Try on the dress in the window, the white silk. It's gorgeous on me, I knew it would be, it's like we're breathing together. Don't ever want to take it off. Tell the salesgirl to wrap it up; she uses sheet after sheet of tissue paper. Love walking down the street carrying the big bag.

See Gary coming back up to the office. He gives me a dirty look, but he's not going to figure anything out—he doesn't have a clue what an Anna Sui bag means.

Keep on touching the dress; I should have clothes like this all the time.

Miss Box down in the dumps. She went to Palm Springs; it got her depressed. Her dad's worse, she thinks maybe she should have stayed down there, blah, blah, blah. "I feel so helpless. I just wish I knew what was going to happen."

Emmett comes down the stairs. He sees Miss Box. He makes it into a big drama. "Oh, honey, what is it, what's wrong?"

She goes into it all again: She's so confused about her life, she wishes she could be sure she's on the right path, yakety-yak.

Emmett, the busybody, starts in. "You know what, sweetie? You should go to a psychic."

Wish he'd shut the fuck up. Who knows what ideas a psychic might put into Miss Box's head. But it's too late, he's got her attention.

"A psychic? Oh, no, I couldn't—I'd be too scared."

Try to head Emmett off, but he's going full steam ahead. He knows this great psychic, her name's Clarice, she tells fortunes with tarot cards, she's never wrong.

Miss Box starting to get excited. "Can she really tell the future?"

Emmett's got center stage, and he's milking it. Clarice told me this, Clarice told me that.

The eyes are huge, the mouth is open. "Well, if she's really that good . . . It couldn't hurt, certainly . . . It might be very valuable; she might have some insights . . ."

She blasts Emmett with the smile. "You've talked me into it. I'm going to go."

Then she looks at me, I know what's coming. "Lori, will you go with me?"

You couldn't keep me away. Call it damage control, I want to hear what this Clarice tells her.

"And you'll have a reading, too, of course—my treat."

Act like I'm thrilled. What choice do I have?

Call the woman, make the appointment. She sounds normal enough over the phone.

I think it'll be okay. Might even be something I can work with. Maybe this Clarice will see Miss Box hooking up with an older man. Even if she doesn't say "older man," I can nudge it, I can put John Bradshaw into her head.

* * *

"Lori, I've got a great idea; let's have lunch together first and then go to the psychic."

Say no, I already have plans, I'll meet her there.

One o'clock, drive to Highland, pull up at the house. Miss Box is in front, pacing around. "Oh, Lori, I'm so nervous! What if she says something awful?"

The house is a dump. The psychic business must be on the skids. I ring the bell, Clarice comes to the door. She's a sad old hack, someone out of a 99 Cents store. She asks which of us wants to go first.

"Lori does," Miss Box says, the same way she did at Ray's.

We go into the dining room, whorehouse wallpaper, sticky plastic chair seats. Clarice hands me a deck of tarot cards, tells me to pick one. I pick one. She deals the rest of the pack. I drink the tea. She keeps staring into the cup; it's making me jumpy.

"I see you're a very determined young woman."

That gets me nervous. Scared she's going to say more, say what it is I'm determined to get, but she's flipping over the cards now.

She starts in—it's all crap, it's just like I thought. It's all a scam, just a story to tell Troy. I tune out what she's saying.

It's almost over now, there's only one card left. She picks it up, her eyes change. She gives me a look, it isn't so funny all of a sudden.

"I see two dark-haired men in your life, very bad men. One has already left through death; the other will be leaving soon."

That night my father died, standing at the top of the stairs and the policemen coming in the front door, *Mrs. Max, I'm afraid we have some bad news.*

The other will be leaving soon.

The woman picks up the cards, puts them away. She doesn't look at me; she knows what she's done.

Smiling at Miss Box. "Are you ready for your reading now?"

Miss Box jumps up. "No, actually, I think I've changed my mind."

She put me through that, but she's too fucking scared to take it herself. I almost can't hold it, I'm so angry.

She pays the woman, we get out of there. I don't say a word, walking to my car. Miss Box stops me, puts her hand on my arm.

"Lori, I can see you're upset, but, remember, she said they were bad men."

Don't trust myself to say anything, just walk away.

The other will be leaving soon. I always knew it, I always knew Troy would leave me in the end.

Pandora

That winter was the busiest of my life. I remember a time of almost constant work—pushing deals through, fussy negotiations, never-ending conference calls. But I was enjoying it, even found myself loving it; and more and more often, as I signed a contract or managed to get a raise for a client, I'd find myself thinking, *Uncle Gene would be proud of me.*

One day in early February, I was waiting in line at the bank when an older, red-haired woman tapped me on my arm.

"Are you Pandora Brown?"

I said I was.

"I'm Alicia Epstein. I was a friend of your uncle's. I heard you'd taken over his agency. How are things going?"

"Pretty well," I told her. "Though I don't imagine I'll ever be the agent Uncle Gene was."

"I hope you'll be a better one," she said.

I was startled. "What?"

"Your uncle was a very charming man, but he lived completely in the past. That's why he was never a first-class agent."

* * *

I couldn't stop thinking about what she said. All afternoon the phrase haunted me. *He lived completely in the past.* And, though I hated to admit it, it was true. There was nothing Uncle Gene liked better than to talk about the grand old days, the big deals he had been part of. After a while, Daddy and I grew to know all his negotiations by heart— it didn't matter that most of them were ten years out of date. At the time, it had been so impressive; now suddenly it seemed a little sad.

I asked Lori if she thought Uncle Gene had been a good agent.

She said, "Oh, yes, the best," but her answer came a little too quickly.

I went home to Palm Springs that weekend. It was an eerie drive down. The 10 freeway slowed to a stop by Pomona, and I sat motionless in the car for three and a half hours while the sky went black around me. Later I heard there was a police blockade. A man had killed his wife and four kids with a sawed-off shotgun. Finally he blew his own brains out, and then the traffic could move again.

When I got to the house, I found Daddy in a lot of pain. Mama and I got him into the recliner, and I rubbed massage oil into his legs. His feet felt so defenseless in my hands, so white and soft.

"That feels just wonderful, Andy-Pandy," he said with a sigh of pleasure. "But I'm much more interested in you. Tell me everything that's been happening. What have you done this week to set the agency world on its ear?"

I knew he'd enjoy hearing about the Honda deal, so I told him about that. When I got to the part about getting the bonus for Enrico, his face turned bright pink. He pushed up the recliner so fast I thought he was going to fly right out of the chair.

"Good for you!" he cried. "That's exactly what your Uncle Gene would have done!"

I thought of what Alicia Epstein had said, and then I pushed her words away. "Thank you," I told Daddy. "That's the greatest compliment you could give me."

"You don't know what a difference it's made to him," Mama said to me later. "All he does is brag to the doctors about all your deals and clients."

It made me want to cry.

After lunch, I went into town to buy valentines. I found a funny card for Lori, a dirty one for Steph, and a beauty for Mama and Daddy, about three feet high, stretching out like an accordion to say, "I love you."

I debated whether or not to get a valentine for Gary, and I finally decided that I would. We'd been sending each other valentines on and off for fourteen years—why break the tradition now?

When I came back to the office Monday morning, I found a message waiting for me on the answering machine. Ginette MacDougal had landed a speaking role on an NBC pilot.

The first person I called was Daddy. The news sent him completely over the moon. When I tried bringing him back to earth, reminding him that we were only talking about six lines and a few hundred dollars, he didn't care at all.

"It just shows what a great agent you are," he told me. "You're the one who discovered her."

And when I called Ginette, she was so excited she couldn't stop screaming.

After I hung up from the two calls, I sat back in my chair, tears running down my face. It was just a contract, just another deal—but I felt crazily proud. My instincts had been right; I was a competent agent, after all.

I couldn't resist going into Lori's office to tell her the news.

"Ginette's landed the pilot."

I thought there might be some embarrassment, some hint that Lori remembered saying Ginette had no talent whatever. But there was nothing.

"Congratulations—that's fabulous," she said, and gave me a big smile.

That afternoon, as I was coming back to the office from a meeting, I saw John Bradshaw half a block away, walking in my direction.

I quickened my steps; I began to fumble about in my purse for the keys, almost frantic to get inside the building before he reached it.

And then I stopped, annoyed at myself. This was ridiculous behavior; I was acting like a child. Just because the man chose to be overbearing, I was no longer going to let him intimidate me.

I found my keys and stood there purposefully, waiting for him to reach the building. I would open the door for both of us, smile, behave like an equal.

John Bradshaw reached the building, glanced at the door, saw me standing there, then continued to walk on down the street.

* * *

Looking back, I can see that it was on Valentine's Day when the machine was set in motion, the turn in my life was taken. And once that day was over and that choice was made, no other ending would have been possible.

I don't know if that's really true or not, but thinking so helps to ease the guilt.

I remember waking up that morning feeling sad. It was definitely hard not having a love on Valentine's Day.

Things cheered up when I reached the office. Lori came in with a big box of See's chocolates, and the mailman brought a beautiful valentine from Mama and Daddy, as well as a funny card from Steph.

But, to my surprise, there was no valentine from Gary. I waited all morning for him to come in with his usual card, but he never did.

Finally I went into the back room where he was working.

"So?" I asked him teasingly. "Where's my valentine?"

He flushed and looked uncomfortable. "Actually, I didn't get you one this year."

The valentine I'd bought him was in my purse, but I certainly wasn't going to give it to him now.

"That's fine," I told him. "It saves me having to get one for you."

I couldn't seem to get over my annoyance. Lori and I had lunch that day, and I ended up telling her all about it.

When I finished, she shrugged. "I'm not surprised. Guys can be awkward in situations like this."

I said, "Situations like what?"

She raised an eyebrow. "Didn't you know? Gary has a girlfriend."

I stared at her. "A girlfriend? Oh, no. I don't think so."

She nodded. "I've seen them together, two or three times outside the office. She's short, with red hair."

"Well, that doesn't mean anything," I insisted. "It wasn't necessarily a girlfriend—it could have been a client."

Lori laughed. "Not the way they were behaving."

I found myself a little knocked off-center by the news. Not by Gary's having a girlfriend, certainly— he deserved someone wonderful—but by his not telling me. It was upsetting to realize how removed I'd become from his life. Or had he thought my ego couldn't take it?

The rest of the afternoon only got worse. After lunch, there was a call from Gnome Productions, saying that Westinghouse wanted to put Tony Mackie on avail for the eighteenth. I called Tony, trying both his home phone and his cell repeatedly, but nobody answered.

Finally, forty-seven calls later, I reached his mother.

"Tony's been put on avail for a Westinghouse spot," I told her. "It's urgent that I speak to him."

"But he's in Sri Lanka, on a two-month camping trip," she said. "Did my bad boy forget to tell you? That's Tony all over."

And then Abe Martin at NBC called. There was a new miniseries coming up, and he wanted to audition Connie Hillbright for a recurring role. I called Connie, euphoric, and told her the news.

There was a pause. "I can't do it, Pandora," she said. "I'm sorry."

"What do you mean you can't do it?"

"I just can't."

"But why not?" I insisted. "This could be the biggest chance you'll ever get. At least give me a reason."

"All right," Connie said. "My husband beats me up. There's permanent damage to the veins around my eye. It shows up on camera through any kind of makeup, and I can't do filmwork anymore. Is that a good enough reason for you?"

After that, I counted the minutes until I could leave the office. At six o'clock I hurried away. Halfway down Sunset, I realized I'd left behind some files I needed, so I turned the car around and headed back to the agency.

When I opened the door, I heard noises, banging and shouting, coming from Lori's room.

I rushed in. Everything was a shambles—files all over the floor, chairs toppled, ornaments smashed. Lori was standing by the window, about to throw a bookend. When she saw me, she froze.

"Just get out of here," she said tightly.

Then she dropped the bookend and put her face in her hands. I hurried over and took her in my arms.

"Lori, what's the matter? Tell me what's wrong."

She kept shaking her head. "Just go, please just go."

But I couldn't just go. I couldn't just leave her like that.

"You shouldn't be alone," I said. "Come over to my place. Spend the evening with me—we'll do anything you want."

Lori suddenly got very quiet. She stepped out of my arms.

"All right," she said in a dull voice. "It's not like I've got anything else to do."

Then I understood. It was the awful boyfriend—he'd disappointed her, let her down on Valentine's Day.

It's strange. When I think about that evening now—and I've thought about it so many times—I'm never quite sure how much of it really did happen, and how much I made up.

Lori came over to the apartment a few minutes after nine. She seemed calmer. She brought some wine with her; I could tell she'd been drinking already.

When she pulled off her jacket, I saw there were bruises around her arm. It was like a bracelet—not as if someone had hit her, but as if she'd been grabbed very hard. I pretended I hadn't seen.

We started in on the wine. I looked at Lori, sitting hunched on the sofa, so beautiful and so sad. I went over and put my arms around her.

"I hope you know how much I care about you," I said.

Then I think she kissed me; or maybe that was a part of the evening I made up. It was over in a moment, if it ever even happened.

I broke out some vodka then and we did some shots. Lori lay down on the rug, and she started talking. It was horrible, what she told me—the things her father did, the things he made her do to him. It was unbearable to listen to.

I lay down beside her and held her. We stayed there on the rug for a long time.

Finally she took a deep breath and sat up.

"Well, this is a lousy party," she said.

The vodka suddenly got to me, and I ran for the bathroom. When I came back, Lori was standing by my computer, going through some papers.

"I didn't realize you actually had a shrine to him."

I saw, horribly embarrassed, that she had found all the articles about John Bradshaw that I'd gotten off the Internet.

"It's not a shrine," I told her. "I've just been doing a little research."

Lori started laughing. "Oh, come off it—you're obsessed with the man."

"No, I'm not."

"Then what do you call it?"

"He just interests me." I tried to say it with dignity. "He's so unapproachable. It's like a challenge, to see if I can get past that. All those thorns he's got up."

"Like Sleeping Beauty."

The thought of John Bradshaw as Sleeping Beauty was absurdly funny. I gave a drunken giggle.

"Well, I have just one question," Lori said. "Once you two are married, will the agency be Brown and Bradshaw, or Bradshaw and Brown?"

"You're crazy," I told her.

"Ah," she said. "You wait and see."

I shook my head. "You can wait as long as you want. He's more than twice my age, he's the most obnoxious man I'd ever met, and he can't even look at me without wincing. Obviously the perfect match!"

We went back to the wine. We finished the bottle.

Lori was rocking back and forth on the floor.

"We can't just let this go, you know. It's too perfect. We've got to do something, get the show on the road."

I didn't know what she was talking about, but I loved seeing her so happy and excited.

She got to her feet and weaved back over to my desk. The envelope with my headshots was on top, and she started pulling out the pictures. When she got to the final one—the one of me with my skirt up, blowing a kiss to the camera—she held it up.

"That's it!"

"What are you talking about?"

"We're sending this to John Bradshaw."

"You're insane," I told her. "Drunk out of your mind."

I got up; I went over; I tried to get the photo away from her, but I ended up tripping over the rug.

And then, as I lay there on the floor, I started picturing the scene: Prissy, prim John Bradshaw, sitting at his desk, opening the envelope and coming upon me with my legs wide open.

I began to laugh. I lay there on the floor and howled until my stomach hurt. I'd finally get myself to stop, even sit up—but then I'd see Bradshaw's face again, and I'd be flat on the floor once more.

"We're doing it!" I choked.

Then I remembered the valentine I'd bought for Gary and never given him. I grabbed my purse and pulled out the card.

"Look! We can send this along with it."

Lori and I whooped and laughed. I was in love with the whole idea. What a payback to Bradshaw for being so rude and pompous.

I whited out the inscription on the envelope and my signature on the card. I tried to write "John

Bradshaw," but I couldn't get the pen to form any letters.

"Let me," Lori said.

She put everything in a big manila envelope, wrote "John Bradshaw, Personal," on the front, and sealed it shut.

I said, "First thing Monday morning, it goes under his door."

"No," Lori said. "We're going to do it now."

"We can't," I told her. "It's too late, and we're in no shape to drive."

"Don't worry," she said. "It's only a few blocks."

She had stopped smiling. There was a look in her eyes that almost frightened me.

"We have to do it now," she repeated.

"All right." I gave in.

We got in the car. It was freezing, but we didn't wait to put on our coats. Lori drove; I kept an eye out for policemen.

We got to the office, and I told Lori to pull into the lot.

"I'm not allowed," she said. "It's for 'tenants only.' "

"As Supreme Goddess, I'll let you do it for tonight," I told her.

It was a stupid thing to say; I could see she didn't like it.

The building was dark, with just the eyes of all those dead movie stars staring down at us. We tiptoed by the agency without making a sound—the last thing I wanted was for Gary to hear us and call the police. But he was probably out anyway, celebrating Valentine's Day with his new girlfriend.

We sneaked upstairs to Bradshaw's office. I got on my hands and knees and pushed the envelope under the door.

As I stood up again, I suddenly didn't feel drunk anymore.

We drove back to my apartment. This drive was a lot quieter. When we got to my place, I asked Lori if she wanted to stay the night, but she said no. She sounded far away, as if she'd already gone.

I woke up at noon the next day and remembered, in one awful flash, everything that had happened the night before.

I got dressed as fast as I could, drove to the office, and ran up the stairs to Bradshaw's agency. For fifteen minutes, I lay on the carpet, trying to retrieve the envelope with a paper knife, but it was pushed too far underneath for me to reach.

I stayed very busy that weekend, doing every errand I could come up with, anything to keep from thinking about John Bradshaw opening his mail on Monday morning and seeing that photograph.

Sunday night, I made my plans. I would get to the office early and wait for Emmett to come in. I'd simply ask for the envelope back and tell him it had been put under the door by mistake.

But Monday morning, even though I was at the office by eight o'clock, John Bradshaw's Mercedes was already in the lot, the door to his agency was open, and the envelope was gone.

The day was endless. There was no word at all from Bradshaw—every hour or so, I'd tiptoe halfway upstairs to see if I could hear anything. I was like a murderer who couldn't leave the crime scene alone.

Lori was very remote all day. Neither of us so much as mentioned Friday night.

When nothing had happened by three o'clock, I began to relax a little. It suddenly occurred to me that maybe Bradshaw hadn't even realized that it was me in the photo. He was an agent, after all; he probably got dozens of glossies in the mail every day, from actresses wanting representation. It was very possible that he had taken one disgusted look at the picture, and thrown it away without ever even noticing who it was.

And I thanked God I'd had the sense not to sign the valentine.

At five, Gary came in, saying he was leaving early that day.

I said, "Going out with your girlfriend tonight?"

He turned a little red. "Yes, actually."

"You could have told me about her, you know."

He nodded. "I was going to."

"Is she nice?"

"Very."

"Well, I'm happy for you."

"Thanks," he said. There was a pause. "Also, Pandora, I wanted to tell you—I'll be leaving here soon. I'm sorry I've encroached on you for this long; I've finally just about got the money together for a place of my own."

"That's wonderful," I told him, but added that he was welcome to stay as long as he felt like it.

"I appreciate that; but I really think it's time I went."

After he left, I sat there at my desk, feeling, for some reason, a little depressed. A few minutes later,

I heard a knock. Thinking it was Gary again, I jumped up and opened the door.

John Bradshaw was standing there. I was so surprised I couldn't say a word.

He didn't speak either. Then finally he asked, "May I come in?"

"Of course."

I was so embarrassed I could barely lead the way. I kept sneaking glances at him, trying to read the expression on his face, but I finally gave it up.

Once we were in my office, he seemed to forget about me. He walked around, taking his time, thumbing through books and looking at all the framed photos.

He said, "I see you haven't changed much around."

"No. I wanted to keep everything the way Uncle Gene had it."

He gave me a small brusque smile. "I can appreciate that—your uncle was a very likable man."

We were standing only a few feet apart. A faint and expensive scent of lime came from his suit. I could see that his eyes were the blue of a shirt washed once too many times. And that his hands were very white, like Daddy's, but beautifully manicured.

There was a pause. He turned from me. He put his briefcase down on the desk and opened it. My heart sank, as out came the manila envelope.

"I'm here about this," he said.

I was too ashamed to look up at him.

"I was a little puzzled when I received it," he went on. "Am I to understand you're looking for artistic representation?"

I was so shocked—it was so unlike anything I'd thought he would say—that I started to laugh.

He put the envelope down on my desk and seemed to forget all about it. He looked at me very intently.

"How are you enjoying living in Los Angeles?"

His tone was kind. It was almost the way Uncle Gene might have sounded.

I said I loved it.

"And being an agent—are you loving that, too?"

"Yes. I've even had a few triumphs lately."

I told him the story of Ginette. He nodded.

"Those moments can be very exciting."

There was another pause; then he looked at his watch and said he had an appointment to get to. I hoped he'd forgotten about the envelope, but he picked it up and put it carefully back into his briefcase. I walked him to the door, and when he reached the hall, he turned around.

"Perhaps one night you'll do me the honor of having dinner with me."

After he left, I sat down at my desk in a complete state of shock.

I couldn't believe what had happened. I couldn't believe that John Bradshaw—haughty, aloof John Bradshaw—had come in just now and been so personable, so warm.

I almost called Lori, but decided not to. Telling her would have made the whole thing into some sort of joke; and it wasn't. I had no idea what it was, other than being the last thing I would have expected, but it wasn't a joke.

I kept thinking of Bradshaw's weary smile, and those sad, beautiful hands. I wondered if he was really going to ask me to dinner.

Gary

That was probably the worst winter I've ever spent. Even today, I don't particularly like to remember those nights in the back room of Pandora's office.

To be honest, I knew, about a week after I arrived in L.A., that the arrangement wasn't going to work out. If I'd been smart, I would have cut my losses right then, gone back to Palm Springs, or found somewhere affordable in L.A. But I've always been stubborn—too stubborn, my dad always said; and I've never been willing to admit when I've made a mistake.

Maybe if I had stuck to Pandora's original idea and only used the office during the day, it would have been all right, but staying there at night was just about impossible. Simple things like ironing a shirt became a hassle, and I got very tired of driving down to the Hollywood Y every night in order to shower. But I kept telling myself that it was only temporary, that I was doing it to save money, and that I could stand anything for a few weeks.

But what really wore me down was being near Pandora again. It was hell, seeing her every day, still feeling those feelings about her and knowing they weren't being returned. I told myself I was crazy for expecting anything else. Right from the beginning, Pandora had made it clear that her offer was a business one, and nothing personal. But, of course, secretly I'd had my foolish hopes that if I came to L.A., if I could just be with her again, I could somehow, magically, bring our relationship back to life. But I couldn't.

Pandora was very kind to me. She went out of her way to show me around town and introduce me to potential clients. But that wasn't what I wanted. I didn't like the idea of being a burden to her, and finally I told her not to worry, that I could manage by myself.

She backed off then and let me alone; and as the days went by I found myself gradually sinking from friend into the role of tenant. That was the worst feeling of all.

It was also hard seeing, close-up, how much the last few months in L.A. had changed her. She had taken on the whole Hollywood lifestyle, and she seemed to care as much about looking like an agent as being one. She was forever concerned with eating at the trendiest restaurants, having lunch with the right people, and dressing like a starlet, with the tight clothes and the streaked hair.

Maybe I was being unfair. I knew how much Pandora wanted to be a success. If she felt that this was the quickest way to achieve it, who was I to say she was wrong? But in my eyes Pandora Brown had always been so special. It hurt to see her now, trying as hard as she could to copy everybody else in town.

Another thing that bothered me was her friendship with Lori Max. Again, I'll admit I was prejudiced—I had taken a dislike to Lori since the very first time I'd seen her at Starbucks.

It was easy at first to dismiss Lori as one of those women who use sex to get what they want—we had them in Palm Springs, too—but as the weeks went on, I started to change my mind about her. I began to wonder if the tight clothes and the makeup weren't just some kind of smoke screen for something else, for something she was trying to hide. To tell the truth, Lori scared me. I got the feeling that everything she did or said had a hidden purpose, was a means to a secret end.

But Pandora thought Lori was wonderful. She had lunch with her all the time, she brought her along to business meetings, they sometimes went out to clubs together on weekends. I could understand where Pandora would value Lori as an assistant, but to me she seemed to be going overboard. I guessed that she was lonely, that she missed her girlfriend Steph and was looking for a replacement in L.A. But as far as I was concerned, she could have chosen a whole lot better.

As the days went by I started getting a better grip on myself. I stopped expecting anything from Pandora and began focusing my whole attention on my work. But that turned out to be another disappointment. It was much harder to establish myself in L.A. than I had imagined, and business was slower than I would have believed possible. None of Pandora's contacts came though, the ads I took out didn't gain many results, and days passed without my getting any jobs at all. Several times I was on the point of giving up and going back to Palm Springs, but then my stubborness would kick in and I'd give myself just one more week. And then another.

Mom and Janine offered to help me out, but of course I wouldn't let them. Nearly a month went by. I felt ashamed that I hadn't managed to do better, and I hated it that I was still living full-time in Pandora's office.

Finally, toward the end of December, things began to improve. Word-of-mouth helped. My business started to move, and, my client list grew. By mid-January I was even starting to save a bit of money, though I was still nowhere near being able to afford a place of my own. Still, I felt encouraged. I told myself that, from a business standpoint at least, the move to L.A. had been justified. The only problem was, I was getting lonelier and lonelier with every day that passed.

After Pandora and Lori left the office each evening, the silence would start to settle down around me. Something about the whole setup—the scratched furniture, the filing cabinets full of ten-year-old deals, those posters of dead movie stars in the hall—brought me right down, made me feel the whole of life was a sorry little waste.

I started taking long walks around the neighborhood—anything to get out of the office for an hour or two. At first I stayed close to the Sunset Plaza area. I'd stroll around the boutiques and restaurants, watching all the people with their perfect hairdos and expensive clothes. It seemed to me they all seemed to walk and talk so much faster than they needed to.

Eventually I got sick of that, and I started going farther afield, driving east along Sunset or down San Vicente to Pico Boulevard. Those were pretty tough parts of town, filled with bars and porn shops, but at least they were alive. I remembered my first trip to L.A. and how shocked I was to find

Hollywood so seedy. Now I was feeling comfortable in places like that—and I wondered if it was only Pandora whom L.A. had changed.

Sometimes I ate dinner in a café or had a few drinks at a bar, but I never went into any of the sex shows. I figured I didn't need to feel lonelier than I already was.

As time went by and I became a regular, I started seeing the same faces night after night. Sunset was where the ladies-for-hire could be found, standing on the corners with their short skirts and big hair. At first, they tried to get my business, but when they saw I wasn't in the market, they still stayed friendly, waving hello, or asking for cigarettes.

One night I noticed a new girl. She was lovely; fresh and clean. She looked like she belonged on a horse ranch in Montana, not picking up men on the Sunset Strip. When I got closer and took a second look, I realized that she couldn't have been more than fourteen years old.

That got me so depressed that for a few nights afterward I didn't go out at all. But in the end the walls of the office started closing in on me, and I came back. I didn't see the girl again.

Sometimes, for a change, I'd walk down Santa Monica Boulevard, where the male hookers hung out. They could tell right off the bat that I wasn't their type, but, like the girls, they were friendly enough, and we got along fine. There was another group on the street, though, that I didn't much care for. Around eleven o'clock every night a dozen or so guys would come out of nowhere and start to congregate, two or three on every corner. They wore black leather and moved very quietly. Whenever a police car cruised down the street they would instantly melt away, only to reappear, like cockroaches, when the cops turned the corner. I made a big point of staying out of their way.

But there was one of them that I couldn't help noticing. Other men's looks don't usually register with me, but this guy was outstanding—tall, dark-haired, with a lean, muscular build. He was handsome enough to have been a movie star. I didn't get it at all. I used to wonder about him, how a man with that kind of looks had ended up on Santa Monica Boulevard, pushing, dealing, doing whatever it was he was doing.

Around midnight, I'd go on back to the office. My head was filled up with music and car horns now, and things didn't seem quite so lonely.

New Year's Day, Tom and Helene got married at the Desert Chapel in Palm Springs. I took my job as best man seriously, spending hours writing a speech that I, at least, thought was amusing.

At the reception afterward I had a good time catching up with old friends. Before I left I wanted to say something to Tom, something to let him know how much he had always meant to me but the feeling was bigger than any words. So I just gave him a bear hug and told Helene to take care of him.

"I will," she said. There was so much love in her voice that I wanted to bawl.

Driving back to L.A., I puzzled over the way life worked. From the time we were kids, Tom and I had been so much alike that people often mistook us for brothers. How had it happened, I wondered, that one of us had gotten to marry the girl he loved and the other had turned into the loneliest man in L.A.?

And then, about a week later, I met Sara.

I had a business appointment at a new travel agency in West Hollywood, and the moment I walked into the lobby I noticed the young woman sitting in the front left-hand cubicle. She was cute, with curly red hair, and hazel eyes. And what's more, she was natural-looking—unlike just about every other girl in town.

She was talking on the phone to someone who was obviously being difficult, but she didn't get impatient. She answered everything politely, and even after she hung up, she didn't complain about the call. I wanted to compliment her on her attitude, but just then the office manager came out from the back, and we went in to our meeting.

Afterward, when I returned to the lobby, the girl was still sitting at her desk. She was doing paperwork now, but I got the feeling she knew I was watching her.

I walked over, trying to come up with a topic of conversation. There were some Swiss travel posters on the wall behind her, and I figured that was as good an opening as any.

"I understand the Matterhorn in Switzerland is even bigger than the one at Disneyland," I said.

She laughed. "Yes, but it doesn't have the Abominable Snowman."

So we got to talking—about Disneyland, and Switzerland, about skiing and chalets and even cheese.

Then, when I ran out of things to say, I asked the girl what her name was.

"Sara," she said.

I felt a jar go through me.

When I was a teenager, my favorite song in the world was an oldie from the seventies called "Sara,

Smile." I'd play it over and over, imagining what the girl in the song was like. I always pictured her as being grave and sweet, a little like this Sara.

"Are you from L.A.?" I asked.

"Yes," she said. "But not Los Angeles. I'm from Lake Arrowhead."

That gave me another jar. Lake Arrowhead was a very special place to me. I'd once spent a week there when I was seven—it was the last vacation my family went on before Dad got sick.

I wondered if Sara had been there the week I'd visited; if maybe she'd been one of the little girls in their bright bathing suits, paddling around in the lake, or eating ice cream on the shore. I might have waterskied right by her without ever noticing.

It was getting late. I had another appointment to go to, but I asked Sara if she could join me for a cup of coffee after work.

"I'd like that very much," she said and gave me another Sara smile.

Driving back to the office, I rolled down my window and began belting out the song. It was the best I'd felt for months, since I'd come to L.A.

That first date with Sara lasted almost five hours. We started off at Starbucks, where we worked our way through two cappuccinos and six biscotti; then after that, we moved on to dinner at her favorite restaurant, The Farm.

I've always considered myself a quiet person, but that night I found I was talking so much I couldn't get the words out fast enough. I guess all those weeks of loneliness had finally caught up with me. And Sara was pretty much the same. Every time we got onto a new subject, we'd both be off, full of opinions, arguing or agreeing with each other about everything.

When the waiter brought the check, he put his hands on his hips and rolled his eyes.

"Newlyweds?" he asked.

Sara and I laughed, embarrassed. And it struck me that in all the years I had known, and dated Pandora, nobody had ever mistaken us for newlyweds.

After that night, Sara and I started seeing a lot of each other. Once or twice during the week, we'd go out to coffee or dinner; on weekends we'd explore the city. As time went by I made the discovery that as long as you have a friend to see it with, L.A. isn't really a bad town at all.

Sometimes we did touristy things, bought doughnuts at the Farmers' Market or window-shopped on Rodeo Drive. Other days, we went on hikes out to the Santa Monica Mountains or up by the duck pond near Mulholland. I even talked Sara into going on the Graveline Tour, where we sat in a hearse and drove by all the places where famous people had died. But she got me back for that one, dragging me into every art gallery on Melrose Avenue.

At night we'd usually wind up at Sara's place, watching videos or listening to CDs. She had a nice apartment on La Peer, very cheerful, full of soft, bright colors. She always let me have a long soak in her tub, and sometimes she'd cook me dinner—I appreciated that more than I could say.

We had good times, sweet and easy and relaxed. In the past, when I'd gone out with a girl, I'd always been impatient for the physical side of the relationship to develop, but with Sara it was different. From the day I met her I sensed that she could end

up as something serious in my life—maybe because
of that song—and I didn't want to ruin things by
moving too fast.

I kept wondering at what point I should tell
Pandora the news that I had a girlfriend. It would
have been the natural thing to do, but for some
reason I kept putting it off. I was getting to the
point with my business where I was almost ready to
move to a place of my own. When that happened,
I decided, then I would say something.

Sara and I had been going together about a
month when I took her down to Palm Springs to
meet my mother. I was a little nervous on the drive
down, wondering how she and Mom would get
along, but the moment I introduced the two of
them I could see that everything was going to be
all right.

We arrived right before dinner. Sara helped
Mom set the table and get the meal ready. The two
of them made fun of me for sitting on the sofa like
a pasha, but I didn't feel like moving. I got a lot of
pleasure seeing them together, coming in and out
of the kitchen, talking and laughing.

After dinner, we watched a little TV, and then
Mom said she was ready for bed. As I walked her to
her room, she said to me, "I like your girl, Gary."

I found myself remembering something from
years back, the day Mom had first met Pandora.
I'd asked what drawer Pandora was in, and my
mother had said, "Top or bottom—I'm not sure
which." With Sara, I knew it was top. I didn't even
have to ask.

Later that night, I took Sara for a walk around
the neighborhood. It was a real show-off evening:

Palm Springs at her best, with 3-D stars popping through a black sky. We didn't say much as we strolled along, but I remember the sound of our footsteps, how peaceful they were, and how well they fit together.

We got back to the house around ten. Mom had given Sara Janine's old room, and she had unpacked her suitcase there; but as we stood together in the hall, I sensed we were both feeling the same way— that it was right for her to come into my room instead.

It was the first time I'd made love to a woman since Pandora. In the beginning, it was a little strange, touching a new body, breathing the scent of a different skin. But I guess that was only natural. Soon Sara became herself to me, smelling of ginger and some mysterious, exotic perfume. Her body was very pale; beneath the tanned, freckled face, her breasts and thighs were startling in their whiteness. It felt very right having her body, compact and strong, beneath me; and as I was falling asleep afterward, the scent of her hair on my pillow, I remembered that waiter at The Farm thinking we were newlyweds.

The next morning, I took Sara out riding in the desert. She'd never been on a motorcycle before— growing up in Arrowhead, it was always speedboats—but she turned out to be a natural rider, with a good sense of balance.

In the afternoon, I took her all around Palm Springs and showed her some of the spots that were important to me: Indian Canyon, the Living Desert, my old high school. But there were a few places I purposefully left out of the list: Taquitz Falls, Katherine Finchy Elementary, the airport. Those were still Pandora's.

Sara loved everything; she told me she couldn't imagine why I'd ever left Palm Springs to move to Los Angeles.

"I wonder that same thing," I said.

We left the desert a little later than planned, and by the time we got back to L.A. it was rush hour. All the noise and the lights were going full blast; the weekend in Palm Springs was already starting to seem unreal.

Sara invited me to stay the night at her place. I told her I would love to, but that I needed to stop by the office first, to pick up some files. I dropped her off at her apartment, and said I'd be back in an hour.

I headed over to West Hollywood and parked the car on a side street about a block away from the office. As I started walking down Sunset, I saw two figures, a man and a woman, about twenty-five feet in front of me. The woman was Lori, and the man was tall, dark-haired, and wearing a black leather jacket. They didn't see me.

They were moving very slowly, talking intently. I couldn't hear what they were saying, but the tone of their voices was clear. Lori's was low and very urgent. It sounded completely different from the voice she used at work—it could have belonged to another person entirely. I heard her say the word *she,* and that caught my attention, but then her voice dropped again. I guessed she was talking about Pandora, but I couldn't be sure.

What I was sure of, though, was the man she was with—when he turned his head to look at her, I saw his face. He was the guy from Santa Monica Boulevard, the one who looked like a movie star. I didn't know exactly what he was—a drug dealer, a pimp, a burglar—but I got a very bad feeling, seeing him and Lori together outside Pandora's office.

I tried not to let myself jump to any conclusions. All that had actually happened was that Lori and a guy were walking together. If it looked suspicious, then that was probably what I was bringing to the party. I decided not to mention anything about it to Pandora.

The next morning, though, when Lori showed up for work, sounding so sweet and mealymouthed, so different from the night before, I decided I couldn't let it go by. I went into Pandora's office.

"It's none of my business," I told her. "But I thought you should know—I saw Lori hanging around here last night with a pretty tough-looking character."

Pandora raised her eyebrows. "And since when have you taken up spying?"

I got the feeling she was definitely interested—that she would have liked to hear more—but she didn't let herself ask.

I went back to my office, annoyed at myself, annoyed at her.

Valentine's Day was coming up. I wanted to make it special for Sara, and I covered all the bases, buying her earrings, flowers, and a bottle of perfume. I also spent a long time at Hallmark, choosing a card, trying to find something that was appropriate for this stage in our relationship. I considered getting a card for Pandora as well, a funny one maybe, but I just didn't do it. I wanted Sara to be my only valentine this year.

* * *

The Monday after Valentine's Day Pandora was in a very strange mood. I'd never seen her so restless. She couldn't seem to sit still or do any work at all.

Around six, I was leaving to get some dinner, and I saw Emmett, the gay guy who worked for John Bradshaw, coming down the stairs. He gave me a big smile.

"Were you in on the glossy?"

I said I didn't know what he was talking about.

He couldn't wait to tell me. I heard all about it, how, over the weekend, Pandora had pushed a porn picture of herself, along with a valentine, under Bradshaw's door.

My first thought was that Lori was behind it, but that still didn't excuse Pandora. I couldn't believe that she'd do such a childish thing.

"What happened when he got the picture?" was all I could think of to say.

"It's hard to tell with Mr. B. All I know is, I didn't see it in the wastebasket when I left." He grinned at me. "Your girl's all right."

I didn't know what made me angrier—Pandora behaving so stupidly, or Emmett thinking she was any girl of mine.

I suddenly didn't feel hungry anymore, so I walked around Sunset for a while, until I was sure Pandora had left the office.

But when I came back, I found she was still there.

"I heard about your glossy," I told her, and her face grew red.

"It was just a joke," she said. "I thought it would be funny."

She was trying to sound breezy, and that made it

worse. I could just picture that poor old guy opening up the envelope and imagining I don't know what.

I grabbed her arm. "Don't be so naive, Pandora—you know better than to lead a man on like that."

Then the oddest expression came over her face. She shook my hand off.

"Who says I'm leading him on?"

I blew up at that. "What's he supposed to think? He didn't know it was a joke."

But she just kept looking at me in that strange way.

"Well, maybe it wasn't."

I was supposed to take Sara to a movie that night, but I canceled the date—I knew I wouldn't be much company. I went out by myself and got good and drunk.

Pandora

The days went by. John Bradshaw never called. I couldn't get his visit out of my mind. I kept remembering his eyes, the tone of his voice. *Perhaps one night you'll do me the honor of having dinner with me.* And then nothing.

I looked him up on the Internet again, as if that might somehow re-start the connection between us. I went back to some early articles, and found another picture of him and his daughter, Amanda. She was sixteen then. That would make her twenty-nine now. Older than I was. I liked the way Bradshaw was smiling down at her in the photo. His expression reminded me of the way he had looked at me that day in my office—and there I was, obsessing about him again.

The following Tuesday I got a call from Steph.

"Clear the decks," she told me. "I'm coming into L.A. for a meeting on Friday. But I'll be free for you to take me out to lunch—somewhere expensive."

I was thrilled that Steph was coming. And it was a relief to have something to think about besides John Bradshaw not calling me. But when Friday came, and Steph and I had our lunch at Trilussa, I found he was the first subject I brought up.

"Do you think there's something wrong with me?" I asked her. "He's old enough to be my father—or worse, my father's older brother."

"It all depends," Steph said. "If he looks like Harrison Ford or Sean Connery, then you're fine; if he doesn't, you're in trouble."

I laughed. "It's more than about looks. I think it would be an interesting experience, going out with an older man. Especially an older man from Hollywood. I'd love to hear all the stories, what it was like back in the glory days."

"Assuming he can still remember," Steph pointed out.

When lunch was over, I asked Steph if she was interested in seeing the agency.

"Of course," she said. "And I guess I ought to meet this girl who's replaced me in your affections."

I gave her a hug. "Nobody will ever do that."

I had hoped Steph and Lori would like each other, but they were cordial and nothing more. Gary was delighted to see Steph, though; when she walked in, he ran out of his office and swung her up in a big hug.

When it was time for Steph to leave for her meeting, I called a taxi for her and we walked outside to the street.

Suddenly I clutched her arm. "That's him!"

John Bradshaw was walking down Sunset, about to go into Le Clafoutis.

"What do you think?"

Steph looked thoughtful. "You're only a *little* bit sick," she said judiciously. "It could be a lot worse."

When the taxi came and we had to say good-bye,

I found I was almost in tears. I hadn't realized just how much I'd been missing my Glorious Girlfriend.

Maybe that was the reason I went into Lori's office later that afternoon and finally told her everything about John Bradshaw's visit.

When I finished there was a silence.

"I can't believe you didn't tell me this before," she said.

I felt terrible. "I guess I was just too embarrassed. I thought you'd laugh at the whole thing." I went over and gave her a hug. "I'm sorry. I'll tell you everything from now on."

"All right," she said. "And don't worry that he hasn't called. He will."

But he didn't call. And eventually I got the point that he was never going to.

A few days later, I saw him outside Chin Chin. He stared right at me, nodded, and then deliberately looked away. He couldn't have been more curt; it couldn't have been more of a dismissal. I walked quickly past. I felt ashamed of myself, for how much I'd been thinking about him, hoping he'd call.

And then, that afternoon, the phone rang.

"Miss Brown? John Bradshaw here. I've just received an invitation to the premiere of *The Weather in the Streets* for the evening of March fifteenth. I'd be delighted if you would accompany me."

His voice was chilly, aloof. For a moment, I thought about turning the invitation down, but from the time I was ten years old, I had dreamed about going to a premiere. I told him I would love to come.

"Then we're all set. There'll be a party following

the screening, and afterward we'll go on somewhere for a late supper."

I hung up the phone.

"Lori!" I started screaming.

The premiere was nearly two weeks away, but ac-
cording to Lori, I needed to start planning for it at
once.

"What are you going to wear?" was her first question.

I visualized my wardrobe. "I don't have anything."

"Then you'll have to get a gown."

That was a daunting thought. I knew what these
premieres were like, with entertainment reporters
publicly criticizing all the women's dresses, and at
that moment I felt very much the little hick from
Palm Springs.

"I wish you'd come shopping with me," I said.
"To give me a little moral support."

Lori smiled. "It would be my pleasure."

That Saturday we met outside Neiman Marcus.

"I've been trying to remember the last time I
bought a gown," I said as we went inside. "I think it
was my eleventh-grade prom. Pale pink tulle. It
cost three months' allowance, and it certainly wasn't
worth it."

"Why not?"

"Rod Starkey asked me to dance out on the terrace, and when it was over there was a big stain
down the front of my dress."

Lori gave a little laugh. "I think every woman
has that story to tell."

"Really? I felt so ashamed, I couldn't even take the dress in to be dry-cleaned. I ended up throwing it away."

"Three months' allowance?" She looked at me a little strangely. "And you threw it away?"

We went up to the third floor. Before we'd even stepped off the escalator Lori was pointing to a silver Prada sheath at the front of the sale rack.

"Grab it," she said.

I tried on the dress; it was ultra-sophisticated and very sexy, and I didn't think it was my style at all. But when I came out of the dressing room, Lori said, "It's perfect. You have to get it."

I remembered the pale pink tulle and wondered if I'd really changed that much since I'd been in L.A.

"It's much more your style than mine," I told her. "You try it on, too. Just for fun."

She came out of the dressing room a few minutes later. I'd never seen anyone look more beautiful.

We shopped around for other choices, but there was nothing quite right. I had the feeling that I was in a chrysalis stage, no longer Palm Springs, not yet L.A.

Lori kept insisting that I had to buy the Prada. "Trust me on this," she said. "Wasn't I right about the headshot?"

I laughed and gave in, and bought the dress. I could see how pleased she was.

As we said good-bye outside Neiman's, I gave Lori a hug.

"You *were* right about the headshot," I told her. "And if it hadn't been for you, I wouldn't even be going to this premiere. So when this whole thing is over, I'm giving you the Prada."

I'd never seen her look so happy.

* * *

As it got closer to the premiere, I grew more and more excited. I kept trying to stay calm, telling myself that it was only a movie and a party afterward. But that didn't make a bit of difference.

And Daddy was no help—the premiere was all he talked about. "I only wish that Gene could be here to see this," he kept saying. I agreed. It would have meant a lot to Uncle Gene, watching me walk down the red carpet on John Bradshaw's arm.

"What are you planning on doing about your hair?" Lori asked the Monday before the premiere.

I said I hadn't thought about it.

"Well, you'll need to get it done Friday afternoon, and you might as well have a manicure and a full makeup, too. I'll book you with Rose Casey and Marie at the Bel Age."

I laughed. "Aren't we being a little excessive?"

But it didn't take much to persuade me.

The next day John Bradshaw called to finalize the arrangements.

"Where shall I pick you up?" he asked.

I was about to give him my home address, but hesitated. For some reason, I didn't care for the thought of him seeing my little apartment.

"Why don't you pick me up at the office?"

He seemed surprised. "Are you sure?"

"Yes."

As I hung up, I thought how inconvenient I'd made things for myself—I'd either have to dress at home and drive over in my gown, or get everything ready in the office. But I still preferred it that way.

* * *

The night of the premiere finally arrived. I ended up getting dressed at home. I was so nervous I could barely zip myself into the Prada.

A part of me longed for the evening to be safely over with. I remembered all those dances I'd gone to in high school, how much I looked forward to them, and how awful they always turned out to be. I cheered myself up by thinking that the premiere couldn't possibly be as bad as that. I was ten years older now. A little perspective had been gained.

But I was still almost too shaky to drive to the office.

At seven o'clock, I could see the headlights of a limo coming down the street. I watched out the window as it stopped in front of the building and Bradshaw got out. He didn't use his key—he buzzed very formally, as though he were a client, and I let him into the building.

He was wearing an Armani tuxedo; he looked elegant and distinguished, the way he had in the old photos I'd seen on the Internet.

I felt very self-conscious beside him. I started flashing back on my life: weeding in the garden, dirt-biking, hanging out by the airport, buying clothes at Gottschalks. It seemed completely unbelievable that I could be standing here now, wearing a Prada dress and going to a premiere with a man in an Armani tuxedo.

He bent down and kissed my hand. "You look absolutely enchanting."

"Thank you, John," I said. It was the first time I had called him—or even thought of him—by his Christian name.

I locked up the office—Gary had said he wouldn't be in until Monday—and we got into the limo. It was beautiful, with a soft gray interior and burled wood paneling; everything was fitted out like a ship's cabin. There was a little bar, filled with decanters and crystal glasses, and John asked me if I wanted a drink. I said no, knowing I wouldn't be able to swallow. But I did take a paper napkin as a souvenir for Daddy.

We talked only a little during the drive. We discussed *The Weather in the Streets,* and I told him I'd read the novel when I was in high school. I knew the moment I said it that mentioning high school was a mistake—it reminded us both of the difference in our ages. Sure enough, he was quiet for a moment, and then he changed the subject.

"Cora Macafee is one of my clients," he said. "She plays Etty in the picture."

I couldn't help thinking that ten years ago John Bradshaw would have been the agent for the leading actress, not the supporting one. But actually I preferred it this way. It was awkward enough being with him now—how much worse would it have been at the height of his fame?

We reached Hollywood Boulevard. I'd never seen such a crowd. The street was solid with cars, with police and blockades everywhere.

"People have been camping out all day," the limo driver told us. "Waiting to see the celebrities."

Kids kept breaking through the blockades and running up to our car. They'd cup their faces in their hands, and press them up to the window. It was eerie—completely impersonal. They didn't care who was inside the car as long as it was someone famous.

Finally we pulled up to the theater. The driver came around and opened the door for me. For a moment, I didn't think I'd be able to get out of the car—it was like entering a nuclear blast, light and heat and noise all around. A million flashbulbs went off as I stepped onto the red carpet. Part of me, the little girl from Palm Springs, hated it and wanted to hide; but part of me loved it, just loved it. I didn't care that I hadn't done anything to deserve being here; I was greedy for all of this; this was what I wanted.

John Bradshaw got out of the car and stood beside me. There were more flashbulbs, more yelling. He held my arm tightly, and we walked together down the red carpet. A crowd of fans, three and four people deep, lined the way, separated from us by the cordon.

I saw one little girl, about thirteen years old. She looked scruffy and tired, like she'd been standing there all day. That could have been me at her age, waiting for Brad Pitt or Tom Cruise. I waved at her and smiled. She clutched the girl next to her, and pointed me out, thrilled. Hopefully, she'd never discover that I was nobody.

We reached the lobby. There were so many celebrities there—I tried to notice every detail, without seeming to gawk. Everyone came up to John Bradshaw. He was elegant, low-key. He introduced me, not mentioning that I was an agent. I tried to look above-it-all and intellectual. It's funny what embarrassment will do.

The lights began flashing, so we went into the theater and took our seats. One of the producers made a speech, and then the director introduced the film. When the opening credits came on, the audience applauded every name. It was fantastic to hear—it was so personal, so rich. I felt forever spoiled; I never wanted to see a movie in Palm Springs again, only here in Hollywood where everybody in the audience knew everybody on the screen.

When the movie began, I found that I was very aware of Bradshaw's presence beside me. He sat completely still, focused on the film, and I realized that he was staring at the screen in the same way he had stared at me that day at Chin Chin. I had assumed at the time that it was curtness, but it wasn't—it was intensity.

I thought the movie was absolutely wonderful. When the final credits rolled the entire audience stood up and cheered. It was fantastic, being a part of all that.

At last, we stood up to go. John took my arm and led me back to the lobby. Outside, the crowd of fans was still pressed behind the cordon. It was unnerving to think that they had been standing there, waiting for us to come out ever since we had gone in.

The party was held across the street. A huge striped tent had been erected over a parking lot, and a parquet floor was laid over the asphalt. As we walked in, nothing seemed quite real, maybe because it was so hot and crowded.

I had one glass of champagne and concentrated on being invisible. People kept coming up to John, and again I was impressed by how regally he behaved—even in the crowd, he managed to seem apart from it all. Only when he spoke to his client, Cora Macafee, did he unbend a little.

We didn't stay long. He congratulated the director and the producers of the film and then asked if I was ready to go.

We walked back out to Hollywood Boulevard. It was still solid with cars. I didn't see how we would ever find the limo, but there it was, waiting just outside the theater like a well-trained dog. When I got in my ears were buzzing from all the screaming. John didn't seem to be affected at all.

"We'll be going on to The Ivy now," he told the driver. "If that's all right with you," he added, turning to me.

I told him it was wonderful. "I've never actually been there, but it was Uncle Gene's favorite restaurant. He always promised he'd take me someday."

There was a pause. I was afraid I'd said something wrong, but John Bradshaw gave me a wry little smile.

"And now I'm keeping his promise for him."

We drove in silence for a while.

"What did you think of the movie?" I asked finally.

"I enjoyed it," he said, "although not to the extent you seemed to."

I suddenly felt gauche, too easily seduced by the film.

"I thought Cora Macafee stole the show," I told him quickly.

"Yes," he agreed. "I was very pleased with Cora."

Then I couldn't think of anything more to say.

We reached The Ivy. It was enchanting, surrounded by a weathered white picket fence and furnished with faded chintzes, rosy bricks, and wrought-iron furniture. It made me think of a French farmhouse, but I didn't like to say so, since I'd never actually been to France.

The maitre d' showed us to our table. The waiter came by to take our drink order, and after he left there was another silence. I started chattering on about the agency—it was the only thing that came into my head. I talked about what was happening with Enrico Morales and Kim Helens, and I told John Bradshaw the story about Tony Mackie going camping in Sri Lanka and forgetting to tell me. I knew I was babbling, but I seemed to be under a compulsion to keep on; I couldn't stop myself.

Then he did it for me. He reached forward suddenly and took my hand.

He said, "I can't stop thinking about you."

I thought I had heard wrong.

I stared down at our two hands. His were cool and white, with those beautifully manicured nails. Mine seemed unformed, too pink.

I looked up at him. He smiled, a rather sad smile; he seemed suddenly much older. He made me think of Daddy.

"I guess it was your valentine."

"I'm so sorry," I said. "It was a stupid, stupid joke."

"Don't say that," he told me.

The waiter brought our drinks, and Bradshaw took his hand away. He drank some wine, then carefully put the glass down. And suddenly all the silence was gone, the words kept coming and coming.

He told me about Lorraine, his wife—how they had first met; how the moment he saw her, it was like being hit by lightning. How they'd been so happy for twenty-five years and how she'd suddenly gotten sick. How much he missed her after she died.

"There seemed to be no point in going on afterward. But I did—for Amanda's sake, if nothing else."

I thought of Daddy, how he would feel if Mama died. And whether he would go on for me.

"It must have been very lonely," was all I could find to say.

"It was. And I never tried to make it less so. I'm not a sociable man. I knew what I had with my wife was never going to happen again." Then he looked at me and said very slowly, "That bolt of lightning comes very rarely."

I felt my face burning. I knew what he was going to say next, and I was too cowardly to let him go on. I excused myself and went into the ladies' room. I stood staring at myself in the mirror, at this unknown young woman in the silver Prada dress.

When I came back to the table he didn't bring the subject up again. Dinner was ordered and served; throughout the meal, he was charming but casual—almost the way he might have behaved to a client. He told story after wonderful story about the grand old days of Hollywood, and, listening to him talk, I was able to relax, pretend that other moment hadn't happened.

At the end of the evening, the limo dropped me back at the office. Bradshaw got out of the car and walked me to the front door.

"Thank you," I said. "It was an unforgettable evening."

He kissed my hand again.

I couldn't get to sleep that night, remembering the look on his face, the coolness of his hand over mine. I kept telling myself I was wrong—that I had misinterpreted what he was saying—but I knew I hadn't misunderstood anything.

I felt so very amazed. And flattered. And touched. But I also knew I didn't deserve any of it. The whole premise was a false one. Whatever John Bradshaw had been imagining, whatever vision he had built up, it wasn't really me. He didn't even know me.

It was just a matter of timing. He'd been lonely. He'd been by himself for so many years, all the walls were up. He said himself that he wasn't a sociable man (number one on the list of Hollywood's Ten Scariest People, I couldn't help remembering). He would be too proud to break out, make the gesture to anyone. And then I came along, sending him that stupid glossy and valentine—I had shaken him up, made the gesture myself.

I finally gave up even trying to sleep. I wondered what I should do now. I felt scared. I wasn't sure how far I wanted this whole thing to go. In spite of Bradshaw's age, I had always found him attractive, with that sense of weary power he gave off. And the vulnerability he had shown that evening had touched me very much. But then there was the other side. I remembered his arrogance, his coldness, the way he had looked at me in Hugo Boss, in the days before he "couldn't stop thinking about me." I also couldn't help picturing the age spots on those beautifully manicured hands.

The thought of going to bed with him . . . I didn't want to imagine it; I shied away from the idea. And yet, the next minute I found myself wondering what it would be like.

Steph and Lori both called the next morning to see how the premiere had gone. I didn't tell either of them what had happened afterward, not even Lori, in spite of my promise to her. I couldn't bring myself to do it—it was all too strange. I simply told them that it had been a wonderful evening.

John called me at home the next day. He sounded in control again, clipped and cool. For a second I wondered again if I might have misunderstood everything he had said.

But then he asked, "When may I see you again? Are you free for dinner on Friday?"

I felt unprepared, but I told him, "Yes, that would be wonderful."

When I came into the office Monday morning, Gary was waiting for me.

"I hear you went out with John Bradshaw on Friday night."

"It was hardly a secret," I told him.

Gary pulled out a magazine—the trashiest rag on the newsstand—and there on the front page was a picture of John Bradshaw and me, coming out of The Ivy. The caption was, "His granddaughter?"

I said, "Shame on you, Gary—I didn't know you subscribed to this kind of magazine."

His face grew purple. "What the hell do you think you're doing?" he yelled. "Why are you leading this poor man on?"

I could feel the anger starting at my feet and continuing to rise, the same way it had when Gary told me I had no business running the agency.

"I'd appreciate your keeping your nose out of my affairs," I told him. "Especially since this happens to be my office."

He threw down the magazine. "Maybe you'd like me to leave it—maybe you'd like me to leave it right now!"

"What a wonderful idea!" I shouted back.

He was gone by noon.

At first I was thrilled—thrilled to have my space

back, thrilled to have that disapproving presence gone from my life—but after a few days, I began to feel a little regretful. Gary and I had been friends an awfully long time, and I couldn't help wishing we had parted on better terms.

I called Steph and told her what had happened. "Don't worry," she said. "Remember that unfinished business." I wasn't sure if that thought was comforting or not.

I hid the tabloid in my bottom drawer, and every so often I'd sneak a look at the picture of John Bradshaw and me. I'd never been in a magazine before, even a rag like this one, and I had to admit, it gave me a thrill.

When I showed the picture to Lori, she didn't even mention the caption. She just said, "I told you you should buy that dress." I hugged her—it was the perfect reaction.

All week long, friends, clients, and even people I barely knew called about the tabloid, asking if the rumors were true. I kept saying they weren't and wondered how honest I was being. John didn't mention the picture—it was even possible that he hadn't seen it.

He was calling nearly every day now, and I seemed to be running into him constantly, in the hallway, and on the street. I knew it was on purpose, and I was never quite sure what to say. He didn't say much, either, but always stared at me so intensely that I was beginning to feel uncomfortable. I told myself that it was only because this whole thing was so new, and that when we got to know each other better, it would start to feel more natural.

*   *   *

Friday turned out to be an awful day, ending with Suzanne Chu being put on avail for a national spot and then not getting it. I was haunted all afternoon by her tearful voice on the phone.

When seven o'clock came I wasn't really in the mood to go out to dinner with John. I tried to be upbeat as we drove to Mr. Chow's, but he noticed that I was distracted.

"What's on your mind?" he asked as we sat down at the table.

I told him about Suzanne.

When I finished the story, he nodded. "I'm afraid that kind of thing happens pretty regularly in this town. And you never get used to it; being an agent means heartbreak on a daily basis. Sometimes we feel like a mother pelican—we'd feed our clients with our own blood sooner than let them starve."

I was touched by the unexpected image.

John looked at me intently. "Are you sure you're happy doing this work?"

I sighed. "Eight months ago, all I wanted was to be in real estate. I love the agency, but on days like this, I think I would have done much better to stay in Palm Springs."

He looked distressed. He said, "I wish I could make things easier for you."

"No," I told him quickly. "It's good for me—I've gotten my way in life far too much as it is."

As we were leaving the restaurant, John told me his daughter was coming down from Ventura the following day.

"Would you be able to join us for lunch?"

"I'm sorry," I said, "I already have plans. Maybe next time she's in town."

There were no plans. I just didn't like the thought of Amanda Bradshaw driving all that way and then finding me there with her father at the restaurant—especially if she had seen the tabloid.

He drove me back to the office. I told him not to bother taking me inside, but he parked the car and walked me into the building. Just inside the hallway he took me by the shoulders and leaned forward to kiss me. His face was blazing, intense.

I found myself stepping back. "Not yet," I said.

The following Tuesday he invited me to dinner at his house.

He lived in Brentwood, in a graceful old colonial. The house surprised me—it wasn't anything like John, not elegant, or spare at all. The living room was warm, even slightly shabby, with almost a mid-western feel. I imagined I could see his wife's touches all around. Her portrait was above the sofa; I went over and looked at it. Lorraine Bradshaw had a kind face, down-to-earth, nothing pretty or Hollywood about her at all.

"Would you like to see the rest of the house?" he asked me.

I told him I would love to.

As we went around the downstairs, he said, "You seem to be noticing just about everything."

"It must be the Realtor in me," I laughed.

"Ah," he said. He sounded disappointed.

We went upstairs, and he showed me his daughter's room. It was the quintessential teenager's hangout, with stuffed animals on the canopy bed and posters of rock stars famous a decade ago covering the walls.

"I should redo it, I suppose—it hasn't been touched since Amanda left for college. But I rather like coming in here from time to time."

He didn't show me his bedroom, and I didn't ask to see it.

Dinner was served by the butler, Stevens, an older man John said had been with him for twenty-five years. I could feel Stevens's dislike for me in the very way he served the vegetables.

After dinner, John and I went back into the living room. He put on a CD of Nat "King" Cole, and lowered the lights. He poured us both a glass of wine, and we sat down on the sofa. He put his arm around my shoulder and started to draw me toward him. I focused on tiny things—the monogram on his shirtsleeve, the golf cuff link in the shape of a star, and, as always, the beautifully manicured fingernails.

"Pandora," he said thickly.

Again I found myself pulling away. "I'm sorry," I said, "but it's getting late; I really should be going home. I have a meeting in the morning with Warner's, and I need to prepare for it."

I stood up, and after a moment so did he. He walked me to the door, and I kissed him on the cheek. "Thank you for inviting me to your beautiful house."

After that night he began calling every day. I felt more and more pressured, awkward. I began inventing excuses to keep from seeing him. I could feel his presence up in his office above me—the intensity seemed to pour down through the floorboards. I told myself I was being childish and un-

fair; that I had to come to some sort of decision
soon.

I went to Palm Springs for the weekend, mainly
to buy myself some time. I was horrified by how
poorly Daddy was doing—the new meds weren't
working, and he was in a lot of pain. I rubbed his
legs, which had helped before, but this time it did
no good at all. I could tell he was just waiting for
me to stop.

After dinner, while we were doing the dishes,
Mama said, "Millie's moving back to Barstow next
week."

I was shocked. "Why?"

"I guess she's just had enough of the desert."

I knew how much Mama had enjoyed having
Millie there and what a help she was with Daddy.

"Do you need me to come back?" I asked her.

"No," she said immediately, "No, of course not."
But her voice sounded remote. And I wondered if,
just a little, Mama resented my being so far away,
leaving her to cope with everything.

Daddy was up all that night, moving around,
groaning. I lay stiff in bed, waiting for the next
noise.

In the morning, we were all exhausted. I stayed
with Daddy while Mama napped, then I took a walk
around the neighborhood. It was unbearably depressing. Weeds were growing through the pave-
ment, the empty lot across the street was trashed,
graffiti was scrawled all over the Dumpsters. And our
house was the worst eyesore of all. It needed painting, dandelions were taking over the garden, and the
fence was falling down.

I drove to the hardware store, bought some paint, some weedkiller and some wire, and went to work.

That night, Daddy had a bad attack. He couldn't breathe; it was terrible, seeing the fear in his face. Mama tried to calm him down by rubbing his chest. Her hand looked so old; his chest looked so old. I couldn't stand it.

I left their room and lay back down on my bed. I had the most wonderful dream. Mama and Daddy were living in a condo in Laguna, all tile floors and wicker furniture. They were both wearing white linen, on their way to have dinner at a country club. Daddy's legs were better; he was able to walk just using a colorful little cane. And Mama was laughing the way she used to when I was a child.

I didn't want to get up, the dream was so pleasant. I thought, *I would do anything for them to have that life. Anything at all.* And then another thought came, the one I had tried to stop myself from thinking: *If I married John Bradshaw, I could give them that life.*

He had the money to make it all happen. He could get Mama and Daddy out of Chia Place, buy them that condo in Laguna. They would never have to worry again. If I married John Bradshaw, we could combine our agencies. We could buy out Aunt Marilynn. We'd make Lori a partner, maybe Emmett, too. It would be a whole fresh start for all of us.

I went into Mama and Daddy's room. Daddy wasn't so white now, and his breathing seemed a little easier.

"Sorry, Andy-Pandy." He reached for my hand. "Didn't mean to scare you."

I sat down on the bed.

"There's something I've been wanting to tell you," I said. "I've been seeing a man back in L.A."

"That Enrico Morales?"

"No. Actually, it's John Bradshaw. The one who took me to the premiere. We've been spending a lot of time together. I think you'd like him—he's bright and good company. And very substantial." The words came out lukewarm. "The only thing is, he's quite a bit older than I am."

I waited for them to ask how much older, but they didn't. Daddy began to cough, and Mama helped him sit up. It was as if they were both so worn out, so beaten down by their own lives, that they no longer had the energy for mine.

"I always thought you'd marry Gary," was the only thing my mother said.

"That was never the plan," I told her.

I left for L.A. that night. I couldn't bear to stay any longer.

I got into work early on Monday morning and went straight up to John's office. It was the first time I'd been there. It was beautifully decorated in plush, dark colors, and filled with antique furniture.

Emmett was at the front desk.

"Hey, beautiful, what's up?"

I tried to sound casual. "I wonder if I could see Mr. Bradshaw for a few minutes."

Emmett gave me a raised eyebrow, then buzzed the intercom.

"Miss Brown to see you."

Then Bradshaw's voice. "Tell her to come right in."

I went down the hall into his office. Like the reception room, it was large and dark and elegant. John was sitting in a leather wing chair behind a mahogany desk.

"Pandora," he said, smiling at me.

I crossed the room and went over to the desk. I put my hands on his shoulders, and then I leaned down and kissed him.

His whole body started to shake. He began to kiss me back—it felt like a piece of machinery coming to life after a long, long time.

Lori

The Prada's hanging in the closet. I go over every few minutes and touch it. Thin and silver and sharp, it's like a liquid knife. I could be anyone when I wear that dress, famous, rich. Someone people would point to, stare at, wish they were.

I willed it to happen, willed Miss Box to buy it, willed her to give it to me.

When she hooks up with Bradshaw, she'll be buying the best of everything, Kenzo, Armani, Stella McCartney. And I'll do okay from it, she won't make a move without me.

Oh, Lori, I'm going to dinner at Spago's on Tuesday; would you help me find a short black dress? Oh, Lori, I'm going to Mexico for the weekend; let's go shopping for cruisewear.

I'll choose everything, all the outfits I want. I have no problem with hand-me-downs.

Don't jump the gun, though; it hasn't happened yet.

Hard to tell exactly what *has* happened. Something's going on; I can see it on her face. And I know Bradshaw's always calling. I see the button lighting up on her private line. But she isn't telling

me a thing. Little Miss Princess, she doesn't talk
about vulgar subjects like that. All I get is, "Everything's moving along fine," in that coy voice.

He takes her to movies. They go out to dinner.
She tells me all about the restaurants. I can't ask,
"Have you let him in your pants yet?"

Maybe it's better if she hasn't; his body's probably crappy. Or maybe he's good; old guys sometimes are.

Bottom line, Miss Box is the sort that if she
screws someone, she's hooked, so the sooner the
better for everyone. For Chrissake, what more does
she want? It's the perfect match—old and rich
with young and stupid. And he's got the hots, he's
hooked, he's completely gaga; I knew we had him
when we sent the photo.

Should be smooth sailing now that Gary the asshole's gone. That was a little gift from heaven—I
didn't even have to give things a push, he did himself in, fucked himself right up with Miss Box.

I'm liking these little hints she's been throwing
out lately. "What would you think if John Bradshaw
and I merged the agencies someday? Wouldn't
that be fun?" Oh, yes, loads of fun. Just keep her
thinking along these very nice lines. When she
asks me to be partner, I'll act so surprised.

Tried the Prada on again. Half-close my eyes,
look in the mirror, just see a silver fog. In it, I almost don't look human; I'm from another planet.

Call Troy; he's home, for a wonder. Picks up.
Say I want to go somewhere special tonight, expensive; tell him I have a surprise for him. He says
okay, he had a good week. He'll take me out to
Yamashiro.

Take my time getting ready. Scared of looking
too long in the mirror, that it's all just a magic trick,

it might go away. The dress, the shoes, the makeup. I'd like to die right now, looking like this.

Troy coming up the steps. I open the door, smile at him, his eyes light on me for a second. Then they're like some goddam bug, flying around, looking for something else.

"So what's the big surprise?"

I want to beat on him, pull out all his hair. "The dress, you shit—it's me in this goddam Prada dress."

He's been drinking, I should have seen it right away.

Feel depressed as hell. When we first met, he was so tuned into me, he noticed everything I wore. We'd pass shop windows, he'd say, "You'd look beautiful in that. One day I'm going to buy it for you."

Turn away, go to the window. He comes up behind me.

"I'm sorry," he says. "It's a beautiful dress. I'm an asshole, I don't know what I was expecting."

His breath on my neck, hot and smelling sour on my perfect hair. I don't mind.

"I'm just in a crap mood, that's all."

"You told me you had a good week." I'm a nag, I'm turning into my mother, I'm trying to trip him up.

He says, "I hear your voice on the phone, it makes me think it's been a good week."

I turn, let him kiss me. He's good about the dress now; he looks at the beading, touches the seams.

We drive to Yamashiro. It's a foggy night; the mist never stops moving across the headlights. Keep imagining something's out there, something's going to jump out of the trees and get us.

We turn up La Brea. We always get lost, going to

Yama-shiro. We usually just give up on some side street, park by the side of the road, a few minutes together in the darkness before we try again. Even in this dress, I wouldn't mind doing it. But tonight he takes the right turn. There's the restaurant.

We're lucky, a lot of cancellations because of the fog. We get the best table, right by the window. All the lights of L.A. are down there, going like crazy, but we can't see them. Order sake, tempura, sushi. It gets me so happy; it looks like origami, all perfect on the little flat plates.

Troy's making up for before, holding my hand. Then at the end, the fog rolls right away. There's L.A. below, a whole blazing little universe. A good omen—it has to be.

Tell Troy all the things I'm planning to do when Miss Box and Bradshaw merge the agencies, when I'm made partner.

He's shaking his head, he thinks it's funny. "You kill me. You're never satisfied. You know what you are? A control freak."

He doesn't get it; he never will. He's lazy, he's spoiled, he waits for things to come along, for someone to help him out. I've had to do it with nobody's fucking help, ever. I've worked my ass off. I had to screw Gene. I have to suck up to Miss Box. Now I'm almost there, I'm finally getting what I deserve, and he tells me I'm a control freak, the prick.

Went to The Paper Place, bought an origami garden kit. Big golden flowers, shiny green leaves, little circles of seeds.

It makes me think about Grandma. I was twelve.

My father had just died. I was over at her house; we're planting sunflowers.

People don't really leave you when they die, Lori. It's like these sunflowers. Up where you can see them, they look like they're apart, but underneath the soil the roots are touching.

She points out two sunflowers. *That one's you; that one's your father.*

I don't want my father touching me even as a fucking sunflower.

Which one is you, Grandma?

She points to one a little way off. She goes in the house to get ice tea. I dig up her sunflower and put it next to mine, I pull up the one she said was my father, and throw it in the compost heap. Grandma comes back out, she sees what I did. She's so shocked she can't think of anything to say.

I miss Grandma, I haven't seen her in a while, I give her a call.

"Grandma, it's Lori."

"Who is this?"

"It's Lori, Grandma, Lori."

"Ann? Is this Ann? Who is this?"

Hang up the phone.

Feel depressed as hell that Grandma didn't know who I was. *A Room with a View* playing at the Nuart. I go down and see it. Don't ask Troy to come. Why bother? He can't sit still if there's no action. I love *A Room with a View*. It's beautiful, everything about it, the old clothes and jewelry, being in Florence, riding in those carriages. I've seen it ten times at least.

Always a big downer afterward, coming back out of the theater to Santa Monica Boulevard, trash and junkies all over the place.

* * *

Miss Box asks what I did last night, I say I saw *A Room with a View*. She starts squealing, "Oh, Lori, that's my favorite film. Why didn't you tell me? Next time you go see a movie, let me know, we'll go together." She's never satisfied, she has to move in on everything.

Get a call at work. It's my mother. "I'm dizzy. I'm having a stroke. I need you to come over right away."

Bullshit; I've been wondering what she'd do for attention now that the cast is off.

Miss Box pouring on the sympathy. "Oh, the poor thing; you've got to go right away—and, here, take this—buy her some flowers."

She pulls out a twenty from her wallet. Put on the humble smile, say thanks, take the money; it will not go to buy flowers.

Get over to my mother's place. The dizzy spell is completely gone, of course. Did her shopping, unpacked the groceries. It wasn't enough, it never is. "Why don't I ever see you anymore? You're always busy. I'm the last one on your list. You don't care about me at all."

If I said, you're right, I don't, what would she do? Plop down, fizzle out, die right there on the linoleum? Or find someone else to torture?

Finally get out of there. It's dark; the fog's come up again. Park the car in front of my building, start to walk down the path. There's a weird feeling around. I stop. I know there's someone there; I can feel it, someone's watching me.

Get to the front door, take out the key. Hear rustling. It's too late, he's got me. There's a mask over his face. I can't breathe; his hand is over my mouth. I'm kicking; he's got me off the ground.

He pulls me over. He takes me around the side of the building. They won't find my body for a while.

"Where the fuck is Troy?"

He's got a knife, I can feel it.

I tell him, "He's gone. The lying scumbag, he left town."

I sound convincing. He believes me. He lets me go.

Get inside the building, up to my apartment.

Fall down when I open the door. Lie on the floor. Can't breathe, can't get up. Crawl to the window and keep watch from behind the curtains. He's a black shadow, he's creeping down the driveway, he finally goes away.

Start throwing up. I can't stop. What the hell has Troy been doing? Got to call him, warn him, but if the feds are in on this, they've tapped the line.

I've got to get to a pay phone. Walk out the building, down the street, real slow, real casual. Keep checking to see if there's anyone following.

Call Troy from the car wash on Santa Monica. Goddam him, he's not in. The machine picks up. There's a new outgoing message. A noise in the background—it sounds like a girl, giggling.

Hang up and head for home. If there was a girl on the message tape, I hope he's put away forever.

The street's dark. I'm scared to walk. Noises from the bushes—I think the guy's back. No, it's only groaning, an addict, we get them all the time.

It's not an addict, it's Troy.

They've cut up his face, they've punched his eyes, his nose is smashed, blood running everywhere. I touch his hand, he screams.

I try to get him to my apartment. There's no way; he can't move. I run upstairs, bring down some wet towels, I try to clean him up; it's no good. I get him into the car, I take him to the emergency room.

We get to Cedars-Sinai. The girl at Reception jumps when she sees him; damn her, they're not supposed to do that. She asks what happened. I say it was an accident. She doesn't believe me, but she can't do anything. Go through Troy's wallet, give her his false ID.

They put Troy in a bed, leave him for dead. A doctor finally comes; Dr. fucking Friendly, he takes X-rays, says the hand's broken in three places, he'll have to set it.

"But I'm more worried about the eyes. Are you seeing any flashing lights?"

"I'm not seeing fucking anything, I can't open my eyes."

The doctor keeps on, all the things that could go wrong. "The retina might detach, you might need plastic surgery, there could be permanent loss of vision," yakety-yakety-yak.

I can't stand this, I don't want to hear it. The doctor finally goes away. Troy and I stay there. I can't do anything. There's no one to tell, nothing to do, just wait.

They bring a little girl in on a stretcher, a car accident. She isn't moving. Her mother's there—she has all these stuffed animals, she keeps dancing them around the bed. "Look, Amy, here's your bear, he's come to see you. Open your eyes and say hello to bear."

The little girl dies around midnight. Her mother packs up all the toys.

The doctor comes back. He sets Troy's hand. I know, Troy knows, that if it's set wrong, that's it, it's all over, he won't be able to work again.

They say Troy should stay the night for observation. I say no, thanks, screw them. I hate this place; I just want to get him out of here.

Take Troy back to my apartment. Tell him he's got to stay with me for a while, it's not safe for him to go home. It takes half an hour to get him upstairs.

Saturday morning Troy's still asleep in the bedroom. Run out early, get soft stuff he can eat, applesauce, oatmeal. Feel tired as hell. I slept on the couch last night, scared I'd knock into his hand.

Bring him breakfast on a tray. Sit and watch him eat. When he's done I ask him the question: "Who did it?"

All night I've been scared to ask.

He says it was a guy he knew. "He didn't like some stuff I sold him."

Begin to bawl; it isn't the worst, it wasn't the feds, it wasn't organized, it's only one guy. Start screaming my head off, tell Troy he deserves everything he gets. He promised and promised he'd stop dealing, and now this. "And it's going to get worse. Next time it'll be two guys—or I'll come in and find you, your knees nailed to the floor."

He's crying. "This is it, I swear. I've learned my lesson, I'm never doing it again."

He's been here a week. I like having him around. I make him meals, I help him get dressed. Funny to think of, the big bad stuntman, he's completely in my power now; it's like he's my child.

He still looks like shit. His face is so banged up, he can't go anywhere. He had a job lined up; he couldn't do it. He called SAG, said he had to go out of town on an emergency—they don't want to hear you're sick.

I stay with him as much as I can. Told Miss Box my mother's had another fall, she needs me at home. Miss Box does the Lady Bountiful act, "Don't worry about it, Lori—of course you have to be with her. Come in when you can—a few hours—and I'll pay you for the whole day."

But Troy's starting to get down, I've never seen him so down before. He watches soaps, reads magazines, nothing much else he can do. He's usually fast to heal, but not this time. Sometimes the hand acts up, and the pain's so bad he hits his head on the wall.

I can't stand seeing him this way. He talks shit, he says he's washed up. Already it's harder to do the stunts than it used to be, it takes longer to get over them afterward. A few years down the road, he'll be through. He says I should do the smart thing, just cut loose.

I've got news for him, I'm never cutting loose.

Other times he feels better, it's okay. We watch TV, we play cards, it's like we're an old married couple. Dinnertime, we eat wearing our bathrobes. He likes pot pies, I get them from Marie Callender's. He's worrying about his weight; he can't work out, he's scared he's going to get fat.

The main thing, I keep telling him, is that he's safe. No one's going to get to him here. There hasn't been any sign of the guy. I don't think he's going to come back. Troy said he took off running, he thought he'd killed him. And that girl giggling on his message, she can't get to him, either; he's all mine.

He says he didn't lie to me, he did stop dealing.

But this one thing came along, and he wanted in on it. "It was all for you—so I could buy you all the stuff you want."

I said, "Bullshit, I don't need anything that badly. You're the one, it's you."

I've seen the way he flips through catalogs, I see the way his eyes get, hot and hungry; he wants it all.

Went to Jerry's Deli, got pastrami, matzo ball soup, lox, scrambled eggs, the works. Troy wouldn't eat it. He says he's sick of takeout, he's starting to feel like a prisoner here. Got so mad, I wanted to break his hand again. Told him the only reason he's a prisoner is because he was fucking stupid enough to get his face made into meat.

Tell him, "Get out, go home, if that's the way you feel." He says, "Calm down, calm down." He eats the pastrami.

Come in from grocery shopping. He's watching *The Munsters*. Tell him I can't believe he'd waste his time on such a stupid show.

He says, "I like Yvonne De Carlo. She was a great lady."

First I've heard of it.

"She was married to a stuntman. He got into an accident. He could never work again. That's why she did this crappy show—so she could take care of him. I bet you wouldn't do that for me."

I tell him, "Of course I would; you know I would."

But later I keep thinking, would I? The one thing I *could* do for Troy, the one thing he wants me to do, I don't do.

An introduction to Miss Box. It would be over in two minutes, no big deal. If she handled him, he'd have things so much easier. He'd have the agency behind him, he could get commercials, it would mean more money. But I don't do it.

Bad night. He's so blue, the worst I've seen him.

"This whole thing's crap. I give up. I've had it with stunt work. I'm leaving town. I'll go to Wyoming, get a job on a ranch."

That's it. I can't stand it anymore. I've got to do it, bring him in to meet Miss Box. It won't be anything at all, I'll laugh at myself for having put it off for so long.

I'll have him come to the office. I'll say he's a friend, a stuntman who needs an agent.

I tell Troy. I can see he's getting excited. He asks me twice, "When are we going?" I say, "Not till your face is back to normal; you still look like shit."

He's all better. He's going back to his own place tomorrow. It's going to be strange; I've gotten used to having him around.

Lunch at Il Sole with Miss Box. She's patting my arm. "I'm so glad you're back, I've missed you."

Coming down Sunset, we run into Connie Ehrhart, I haven't seen her for almost three years. She looks good, says everything's great, she's very busy, working a lot, yakety-yakety-yak.

Afterward, Miss Box says, "Who was that?"

Tell her Connie's an actress. She used to be with the agency. Miss Box turns into Little Miss Professional. "But why isn't she still with us? What happened?"

I say it was her morals—it's the first thing I can think of. "Your uncle let her go; he didn't like some of her morals."

Miss Box looks surprised, like she didn't think precious Uncle Gene was such a prude. The truth is, Connie was the one Gene was screwing before me, and when I came along she got kicked out of the picture.

Telephone call this afternoon—surprise, surprise, it's Connie. All sweetness and light, inviting Miss Box and me to a party at her house next Friday night. Can guess what the angle is. She was giving us a load of crap this afternoon. *Busy working,* bullshit! She wants an agent.

Well, it's no skin off my ass. Gene's gone, why not? We could do something with Connie; she's got some talent. And this party we're invited to— that might work out just fine. A nice easy way for Troy to meet Miss Box.

Tell her about the party. "It'll just be a casual thing, but Connie would love it if you could come." Miss Box twittering, of course she'll be there, she's sorry the agency lost Connie, she'd love to get her back.

Ask her if she's going to bring John Bradshaw. She gives me a little frown. "I don't think so; he wouldn't exactly fit in." No, he's about thirty years too old. Decide not to push it, but I'd feel better if he were going.

Go over the plans with Troy. He'll show up at Connie's at eight, Diesel jeans, Burberry jacket. He'll come up to me, "Hey, how have you been, haven't seen you in ages."

I'll say, "What happened to your hand?"

"I got ripped doing a stunt."

With any luck, Miss Box will start in. "A stunt? You're a stuntman?"

Then Troy can work it, all the things he's done,

say he's SAG, thinking about a commercial agent. And just take it from there. It'll be fine. It's stupid to worry like this.

Call from my mother. I've got to get out to Kester right now, Grandma's dying. Probably a lie, but I go. Get to the place, run up the stairs to Grandma's room. It's like a scene from a play; all the relatives around, it's like some reunion of vultures.

Grandma's on the bed. I stay away from her. I never want to see anyone die. Try to get out of the room. Mother won't let go of me; she's clutching my arm. I pull away, she pulls me back.

Grandma seems like a ghost already. I try to remember all the things about her: planting sunflowers in the garden, drinking juice at her table, sitting on her lap. None of it seems real. She was a ghost all the time; I sat in a ghost's lap.

The nurse is waving at me. "Are you Lori?"

Grandma wants me, I've got to go up to the bed. Can feel my mother behind me. She's furious—Grandma doesn't want her.

Up close, it isn't as bad, Grandma smiles at me. She says, "My good girl," in her old voice. She pats my hand. It feels like her real hand, the one that used to give me juice.

Can hear Mother sobbing. Big phony look-at-me sobs. The nurse says it won't be long now; it's long. We wait and wait. Keep looking at my watch. I've got a date with Troy at eight—when is this going to be over?

It's seven. I've got to call Troy. Leave the room, go down the hall to call from my cell phone.

My mother comes rushing out. "It's over—she's gone." She's happy because she was there and I missed the big moment.

Go back in the room. Grandma lying there sleeping. I've seen her look like that a hundred times, Sunday mornings when I'd tiptoe into her room to see if she was up yet. And she'd be sleeping, just like this.

My mother says, such a hypocrite, "She's at peace now."

I always figured the moment before you die you can see into everyone's heart, you know what's really been going on. Wonder if Grandma still thinks I'm her good girl.

Canceled the date with Troy; don't feel like doing anything. I don't want to get old. I don't want to die.

Connie's party's tomorrow.

"Oh, Lori, I'd love to drive over there with you," Miss Box starts in. "Won't that be fun?"

Put on a big smile. "Sure, that'll be great."

I had plans with Troy, after. Now I'll have to cancel them. Shit.

She picks me up at six, Little Miss Matching Shoes and Purse. The party's in Silver Lake, to hell and gone. The bright side is, I've got time to pump her during the drive.

"So how are things going with you and John Bradshaw? You haven't said much lately."

She doesn't smile right away. That's a bad sign.

"It's going fine." The prissy, careful voice. "He's going to take me to the opera next week. I've never been to the opera."

Like I give a rat's ass about the fucking opera.

"That's great. But what about . . . ? Have things . . .?"

She frowns. I've gone too far. She's going to say it's none of my business. But she sighs and says, "No. Well, to some extent, yes. But not what you mean."

They're not screwing. Shit.

"Oh, Lori, it's just so confusing. I do like John a lot; and it's an honor that he's interested in me. But then I think, what am I getting myself into? I mean, what about in ten years, when he's . . . older? What will things be like then?"

I say that's ridiculous. I lay it on thick. "John Bradshaw's a legend. It's a privilege to be in his company. Age doesn't matter with someone like him."

"I know, I know." But she doesn't sound happy.

I say, "And then there's the practical side."

She frowns again, I shouldn't have said that. She's offended.

But, no, she's not. "I know that; and I won't pretend it doesn't make a difference. I think about my parents, and everything he could do for them. And there's the agency to consider, too."

Then the big-eyed look. "Do you think I'm cynical?"

"Of course not. You're just realistic."

"I guess you're right."

But the doubt in her voice, I don't like it.

We get to Silver Lake. God, it's dreary, block after block of little crap houses. Connie's is the one with balloons on the mailbox. Isn't that cute— I could puke.

Go inside, it's a little crackerbox, depressing as hell. She might as well put up a big sign, *I've given up, this is the best I could do.* If I couldn't afford a decent house, I'd rather live homeless on the streets.

We go inside. The place stinks with actors. Connie bounces up, introduces us around. She doesn't say we're with an agency, but everyone knows. They're being way too friendly, big clammy handshakes, asking how our drive was.

They're buzzing around Miss Box, take her off to the bar. Do they think if they get her sozzled, she'll give them a contract? Can hear her laughing, she's having a good time, she doesn't have a clue why they're being so nice.

Party games now. We're supposed to guess the number of pennies in the jar. "Being actors, this is probably the most money you'll see all year!" We're supposed to laugh.

Eight o'clock, where the hell is Troy?

Go out to the pool in back. It's covered in dead leaves. Sit down and touch the scum on top, watch it make oily rainbows. It's creepy, like something's dead underneath; I think of Grandma.

What's going to happen now? I can only sit here and wait.

Troy's come, I can feel it. Look through the sliding door, he's there, standing in the hall. Get up fast, go inside the house, back to Miss Box.

"Lori, where have you been? I was looking everywhere for you."

She hasn't noticed him yet. I have a few seconds left of watching him, of it still being the same.

Then she turns and sees him. I watch her face. I watch his. It's all over.

They're staring at each other. They're not moving. I could holler and scream, I could run around yelling I'm on fire, they wouldn't even hear me.

Pandora

It was one of those moments. All your life you remember them, and no matter what happens afterward, nothing can take away their completeness.

"Hi, I'm Troy," he said.

It was the bolt of lightning John Bradshaw had spoken of. I stared at him and felt my heart shake.

"Hi, Troy," I said. "I'm Pandora Brown."

Coming home from the party, I felt giddy and dazed. I was dying to ask Lori everything she knew about Troy, but I felt I couldn't. On the drive over, we'd done nothing but discuss John Bradshaw—I would have been indecent to bring up another man on the way back. And I could see Lori didn't feel like talking. She was silent the entire drive. I wondered if something had happened to upset her during the evening.

The days went by; I heard nothing from Troy. I tried to keep things in perspective. I told myself that it was easy to be charming for an hour at a party, and that it didn't mean anything. I also reminded myself that Lori had known Troy for years. If he were really that wonderful, she would surely have gone after him herself. No, Troy was just a tempting blip on the screen, a red herring, a schoolgirl's fantasy. It would pass.

But all that week, his image hovered in my head. I'd be in the middle of a meeting, and his face would appear like a hologram on the contract. Or a client would shake my hand, and I would suddenly see Troy's hand instead, warm and tanned.

The last thing he said at the party was that he would come by to drop off his headshots. Every morning I would wake up and wonder if this would be the day. I couldn't believe I was acting so stupidly. I thought I had put high school crushes behind me long ago.

Lori didn't come in until Friday that week—she called in sick every day. I wondered what was up. She sounded strange, but, once again, not particularly ill. I didn't mind the extra work, though—it kept me from thinking about Troy.

Tuesday morning John Bradshaw came by the office, asking if I was free for lunch. I caught myself wondering if Troy might be coming by with his headshots, and then pushed the thought away.

"I'd love to have lunch with you," I said.

We went down the street to Cravings and were automatically given the banquette by the window, the one Lori and I could never get.

"I have some good news," he told me. "I've signed a new client, a very talented young woman. I think she's going to be the next Julie Christie."

We talked about the client for a few minutes more, and then the conversation lagged. John took my hand and started to stroke it under the table. I found myself continually looking out the window, glancing at every dark-haired man who came down the street.

"You seem a little distracted," he said finally. "Is anything wrong?"

"No, nothing at all," I told him.

Out the window, I could see yet another young man nearing the crosswalk.

We left the restaurant and walked back toward the office.

"My daughter was disappointed not to have met you."

"I'm sorry," I said. "The next time she comes into town, we'll have lunch, I promise."

We reached our building and stood for a moment in the hallway.

"Are you free to have dinner with me on Saturday?"

"I'm not sure," I told him. "I'll have to check. I think I've already made plans."

His face grew diffident; he stiffened slightly.

"You know I'd never push you into anything, Pandora."

"I'm not being pushed," I told him quickly.

The shadow over his face wavered, then cleared.

"Let me know about Saturday, then." He smiled at me and pressed my hand. "And perhaps I could have a little kiss to tide me over."

I kissed him. It lasted too long. He let me go finally; we said good-bye and went to our separate offices. It made me feel uneasy, how much those kisses seemed to mean to him.

Troy didn't come by that day, or the next. Wednesday night, I called John.

"I just wanted to let you know that I'm free for dinner on Saturday."

"You were able to change your plans?"

"Yes; it wasn't a problem."

If he suspected that those plans had been fictitious, he didn't let it show.

"I'll be looking forward to seeing you then."

"I know it's just a matter of time now," I told Steph on the phone that night. "We've been going out more and more, he kisses me for longer and longer. So far he's been very patient, but that's not going to go on forever."

"And you wish it would?"

"No, of course not," I snapped. "That's not what I meant. I'm looking forward to it—really. It's just that once we finally do it, I don't know what will happen; I can see us getting married in six months' time."

"Well, isn't that kind of what you're aiming toward?"

"I'm not sure *what* I'm aiming toward anymore," I confessed. "I mean, he's a lovely man, he's wonderful company, and I know what an opportunity this could be. But for some reason, I'm getting less and less sure about everything."

Steph sounded annoyed. "Just please don't tell me this has anything to do with the guy you met at that party."

"Don't be ridiculous," I said irritably.

The following day I had a surprise visit from Aunt Marilynn. I offered her a chair and some coffee, but she shook her head.

"I've come for Gene's Oscar. Just give it to me, and I'll be on my way."

"Gene's Oscar?"

"The Oscar Mack Sennett gave him," she said impatiently. "It should belong to me now, not you."

"But I don't have it. It isn't here."

"Of course it's here."

"Look for yourself," I told her. "I haven't seen it since I came to the agency. It must be at your house somewhere."

She didn't believe me. Her eyes were careening all around the room, trying to find the Oscar. Finally she left, still unconvinced.

I called Lori at home and asked if she had seen the Oscar. She said she didn't know what I was talking about—so it must have disappeared a long time ago.

That made me very sad. When I was a little girl, I used to spend hours holding up that Oscar and making speeches to a cheering imaginary Academy Award audience. And now it was gone. I felt ashamed that I hadn't even noticed.

That night I had a dream. I was sitting in a large, empty room filled with packing boxes. A cold wind was blowing through long white curtains. Troy walked in. He nodded and sat down a few feet away from me. We stayed there, staring at each other, but not saying anything.

When I came into work the next morning he was sitting on the brick wall in front of the building.

"Hi," he said. "I've brought you the headshots."

I felt myself heating up, my cheeks starting to sting. I couldn't look at him.

"Yes, of course," I stammered. "Why don't you come in?"

My voice sounded thin and unnatural. I walked ahead of him into the office like a remote-controlled doll.

He put his briefcase down on the desk and pulled out the pictures. His hand was still bandaged. I watched as he teased the envelope up the side of the leather.

The headshot was absolutely gorgeous.

I turned it over. On the back, along with his résumé, were action pictures of his stunts, shots of cars smashing into bridges or colliding with trains.

"As you can see, my specialty is crash work." The way he said the words, softly, almost seductively, made the hairs on my arm begin to rise.

"That's very unusual." I tried to keep my voice professional. "What's generally called for in commercials are falls and aerial stunts."

"I can't fall," he said. "It's the one thing I don't do."

I thought he was kidding.

"No," he said. "I really can't. I have a problem with aerial awareness."

He was standing very close to me now. Talk about awareness—it was all I could do to get out a coherent sentence. I stammered out that it was a pity, his not being able to fall; that it would limit the number of jobs we could send him out on.

"Have you thought about taking gymnastics classes, or maybe doing trampoline work? That might help you get over it."

He smiled. "When I was a kid, my father threw me down a flight of stairs. Since then I've never been real crazy about having my feet higher than my head."

He spoke so lightly, I didn't know what to make of it.

I tried to be light, too. I joked about it being just my luck to get the one stunt man in the world who couldn't fall.

He was looking down at me—it was like a sun lamp. I found myself blushing, staring down at the headshot, searching for something casual to say.

"Well," I told him finally, "your car crashes certainly look impressive."

"They are," he said. "Saturday morning I'm doing one downtown for an Eddie Murphy film."

There was silence. I knew what was coming—I tried to stall for time.

"Do you think your hand will be well enough by then?"

He ignored the question. His eyes never left my face.

"The filming starts at ten, by the Sixth Street bridge. Why don't you come and watch?"

My cheeks began to sting. Endless time went by. He stared down at me.

"I guess I could try to be there."

The next day Amanda Bradshaw came into town again. I met her and her father for coffee at Le Clafoutis after work. She looked different than I had expected; she had changed a lot since those photos I had seen of her as a teenager. She had grown up to be gentle and unobtrusive, a little careworn.

I could feel how anxious she was, meeting me, but she made a point of being very pleasant. I was

impressed by that. In her place I knew I would
have been a raving harpy. If it were Daddy going
out with a woman less than half his age, I'd have
done anything to stop him, to keep him from making a fool of himself. But Amanda behaved beautifully. She only asked me a few questions, innocuous
ones: where I'd come from, how I was enjoying living in L.A. I answered everything very blandly, as if
I were being interviewed for a job.

I made a point of not doing anything to upset
her. I didn't take her father's hand or mention any
dates we'd been on, or kiss him good-bye.

As I walked back to the office, I thought about
how much I'd liked her. I found that ironic—if she
weren't John Bradshaw's daughter, I could see
Amanda being someone I would very much like to
confide in.

Lori came back to work Friday morning. She
was very quiet. I didn't ask if anything was wrong,
and she didn't say. I decided not to mention Troy's
visit or tell her that I might be going to watch him
do a stunt the next day. There was no reason I
should. Troy was a potential client, and it was simply my professional responsibility to check out his
work.

Before I left the office, John called to confirm
our dinner date.

"I've made an eight o'clock reservation at Mr.
Chow. I'll pick you up at seven-thirty. Perhaps this
time it could be at your apartment?"

The suggestion was made lightly, but I knew
what it meant.

"All right," I told him.

I hung up the phone. So it looked like tomorrow

night would be the night—his picking me up at my apartment, and his bringing me back again later.

It took some time to sort through all my feelings. There was excitement, a little dread, and, mainly, a sense of inevitability. I remembered what I'd said to Steph, about how six months down the line we'd probably be married.

I went on with the fantasy, conjuring up wonderful images: a honeymoon in Europe, Mama and Daddy in their condo by the sea, the two agencies officially merged. I'd try to be a good wife to him—I'd do my best to make him happy.

And then I thought about Troy. I remembered the smile he'd given me when he left the office, and I knew there was no way I could go see him do his stunt tomorrow. I had made certain choices about what I wanted for my life, personally and professionally, and I wasn't about to sabotage myself now. I went to bed that night feeling very peaceful and strong.

And the next morning—big surprise—I woke up at seven and went to watch Troy do his stunt.

There was construction on the 110 heading downtown; I took the detour and got lost. When I found the Sixth Street bridge, the entire street was blocked off. I was reminded of the night John had taken me to the premiere, and I buried that thought.

I finally found parking in an alley nearby. Everything was chaotic, with trailers, cables, camera equipment everywhere. A security guard came up to me and asked for my name. If I wasn't on the list, I decided, it was a sign that I should just turn around and go back home. But he found my name and let me in.

I walked onto the set. I didn't see Troy anywhere, and part of me hoped that he had already
gone. But then I looked over by a trailer and saw
him standing there.

I felt an overwhelming shyness; I almost walked
away. Then he looked up and saw me.

"You're just in time," he said. "I'm due in hair-
dressing. Want to watch?"

"Sure," I told him.

He strode over, took my hand, and pulled me
up the stairs.

The hairdresser was a tiny older woman. She
looked at me sharply as I came into the trailer.

"I hope you don't mind my being here," I said.

"It's all right," she told me. "I'm used to groupies
hanging around the stuntmen."

I didn't know how to answer that.

On the counter was a still of the actor Troy was
doubling for. The hairdresser sprayed Troy's hair
platinum to match, moussed it into the same style,
then trimmed it. It amazed me, all that care being
lavished on something that would last, at the most,
half a second on the screen.

When the job was done, Troy bent down and kissed
her on the cheek. "Thanks, Addie." He took my arm.
"Next stop, wardrobe."

We went into the adjoining trailer, and Troy
showed me the costume he was going to wear. On
the outside, the clothes looked like a regular pair
of jeans and a jacket, but underneath was padding,
several inches thick, and a whole set of hand, knee,
and ankle braces.

Troy got dressed in the trailer while I waited for
him on the steps. I thought of nothing, made sure
I thought of nothing. When he finally came out I
hardly recognized him.

"And now it's time to check the car."

We walked over to a shed behind the trailers. The stunt car looked at first like an ordinary red Mustang, but inside were hidden roll cages, extra inches of steel framing, and a five-point safety harness.

Troy was very quiet as he went over the car. He checked everything, the meters and fastenings, the tire pressure, the channel on the walkie-talkie. I remembered what I had once read about skydivers—how they folded their own parachutes before the jump, trusting that job to no one but themselves.

At ten-thirty a muffled announcement came over the loudspeaker.

"Safety meeting," Troy said.

We hurried across the set. The stunt coordinator was standing on a ladder by the bridge, talking and gesturing to a circle of stuntmen. I couldn't understand a word of what he was saying, but Troy was nodding, completely focused.

When the meeting ended, Troy smiled down at me. He put his hands on my shoulders—I could feel their warmth through my dress. He led me over to a director's chair.

"I've got to go now," he said. "You stay right here; you can watch it all on the monitor."

I wished him luck. He waved and took off.

Over to the right I saw an ambulance waiting and two medics standing by. Everything was very quiet.

"Action," the director said.

The AD spoke into his walkie-talkie. "Action. Stunts."

There was a pause, and then Troy's red Mustang came roaring down the road. He reached the bridge and started weaving in and out of the pillars, almost invisible in the clouds of dust.

The car rose onto two wheels, staying, for a long moment, suspended, almost vertical. Then just when it looked as if it were going to flip over, it crashed back down.

Two police cars came roaring into the intersection. Troy rammed into one, backed up, then jerked ahead. As he ran the red light, another car came from the left and smashed into him. The Mustang flew up into the air; the hood crumpled, the windshield shattered. And then there was silence.

The seconds passed. Everything was deadly quiet. The medics were standing poised, staring at Troy's car.

Nothing happened. There was no movement of any kind. I felt the blood start to leave my head.

And then suddenly there was Troy, springing out of the Mustang, running out of the shot.

"Cut!" the director yelled.

I started forward, but someone grabbed onto my shoulder, pushing me back.

"Don't move."

The medics were running up. I couldn't see Troy, only the circling huddle. Then there was a shout—the medics backed away, and Troy was standing there, grinning, giving a thumbs-up. Everyone on the set went wild, screaming and clapping.

I couldn't stop shaking, I couldn't move from my chair, I couldn't go up to Troy. It took a while before I could even look in his direction. We met halfway finally, him walking toward me, me walking toward him.

I wanted to tell him how incredible it had

been, that it was the most thrilling thing I'd ever seen. But I couldn't. I could only stand there and look at him.

He lifted my chin. He put his hands on my shoulders, and then he leaned down and kissed me.

He showered and changed. I sat outside the trailer and waited for him. I watched the grips packing up the cameras and cables, and again I didn't let myself think, didn't let myself think about anything at all.

At last he came out of the trailer, his hair back to brown, his clothes his own.

"What do you want to do now?"

There was only one thing I wanted to do, and I tried not to let it show. "It's up to you."

"Well, first of all," he said, "I'd like to get something to eat. I never have breakfast on days when I'm shooting."

I followed him to the Farmer's Market, and we had lunch at the Cajun restaurant. I'd eaten there before, so I knew how spicy the food was, but that day I was so nervous I couldn't taste anything at all.

"Do you come here often?" Troy asked me.

"It's one of my favorite places. My Uncle Gene used to bring me here when I was a little girl."

He laughed. "I can just imagine what kind of little girl you were."

I wanted to know what he meant by that, but he didn't say anything more. There was a pause. I asked him the same question—if he came here often.

"Yes," he said, "it's convenient; I live close by."

"Oh," I said, and couldn't think of anything to add.

We kept trying hard, both of us, but we never managed to get any real conversation going. It was all that sort of inane talk, wandering down little roads, meeting dead ends.

But then I asked him about his stunt, and things suddenly got much easier.

"I loved hearing that safety speech," I said, "but I couldn't understand a single word of it."

Troy's face lit up. "What didn't you understand?"

"I can't remember the exact phrase, but I'm sure I heard something about a steak."

He laughed. "A T-bone. That's when one car rams another square-on from the side."

"And there was another—it made me think of sushi."

I remembered the phrase—it was "fishtail"—but I wanted to make him laugh again.

And he did laugh. "Fishtail—that's when I was driving by the pillars, and the car started flipping back and forth."

I said I hadn't realized that had been on purpose. It had looked as if he'd completely lost control. But Troy told me that every part of the action, even those moments when he was up on two wheels, had all been planned out, frame by frame.

We went through the rest of it. He told me about "sliding nineties" and "playing chicken" and "doing a hundred and eighties." I could see he was relaxing now; I was, too. We were starting to have a good time.

And then we finished eating. Troy looked at me and said, "Where to now?"

I didn't answer. I suppose I thought if I stayed silent, that made it all his responsibility.

He said finally, "I live near here."

"Yes." I kept my eyes on the table. "You mentioned that."

I followed him to his place, an old apartment building on Fairfax. It had probably been charming once, but now the white stucco was peeling, and the lawn in front was burned dry.

We walked up the stairs to the first floor. When we reached the apartment, Troy put his hand on my arm. "Just give me a minute," he said. "I'd like to clean up a few things."

I waited in the hall. Once again, I tried not to think about anything, anything at all. Finally he unlocked the door and I went in.

The apartment was very sparse, one of the emptiest places I had ever seen. I thought of the dream I had had, with the two of us sitting on packing boxes, and the white curtains blowing.

I looked around for something I could comment on, some point of contact with him, but there was nothing. There was no book I recognized, all his videos were action films, his CDs were bands I'd never heard of. There was simply nothing to say. It hit me again that I didn't know him at all.

Then he came over and took me by the arms and pulled me down onto the sofa—and none of that mattered anymore.

I stayed with him for the rest of the day. We never stopped making love. There were breaks, when we had coffee, when we took a shower, but it was always him touching me, me touching him.

His hair was thick and springy under my hand; his body was hard and driven. His skin tasted like bitter almonds. We couldn't stay apart; we were locked, tireless together.

But we didn't speak. There was no need to, now.

Our bodies had become best friends, twins, and nothing we could say could ever match that.

Once he cried out and called me Beauty. That pleased me. Black Beauty, Beauty and the Beast—I liked being someone from a fairy tale.

It began to grow dark outside, but we kept the lights off and made love in shadow. At around seven Troy said he was starved; we sent out for some Chinese food. We ate it in bed, still in the dark. It ended up all over the quilt.

At ten o'clock I said I ought to be getting home. I asked if I could take another shower—alone, this time. I was standing under the water—I put the pressure up so high it hurt—and then I remembered my date with John Bradshaw.

I jumped out of the shower. I tried to get dressed, but my body was so used up, I could only move in slow motion. Troy lay on the bed, laughing at me.

"I need to go," I told him. "I forgot an appointment."

He helped me get my things together. Then he took me out to my car, and kissed me and kissed me until I pulled away.

On the drive home, I turned the radio up loud, so I wouldn't have to think. The car smelled different, I smelled different.

I got to my building and ran up the stairs. I went inside, and saw the red light blinking on the answering machine. There were three messages. The first was John, calling at two o'clock, confirming our date. He said how much he was looking forward to seeing me.

The second message was at seven thirty-five. He was calling from his cell phone, outside my apartment. I hadn't answered the bell—he was wonder-

ing where I was; maybe I was in the shower. He
would try again in a few minutes.

The third message was at eight forty-five. He
had gone back home. Would I please call him
when I returned, no matter what time. He would
be waiting for my call.

He picked up on the first ring.

"Pandora," he said. His voice sounded thick
with relief. He didn't ask me why I had broken the
date—he just wanted to know if I was all right.

I cut through it. I told him he was a wonderful
man, and how grateful I was to him for everything—but that I couldn't go out with him any
longer.

"I'm sorry," I told him. "I made a mistake. I'm
sorry." I said it again, into the silence, then hung
up.

I took another shower, mainly for the noise of
the rushing water. I couldn't stand the silence.

I kept seeing John's face, the way it had looked
after I kissed him that first time; the happiness in
it. It hurt to think about that now. Gary was right—
I hadn't loved him; it had all been a fantasy.

But I hadn't meant to lead him on—not for a
moment. I had been fooling myself just as much.
But now that was just no longer possible.

I got out of the shower and looked at myself in
the mirror. My whole body seemed to have changed.
I wasn't the same woman anymore. It felt like I was
breathing sharper air; it was like breathing rocks.

I got into bed. I thought of Troy with my whole
body. I stared down at my arm—it was ringed with
bruises, he had held me so hard. I remembered
that Lori looked like that on Valentine's Day. Her
boyfriend had bruised her, and I had felt so upset.

I closed my eyes and tried to think of the future,

but no images came. I started to feel frightened. I knew this whole thing with Troy was insane. I'd met him three times. We didn't talk. We didn't have anything in common. But none of that mattered. This feeling—it was like nothing I'd ever had before.

And, insane or not, I had to see it through. I was giving myself that. If it blew up, I would deal with it. But it wasn't going to blow up. It couldn't. Not when it felt like this.

Lori

The words she was saying to me drying up in her mouth. Seeing him look across the room, stopping when he saw her.

Walking toward each other.

"Hi, I'm Troy."

"Hi, Troy. I'm Pandora Brown."

I am invisible to him.

"What a beautiful name; it's from the Greek myth."

"And so is yours."

He touches her hand.

Can't get out of bed, can't go to work. Call the office, say I'm sick, I can tell Miss Box doesn't believe me. I should go in, but I can't. She'd guess, she'd know.

Scared to make a move, just sit tight. Troy hasn't called me. It's never been this long before.

The last thing he said to her, he'd come to the office, bring in his headshots. Can't let that happen, got to find out when he's coming, got to be there, make sure the two of them aren't alone.

But I can't move from the fucking bed.

Troy said I was a steamroller, I'd run over anyone to make what I want happen. Now I'm the one being run over.

Get to the chair. Stare out the window. Find some vodka left over from New Year's; that helps float things along.

Pull out all the presents he gave me; the earrings, the lingerie, the perfume, the little teddy bear. Put them around me in a circle, I'm in the middle.

Go through the album, all the pictures of Troy and me.

The first time we met, him coming up to me at Flings; I knew how it would be the second I touched his hand.

The night at Wolfgang Puck's. He asked the waitress for uncooked pizza dough. He made two little shapes out of it. One was a man, the other was a woman. He laid them down, put the man on top of the woman. We didn't wait for the food.

Cambria, that first Memorial Day. The cabin window open, the breeze blowing the curtains. Him picking me the flowers by the side of the road.

The first stunt I saw him do. The crash for the James Bond movie. The car went over a bridge, into the water. I thought he was dead—he didn't come up. He laughed at me later, called me a baby. I hated watching him do stunts, hated it, but I always went anyway.

He has a stunt this Saturday for an Eddie Murphy movie, down by the Sixth Street bridge. I'll go see it, it'll be like old times again, everything's going to be all right.

Keep telling myself that. Keep up with the vodka. Somewhere in the bottle I'm going to stop seeing their faces, him and Miss Box.

It's like being at a funeral, remembering what isn't anymore.

My mother calls. "You were supposed to bring me groceries. It's Friday, I could starve, you wouldn't care."

Get the goddam groceries, drop them off. She's fucking plastered.

She's going through a photo album, she's showing me these pictures. "Here's your father and me, the time we went to Barbados. Look what a handsome man he was. The hotel had a dance contest. We won it. He said, Ann, you're so graceful, you could have been on the stage."

She's slopping her drink all over, she's crying. "But now—what would he think if he could see me now?"

She looks up, she jabs a finger at me. "And you; you'd break his heart. He was so proud of you, and now the way you dress, the language you use, he'd be so ashamed."

I look at the picture of my father, his eyes and my eyes meet. *You're dead and I'm alive*, is what I'm thinking.

There's another picture below it on the page. It's of me. I'm ten years old. I want to rescue it, I don't even want it to be on the same page with my father.

"Can I have this one?"

My mother shrugs. "Take it, take it."

She could care less; it doesn't matter to her, losing the picture of me.

I pull it out. It leaves four spots where the glue dried. Now my father is alone on the page.

*   *   *

I get home. I keep looking at the picture.

I'm in my spangled tutu, with a little crown on my head. It's the day of the ballet recital. I'm so excited, more excited than I've ever been about anything. I was good, I was the best in the class, the teacher gave me the solo.

I practiced every day. I would get on that stage, and everyone would know I was somebody special. My whole life was going to change.

Every night I'd do my good-luck pretzel. I'd lock my fingers together, twist my arms, I'd make a wish: *I want to be a star, please let me be a star.*

Grandma visited. I'd take her up to my room, show her some of my dance. My mother was jealous. "How come you let her see your dance? You never let me see."

Grandma would hug me. "My little Lori, my talented little Lori, I can't wait to see your show."

It was the night before the recital. My mother says, "I have good news, a surprise, your father's taking off from work tomorrow. He's coming to see your show."

I don't want him there, I don't want him seeing me dance, I don't want him seeing me in my tutu. I start screaming, "If he comes, I won't go."

My mother's yelling back, "You can't talk to your father like that."

"It's all right," he says. "If she doesn't want me, I won't come."

The bastard, the martyr.

My mother looks at me. "You're killing your father, you know that."

The next morning, I'm up at six, I can't eat, I'm too excited. I get dressed, I'm ready to go.

My mother's supposed to drive me to the theater. She's futzing around, the show's at ten, she isn't leaving enough time.

I'm screaming, "Hurry up, hurry up." She ignores me, she just goes slower, she doesn't care, she wants me to miss the show.

Finally we get in the car. There's a wreck on Wilshire; the traffic isn't moving. I open the door, I jump out of the car. I start running, running down Wilshire Boulevard in my spangled tutu and ballet shoes, all the way to the Wilshire Ebell Theatre.

People are pointing at me; they're smiling, they're hollering, they're clapping. I run and run forever and don't get tired.

I'm the best in the show, everyone says so, but it's all over so soon.

People are coming backstage afterward. My mother's there. She's not who I want.

"Where's Grandma?"

"I don't know. She didn't come."

I get home, I call her. "Grandma, where were you? Why didn't you come?"

"I don't understand. Your father called last night; he said there was a fire, the theater was shut down, the show was canceled."

I wait till my father gets home from work. I jump out at him, I claw his face.

He catches my hand. "Whoa, whoa, whoa." He's laughing.

Vodka and more vodka. Keep thinking of that picture. I want to cry and never stop. Me in my tutu and sappy smile. See if I can still do the good-luck pretzel. I can. It was supposed to keep me safe, keep all the crap from happening.

Hold the picture up to the mirror, put our faces together. It's scary how different we look now. I don't know what happened. One minute, I had it all figured out, I was going to be the winner, the star, have all the solos. But somewhere along the line, the little girl got fucked, it dried up, it all just never came true.

My life's shit, I hate it. It's so far from what I want. You keep bargaining, if I only had this, or that, then I could put up with the rest, but everything keeps getting taken away anyway.

I guess what it all comes down to now is Troy. If I still have him, I'm all right; if I still have him, all the rest of it can go to hell.

I fell asleep. I woke up, and the machine was blinking. He called; he left a message: "I just wanted to tell you the stunt on Saturday's been canceled. But maybe we can get together later. I'll call you."

Stunts get canceled, that happens sometimes, it doesn't mean anything. Keep telling myself that.

I'm so calm. I can't believe how calm.

I get to work Monday morning. She's waiting for me. I knew, I knew before she even said a word.

"Oh, Lori, you'll never guess—oh, Lori, I'm almost afraid to tell you."

She didn't have to tell me. When she said his name, I said it right along with her.

She's pinkie-white, blushing bride. "It was just so unbelievable. I'm sorry I didn't let you know before; I wasn't trying to keep anything from you, I promise; I didn't even think I was going to go see his stunt—and then at the last minute, I changed my mind."

I tune her out, I just hear the blips of her voice. I'm nodding like a doll. I knew the stunt wasn't canceled; I knew he was lying.

"Lori, it was incredible; you should have seen him drive!"

Her face shiny pink, the little dimply hands bouncing up and down.

"We spent the whole day together, but it was so awful—I forgot all about my date with John. But it's all right; I've broken everything off with him. It was the only decent thing to do—now that there's Troy."

She comes over, she throws her arms around my neck.

"Oh, Lori, I think I'm in love."

I want to kill her, put my hands around her throat, squeeze it until she turns black and dies. She's killed me, she's taken Troy, she's taken my one thing, my only thing, she's smiling as she tells me.

I can't hear what she's saying. I just see the kewpie lips munching up and down. Squeal, squeal.

Don't think. The trick is not to think now.

Go home. Sit on the floor, look out the window. I'm dead. This corpse on my hands, I don't know what to do with it. Can't keep it at home, it's going to start to rot.

Got to get out, get away from the corpse. Walk down Santa Monica. There are shops, movies, restaurants, windows full of things to buy. All the things for the living. Can't imagine wanting any of that again. There is nothing left, nowhere to go.

Get to San Vicente. Everyone's out; it's a warm day. Jessa's sitting at her corner. I'm tired, all I want to do is rest. I sit next to her, she doesn't move, it's like I'm not even there.

Just sit for a while, breathe in and out. Watch a piece of paper blow across the street.

The woman next to Jessa keeps staring at me. "Who are you? You don't belong here. Get along, go away." She rattles her cart.

Jessa should say something, say I can stay if I want to; she doesn't say anything, I'm on my own.

"Fuck you."

I get up, I walk away.

I am nothing, I am lighter than air. I am not in my skin anymore, I have left myself.

I go home before I dry up and blow away.

Dark, buried. Black all around, silent.

In bed, I don't remember getting here.

There's a noise, I don't know what it is.

The phone.

Troy.

It rings and it rings. It rips through me, I won't pick it up, I won't. I have too much pride for that.

It starts again. He will not win, he will not wear me down. I'm screaming, "Shut the fuck up!" The neighbor downstairs starts hitting the ceiling. Jump out of bed, jump up and down on the floor. "Shut the fuck up!"

There's no more ringing now. It's quiet.

Go over, grab the phone, but there's only a dead noise. It's all over. Standing there with a dead noise. Keep standing there. I don't ever want to move again. If I move, if I put down the phone, it means he's given up trying, it's over.

Pounding, pounding on the door. I run faster than I ever ran before, throw it open. Troy grabs me, his arms are suffocating me. He came, he's here, everything's all right. I don't care that he fucked Miss Box, I don't care about anything, all that matters is he's here.

I look at him sleeping, smelling like Troy, like us together.

All night long, better than the first time, better than Cam-bria, better than it ever has been. Some tiny bit of him that he's never given me, he's given me now. Tried to cram him into me so hard he'll never get free again.

He said he had been crazy. He couldn't live without me. He'd go out of his mind if he ever lost me.

Looking at him now. I just want us to be peaceful. We almost wrecked, but now we're washed up on this pale shore. I want quiet things, nothing too fast, too big. Talking in whispers. Just him and me. Little animals living in a green peaceful forest.

I get out of bed. He's a baby I don't want to wake.

He gets up at last, sweet smiles. I make him breakfast. He's at the table, drinking coffee. There are fuzzy edges to everything. I break the eggs into the bowl, I think if the yolks break, so will the spell, but they don't break.

He says it again. "It didn't mean anything, I swear to you. It was just to get an agent, to get work, I thought it would help."

I can't hear it enough, it sinks all over me, like a beautiful cloud. I'm looking at the two round yellow egg eyes in the bowl. I ask him if he's going to see her again.

He says no, he isn't going to see her again. The two eggs float into one big one now, like the sun shining.

He comes over, puts his arms around me.

I ask, "When are you going to tell her?"

He says maybe he won't even have to tell her. They were supposed to go out Friday night; he just won't show up. She'll get the point.

Miss Box all dressed up, waiting by the door, and his never showing.

I say, "No, that's not good enough, you have to tell her."

He says all right, he'll call her. He'll break it off on the phone. He'll tell her he's sorry, he got carried away. It was all a mistake.

Get into work early. Miss Box comes in, twittering, flitting. None of it bothers me now. I know the truth. I know the thing she doesn't know.

I am cat, she is mouse. I say, "Did you see Troy last night?"

"No. I called but he wasn't in. We have a date on Friday, though."

Or so you think, Miss Box.

A sweet, sweet day. Yesterday, here in this office, here at this desk, I was dead, decomposing. Today I am all together, the winner, alive.

Troy takes me to dinner, we go to Wolfgang

Puck's. It's not as good as it was last night; he's pre-
occupied.

I say, "You should marry me, I'll take care of
you."

Can't believe I said that, I'm usually more careful. He doesn't like it. He says marriage isn't in the
plan right now. I say, "No, we're not ready; I don't
think you'll ever be ready."

I'm crazy tonight. Shouldn't have taken the lid
off that one, but it's something I think about, I
can't help it. Other people get married; it's not so
fucking impossible.

Let it go for now, change the subject. After dinner, we see a movie. We laugh, it's fine again.

Ask Troy if he's called Miss Box yet, canceled
their date for Friday. He tells me he'll do it tomorrow.

He comes over after work. We watch some TV.
He's feeling lazy. We're lying in bed, he's rubbing
my back. Ask him how the call to Miss Box went.
He said he hasn't called yet. I tell him he can call
right now, she'll still be awake.

He stops rubbing my back. The air gets cold between us. He says he'll call when he feels like it.

Friday morning. Miss Box fluttering around the
office, she's screwing up the work.

"Oh, Lori, I'm sorry I'm so distracted—I know
it's ridiculous, but all I can think about is tonight."

My eye on the clock. Hear the phone ringing in
her office.

It has to be Troy. Wait for her to come crying to

me, "It's all over, he doesn't want to see me anymore"—but she doesn't come in.

Lunchtime. She says she isn't eating, she's going shopping for something to wear tonight, she wants to knock Troy's eyes out.

Wait by the phone to take the message.

At three, I call him, get his machine. He doesn't call back.

Five o'clock, she leaves the office early. "Sorry to bail, but I know you understand. Have a great weekend—see you on Monday!"

She's sailing away.

Go home, wait. Wait till seven, go over to her place. Turn my lights off, cruise down the block, park around the corner.

Shaking so much I can't get my fucking legs to move. Get out of the car finally, walk around the corner. Keep telling myself he won't be there.

His car's in front of the building.

Go up the stairs to Miss Box's door. She opens it. Her hair's down, her blouse is out of her skirt, I can smell him on her.

She's embarrassed, she's shocked to see me. "Lori, I didn't know you were coming by."

She gives me a little thumbs-up. She smiles at me, nervous. I can see his shadow in her bedroom. His eyes are looking at me—hard, cold animal eyes, glittering.

Up all night, but it's done.

Dear Mr. Bradshaw, I think there are a few things you should know about the man your girlfriend is fucking.

I wonder if Troy has any idea how much I know, or what I've guessed. Writing the letter, even more things come back. Things I hadn't put together when they happened.

Did he really think he could do this to me? Did he really think he could get away with it?

Go to the photo album, rip out the pictures, pull them out of the frames. Cut up the lingerie, smash the earrings with a hammer. Save the bear for last. Slit its throat.

Pandora

I keep on having dreams about Troy. They start off very happily—we're at an amusement park or a fair of some kind; he's relaxed, he's showing off for me. Then I begin to be puzzled by his presence. I tell him, "I don't think you should be here." He stares at me, turns away, and is lost in the crowd.

Last night I dreamed we were together in Carmel, sitting on the beach and watching the sunset. He was wearing the blue silk shirt I bought him; his arms were around me. The sound of crying finally woke me up—I found my face glued to the pillow with tears.

All day long, it keeps coming back to me, those days with him in Carmel. That happy, happy time.

It started on Sunday night, our second week of being together. We had spent the whole weekend with each other, seeing movies, going to restaurants, staying in and making love. I had never felt so content in my life; for the very first time, there was nothing I wanted that the present moment didn't hold.

"I wish this weekend never had to end," I said with a sigh.

Troy pulled me back into bed. "It doesn't. Call in sick tomorrow—say an emergency came up. I'll take you away for a few days. Anywhere you want."

Monday morning, after he left me, I fell back into bed. I could feel the weekend unraveling, beginning to lose reality. I was already planning the workweek, with its conference calls and business lunches. It was like being forced back into a stale, sweaty dress after I'd been running naked on the beach.

I thought about what Troy had said, about taking me away for a few days. How I wished I could go.

Then, as I was brushing my hair, I suddenly wondered, Why *couldn't* I? It was my agency—I'd been slaving at that office for nine solid months. Surely I was entitled to a few days' vacation.

I picked up my planner and quickly looked over the page. The week was full. There were lunches, conference calls, meetings—but nothing so vital that it couldn't be postponed.

I knew Lori could cope with the day-to-day routine—she had handled everything on her own before I even came to the agency. And I didn't feel guilty asking her—I'd given her so much time off lately, whenever she'd wanted it. If she needed me for anything, she had my cell phone number—as did all the clients—and I'd check in several times a day to see how everything was going.

I couldn't believe I did it, but I did it. I called the office and left a message on the machine.

"Hey, Lori, it's me. Something's come up, and I'm afraid I won't be going in to work for a few days. I'm canceling all my appointments until Friday. If you could just handle the daily stuff, that would be great; I'll call back later."

I could have told Lori the truth, that I was going away with Troy, but I wasn't sure I wanted to. On Friday night she had suddenly shown up at my apartment while he was there—it had been very eerie.

I made several more calls, leaving messages to cancel all my appointments, and then finally I dialed Troy.

"I'm free!" I told him. "And I'm taking you up on your offer."

There was a long silence. I realized that Troy had never given his suggestion another thought.

I was mortified. "Forget about it," I said quickly. "It's crazy, anyway."

But he broke in. "No, it's not—it's a great idea. I just can't believe we're really doing it." Now he was laughing; he was starting to get excited. "Let me get a few things settled. I'll pick you up in an hour."

I started to pack. I felt giddy, like a kid escaping to summer camp. I didn't know where we were headed, so I threw just about everything I owned into my suitcase.

At nine o'clock Troy knocked on the door.

"So, beauty," he said. "Where am I taking you?"

It was a fantastic moment—I couldn't remember another like it in my whole life. We were free to do anything in the world we wanted.

"What about Carmel?" I said finally. "I've wanted to go there my whole life."

He smiled. "Then that's where we're going."

I called Mama and Daddy and told them I was going away with a friend to Carmel for a few days. They told me to have a wonderful trip.

"Carmel was where I took your mother for our honeymoon," Daddy added.

So that was where the feathered Christmas doves had come from. It was an extra little golden surprise in the day.

Troy and I packed up the car and started off. We stopped to get gas at the station on Barrington, and I suddenly caught sight of Gary walking down the street. I almost called out to him but didn't. We hadn't spoken in months, not since he'd left my office after our fight. Seeing him now, I felt a little guilty. He had been right about John Bradshaw, and I had never apologized. I told myself that as soon as I got back from Carmel I would give him a call.

Troy saw me staring out the window.

"Who's that?" he asked. "Should I be jealous?"

"No," I told him.

He leaned through the window and kissed me hard.

We started north, up the coast. I opened the window, waving my arms around in the beautiful, blue, blowy weather. I couldn't think of when I'd been so happy.

When we reached Santa Barbara, we took a break and strolled up and down State Street. Troy teased me for wanting to go into every store.

"Just one more," I begged, spotting a small antique shop. "I love antiques."

"As a matter of fact, so do I."

We went into the store, and I watched Troy as he walked around. Every now and then, he'd stop and touch something: an old Blue Willow plate or an antique rocking horse. It made me feel weak, seeing the tenderness in his fingers.

At the back of a bookcase, I found a crumpled little glove. I showed it to him. "How sad, to be left abandoned like that."

Troy took the glove from me. "Say something nice about it."

I said, "You're a very well-made little glove, and the stitching on your back is beautiful."

"That was perfect." He smiled at me. "You've made it very happy. Now it will spend the rest of its life remembering what you said."

That made me want to cry.

Several times that morning I tried calling the office, but Lori didn't answer.

"Wait until tomorrow," Troy told me. "We're on vacation."

Around noon we passed through San Luis Obispo, and I saw a sign for the Madonna Inn.

I clutched Troy's arm. "Oh, please can we have lunch there? I've always wanted to go!"

Troy groaned, but pulled obediently into the parking lot.

The Madonna Inn lived up to expectations. It was an absolute riot, decorated to the teeth with colored fountains, plastic flowers, cupids, and animated dolls swinging from the ceiling. And everything was pink—from the sugar on the table to the rotary sign out front.

"So when do I get to see the waterfall?" I asked as soon as lunch was over.

Troy groaned again, but took me downstairs to the men's room. He stood guard while I went inside and watched the famous flower-decked waterfall splashing about in front of the urinals. I couldn't have loved it more.

After lunch, we sneaked around the property, peeking in windows, seeing some of the "theme" bungalows. My favorite was the Caveman room, with its leopard-skin bedspread and rock walls. Troy thumped his chest à la Tarzan, and asked me if I wanted to stay the night, but I said I had no wish to be Wilma Flintstone.

"Though imagining you as a caveman is definitely an intriguing idea!"

We got into the age-old debate then: the Flintstones versus the Jetsons. Troy admitted that when he was nine years old he'd had a big thing for Judy Jetson. I could imagine him at nine—a shy, dark-haired boy, wearing a plaid shirt and a baseball cap.

I felt a little wistful as I put my arms around him. "I wish I could have known you then."

He kissed the top of my head. "Things are better now."

Around two o'clock, we reached Cambria. It was an absolutely endearing place, like a town from a hundred years ago, everything single-story, with wooden storefronts and raised porches. And Troy seemed to have a second sense about where to go—it was amazing. I asked if he'd been to Cambria before, but he said no, never.

"Maybe you lived here in a past life!" I teased.

"Maybe that's it."

We found the most enchanting little garden shop, selling homemade soaps and perfumes. Troy bought me a box of jasmine-scented potpourri.

Then we walked to the back of the shop, to a little herb garden, and he kissed me under the trees.

Afterward we drove up to Hearst Castle. I'd grown up with the movie *Citizen Kane* and had always wanted to see the inspiration for Xanadu. But

Troy, who had never seen the film, ended up liking the castle more than I did. I found it overwhelming, with its heavy furniture and baroque frescoes—a humorless version of the Madonna Inn.

"How would you like to live here?" I asked Troy.

"I'd like nothing better," he said.

I couldn't tell if he was kidding or not.

At sunset we drove back to Cambria and checked into the Cambria Pines Hotel. It made me think of an old-fashioned camping lodge, somewhere Teddy Roosevelt might have stayed at.

The next morning we got up early and had breakfast in town. I tried calling the office again, but no one answered. I left a message saying I'd try back later. I had the strangest feeling that Lori was there but just not picking up.

"I hope she's not upset at me for taking off."

Troy shrugged. "So what if she is?"

I thought his tone was a little odd. I'd noticed that before, other times when I'd brought Lori's name up. He had told me that he knew her only slightly, but I suddenly found myself wondering if there was something more to it than that.

"What do you think of Lori?" I asked him. "You've never really said."

He gave another shrug. "She seems okay. I don't really know her very well."

"Have you ever met the evil boyfriend?"

"No," he said. "I didn't know there was one."

I let it go. If there *had* ever been something more there, it certainly didn't seem to matter now.

The scenery going up to Carmel was intoxicating. Pale sky, tiny twisted cypress trees, and just the one narrow band of road sailing over the mountains.

When we reached Big Sur, I asked Troy to pull

over. I got out of the car and walked to the edge of
the cliff. The water below was like spilled oil paints—
royal blue, turquoise, lavender, every shade of
green. I wanted to dive into it, eat it—I wanted to
shout into the wind, fly up into the wisps of cloud,
twist around on top of the world.

Troy took a picture of me there at the edge of
the cliff. It made me sad to think that by the time it
was developed all this would be over, just a memory.

Finally we reached the outskirts of Carmel.

"When I was a little girl," I told Troy, "I thought
it was 'Caramel,' and that the whole town was
made of candy. I'm scared I'll be disappointed."

Troy smiled. "You won't be."

We drove into the little town, and I caught my
first glimpse of the handmade cottages, the leaded
windows, the cobbled streets, and the geraniums
hanging from every lamppost. It *was* a town made
of caramel.

We decided to stay at the Hansel and Gretel
Motel, with its bungalows like enchanting little
fairy-tale cottages. We stayed in the room all afternoon, making love. Then just before dusk, Troy
said, "Time to get up, Beauty. There's something I
want to show you."

We dressed, and drove in silence down a little
rutted road. It seemed like the world's end. Troy
parked the car and led me down a steep path. It
had gotten cold, and he put his jacket around my
shoulders.

The path ended at the ocean. The beach was
filled with people, maybe a hundred, standing in
groups or sitting on blankets, quietly looking out
to sea.

"It's a tradition here," Troy said. "Everyone comes down to watch the sunset."

He took my hand, and we went down in the silence to join them.

The next morning we woke up early and went back to the beach. There was nothing solemn about it now. It was cheerful, simple, washed with bright colors. We had races in the sand, and Troy let me win.

Afterward, we went in to town and browsed around all the little boutiques. Troy bought me some jasmine cologne and a mug that said "Carmel." I got him the blue silk shirt and a few of my favorite Randy Newman CDs.

All morning long I kept checking my cell to see if there were any messages. There were a few from clients but none from Lori, and every time I called the office I got the recording.

"Where could she be? Why isn't she answering?"

Troy shrugged. "I don't know."

"Do you think I ought to just go back to L.A.?"

He looked at me. "Is that what you want to do?"

I pushed the guilt aside.

"It's the last thing I want to do."

I didn't let myself worry about it anymore. Troy and I strolled along through town, holding hands, chatting sometimes, and sometimes relaxing in the silences.

"I keep thinking about our first date," I told him. "That lunch at the Farmer's Market, and how we didn't have a single thing to say to each other. I'm amazed we ever got beyond that day."

Troy stopped and looked down at me. "Oh, I'm not," he said softly.

After lunch, we decided to take the 17 Mile Drive. It was unbelievably beautiful, too beautiful for us to speak about. We just sat silent in the car as the sky, the earth, the sea, the blues and browns and greens rolled by.

We spent the afternoon in Monterey, walking around the wharf. It was a tourist area now, full of shops and outdoor restaurants, but there still seemed to be a gritty sadness left over from the days when it had been a cannery town.

It made me think of Dream Homes.

I told Troy about my parents' house, and how much I hated it.

"But one day, I'm going to get them out of there—buy them a condo in Laguna."

He smiled at me. "Tell you what, when you get me a series, I'll buy them one myself."

I squeezed his hand. We walked along in silence. "Is that your big dream? A series?"

He shrugged. "Mine and everyone else's." Then he added, "At least it would get me out of a few things."

I wondered what he meant by that. "What sort of things?"

"Nothing important," he said lightly. "Let's just say you've been a good influence on me. Now that I've met you, there are a few aspects of my life I'd like to change."

I sighed.

"What's wrong?"

"You're always so secretive," I said. "Sometimes I feel I don't know anything about you."

He gave me a little smile. "What sort of things do you want to know?"

"Everything. From the beginning," I told him.

He laughed. "Well, I was born in Chicago, I

lived on the south side in a railroad flat, and I went
to school. Nothing very interesting."

I pressed his arm. "Go on. Did you like school?"

"I hated it." He was quiet a moment. "It was full
of bullies. They'd rough up the kids. Every morning I'd beg my mother not to make me go. Finally,
my dad taught me to fight; that made things better."

I remembered the only other story Troy had
told me about his father, about how he had thrown
him down a flight of stairs.

"What was he like, your dad?"

"I don't remember too much about him. Mainly
him drinking." His voice flattened out. "He died
when I was ten. I came home one day, and my
mother said we had somewhere to go. I thought I
was in trouble at school, but we went to the factory
where my dad worked. They'd laid him out on a
table. He'd fallen from a girder and broken his
neck."

Troy held out his hand. He took off the topaz
pinkie ring he always wore and passed it on to me.
The ring was warm.

"This belonged to my dad," he said. "It's the
only thing of his I have."

I touched the ring, trying to imagine the man
who had owned it, but I could feel nothing, just
the warmth from Troy.

I put my arms around him and held him for a
long time.

We drove back to Carmel. At sunset we went to
the beach again, had dinner, made love. It was better than ever before—there seemed to be a new
closeness between us.

I said, "Thank you for telling me those things today."

He kissed the top of my head. "That's okay. It wasn't all that painful. One day I may even work up to telling you about Fanny."

"Fanny?"

The name shimmered in the silence.

"Why can't I hear about her now?"

Troy sat up in bed. I could barely see the shape of him in the darkness.

"Please," I said. "I'd like to hear about Fanny."

"All right," he said after a long time. "Fanny was my little sister. I was four when she was born. The thing about Fanny, she was one of those kids everyone loved. I was nuts about her, looked after her when my mother was too busy. I used to take her places after school, help her out."

His voice grew remote. "When she got older, all the guys used to come buzzing around her. She always fell for the wrong kind. I'd warn her about it, but she didn't listen. Then she got knocked up— she was scared to tell Mom. She didn't tell me, either. She went downtown with some girlfriend and got an abortion. Something went wrong, and she died. She was sixteen."

He began to cry. I'd never seen anyone cry like that in my life.

"I was there," he kept sobbing. "I watched her bleed to death. I couldn't do a fucking thing."

He kept going over and over it, how, if only he had known, he would have been able to do something. Stopped her. Talked to the guy. Given her money for a better doctor. I couldn't think of anything to say. I just kept holding him.

Finally the sobs began to grow less, and then

they stopped. "I'm sorry," Troy said into the silence. "Can we please just forget all that?"

"I don't want to forget it," I told him. "It's made me love you more."

I asked if he had a picture of Fanny. He turned on the lamp and got his wallet from the bedside table. Looking at the snapshot, I felt a lump come into my throat. Fanny was so pretty, so bright-looking with her long black hair and her little yellow sweater. One of those girls who just makes you smile.

We lay back in bed, our arms around each other, not saying anything. But right before we went to sleep, I said to Troy, "Describe your perfect day."

He squeezed my hand in the darkness and whispered, "This was it."

The next morning our beautiful trip was over. We packed, paid the hotel bill—and started for L.A. right after breakfast. As we drove down the cobbled streets for the last time, I shot a whole roll of pictures from the car window.

Troy suggested that I take a nap on the way home, but I told him I was nervous about sleeping in cars, especially on roads this twisty. He thought that was hilarious. "I'm a stunt driver," he reminded me.

So I lay down on the backseat and closed my eyes. The next thing I knew, I heard his voice saying, "Time to get up, beauty," and we were back in Santa Barbara.

When we reached L.A. Troy dropped me off at home. I asked him if he wanted to come over later and spend the night, but he said he had some things to catch up on.

We kissed and kissed, and the trip was over.

* * *

I unpacked and took a shower, and then I went straight to the office. When I got there I found a note on my desk from Lori. She said she was out running errands, and then going home—she'd see me tomorrow. I could tell that she had been coming into the office every day. Everything was up-to-date, organized. The mail was taken care of, faxes were stacked.

I decided to stay awhile anyway, to make a few calls, and get my hand back in. I was there about an hour. I was just about to leave, when I heard footsteps coming down the stairs. I heard a knock, and opened the door.

John Bradshaw was standing there. He seemed horribly embarrassed; he wouldn't even look at me.

"I'd like to talk to you, if it would be convenient." He held out a paper. "I received this letter," he said. "I don't know from whom."

I looked through it. It was about Troy, full of the most insane, contradictory things—that he was a Mafia hit man, a drug dealer, a spy wanted by the FBI.

"I didn't know what to do about it," John went on. "I thought it would be best if I came to you. I don't mean to hurt you, but I thought you should know—in case any of it turned out to be true."

I gave him back the letter without a word. He dropped his eyes, and left.

I went back into the office, shaking. I didn't know who could have written such a letter—who hated Troy that much. Or me.

I drove back home. Troy called, and I let the machine pick up.

"I've changed my mind about coming by," he said. "I miss you too much to stay away."

Hearing his voice made me feel weak, but I didn't want to see him—not that night. I wouldn't be able to hide how upset I was, and I knew I'd end up telling him about the letter.

But I couldn't hold out for very long. Before Troy even finished leaving the message, I picked up the phone and told him to come over.

It was a glorious reunion, as if we'd been apart for three months, not three hours. And the minute I saw him walk in the door, I was able to laugh at the letter, just let it go completely.

As we were getting into bed that night, Troy said, "I have a present for you."

He reached into the pocket of his jacket and pulled out a little box. Inside it was his father's ring.

Lori

It's closing in on me. Not a word, all weekend without a word.

Saturday night I go by his apartment. The car is gone. I drive to Miss Box's; it's there in front of the building. Watch from the bushes. They come out together, holding hands, no space between them. Her voice is tinkling, a little scalpel, drawing blood from me.

They drive away, I go back home. Got to stay calm, there's nothing I can do yet. Got to stay calm, got to ride this one out. This will pass, she will not take Troy from me.

Sunday afternoon, no call. Sunday night, no call.

Monday morning I can't stand it anymore, I have to know. Get to the office. Miss Box isn't there. The red light's blinking on the answering machine.

"Hey, Lori, it's me. Something's come up, and I'm afraid I won't be going into work for a few days . . ."

Rip the machine out of the wall; the lying little bitch, what sort of imbecile does she take me for?

Go to the office. I feel calmer there. Stay cool, don't do anything yet. Better just stay put, do the work. Don't give her a chance to get rid of me.

"Hello, Mrs. Brown, this is Lori Max from the agency. A client had a question, and I needed to talk to Pandora—I was wondering if she's in Palm Springs with you?"

Just sitting. Can't move. Carmel, he's taken her to Carmel. How could he have done that? It was our trip, our best time together. That Memorial Day, the Hansel and Gretel Motel, going down to the beach to watch the sunset, we've never been so happy.

He couldn't have taken her there; her fucking senile mother must have gotten it wrong.

Go over to her apartment. The car's gone.

My body is burning under me.

I can't move, I can't get up. She'll be paid back. I'll destroy him. I will not lose Troy to her, she cannot get away with this.

My head hurts, like mines exploding. I'll go to Carmel. I'll track them down.

But I can't think, I'm so tired, I can't think.

Go to the office. I feel calmer there. Stay cool, don't do anything yet. Better just stay put, do the work. Don't give her a chance to get rid of me.

Take everything out of my office and put it in Miss Box's. Sit at her desk, stretch my legs out. This is how it was meant to be, how it should always be. The big room, the big desk, the big window for me.

Do the work, do it better than she does. The clients call. "Is Pandora there?"

"No, she's away for a few days—but I'll be happy to handle any questions."

It clicks. I'm wonderful. Everyone can see I'm wonderful.

She calls all the time, I let the machine answer.

"Lori, it's me. Are you there? Pick up if you're there." I don't pick up. Stupid not to answer—it could get me fired. But I can't take it anymore. *I'm not your slave, Miss Box. I'm not your fucking slave, and I'm not picking up your fucking phone.*

Run into John Bradshaw coming down the stairs. He looks gray, all shriveled up. Feel good. It was my letter that did that to him.

"Ah, Miss Max—is Miss Brown here?"

"No, she's not. She's gone to Carmel with a friend."

He shrivels even more. He can guess who the friend is. "Do you know when she'll be back?"

"She says Thursday afternoon."

"Is the agency being taken care of in her absence?"

Yes, you bastard, better than she ever took care of it.
"Oh, yes, everything's fine."

"If you should run into any problems, please feel free to contact me."

Pathetic old man, I don't need your help, you're the one who needs my help. Thinking about writing another letter, giving him a few more details; but for the moment, this is good. He's going to do something, I can see it in his face. He's hooked, he's wrecked by my letter, by what she's done to him. There's still a chance, I still have a chance.

Home. The silence, drowning in all that silence, I can't stand it.

Troy's cache in the bottom cabinet, he didn't know I even knew about it. White pills, green pills, yellow pills. Take a few of each, play fair. Keep the ceiling from crashing down, keep the silence from smothering me.

Get out, get in the car, the air won't fit in my lungs.

Go to Shirley's. Standing by the bar. Music swirling around, I want it to suck me away. I've never been alone here before, Troy never let me come. Always so jealous of the girls, what they could do for me.

Now they're smiling, they've seen me, they're buzzing around.

"Can I buy you a drink?"

Sure. Take the drink; play along with it.

A girl comes up. Dark red hair, knockout, expensive dress. Low voice, a drag queen maybe; no, those aren't a man's hands. Good at touching, knows where to touch.

"I haven't seen you before. Where are you from?"

"Nearby. I've just never come here alone before."

"Why now?"

"To take my mind off something."

"Or maybe someone?"

The hands get busy, a life of their own.

"I'm good at helping people take their mind off things."

Follow her into the bathroom. A little pillow of pills hidden in her bra. Smells like her perfume. Swallow them down.

She says, "I live near here."

She has a little red Mazda. I knew a boy in high school, he had a little red Mazda. We would fuck in the backseat. It wasn't pleasant. It wasn't comfortable. This girl is too tall; it would hurt on the steering wheel.

But she's only driving; she's touching me, but that's all right, that she can do.

"I can't wait for you, Lori. I just can't wait." She's panting. She's driving so fast, she's on the wrong side of the street. "Don't worry—I know what I'm doing. I could be a stunt driver."

Don't tell me about stunt drivers, I know about stunt drivers.

Pull up at her place, it's on Hayworth. The building smells like old grandmas. I'm cold, why the hell am I here? *Troy, come and get me; come pounding on the door like you did before and take me away.*

We go up the stairs. She takes me into her apartment. It's a page from *House Beautiful*. I'm trapped in all the little wreaths and candles.

"Do you like it, Lori? I hope you like it."

More pills, this time from a silver tray.

Go on a little trip, in the Candyland car. Driving down a rainbow road. Glass on the side of the road, better drive carefully. I could be a stunt driver. Go too fast, shoot off the rails. There's the glass coming, get cut to pieces. But, surprise, it's great, it doesn't hurt a bit. Blood spurting like ribbon candy; when I bend my knee, it sprays out designs. I'm a hydrant, people come, they dance around in my blood.

She's smiling, stroking my hair. "Did you have a nice trip?"

I start to cry. She's kind. My mother never stroked my hair like that.

She keeps stroking, then my shoulders, then down and down.

In her bedroom all the sheets match.

At first it's okay, but then it starts to drain away.

It isn't any good. I don't want this, I want Troy. She keeps on, she's moaning. She lied to me—she promised she would make me forget; I'm not forgetting anything.

But I'm too tired to fight it, just get it over with.

Stale gray morning air. She's lying next to me, smiling in her sleep. Her breasts are huge grandma breasts. Rumply bed, noises like whispers. Got to get out of here.

Get dressed. Don't make a sound. Breathing in the smells, her perfume, her ticky-tacky apartment, her little wreaths.

Stand over her before I go, look down. She tried, I'll give her that.

She turns over, I don't want to wake her, don't want to have to see her with her eyes open. Can't remember her name, anyhow. Take an ashtray on my way out.

"Lori, if you're there, pick up. I guess you're not there. Just to let you know, I'll be back tomorrow afternoon. Hope everything's okay."

Thursday afternoon I'm at Miss Box's. Parked around the block, waiting by the bushes. Two o'clock, she's not here, I go away, come back at three.

Four-fifteen the car comes in. They've got the top down. Troy's driving; he's laughing, he's taken his hands off the wheel, he's all over the street. The backseat's full of packages, it's Santa's fucking sleigh. I see his suitcase, the one I got him for our trip to Mexico. Can't believe he took that suitcase on a trip with her. Want to beat him over the head with it, beat him over the head till he drops down dead.

He pulls up, stops the car. They're laughing, she's batting at him, he kisses her.

Turn and go away.

I call him, I can't help it, I hate myself, I keep calling. Crying, tears in the phone. It rings and rings and he picks up finally—I know he knows it's me.

I don't ask where he's been. Just say I need to talk to him. Right away. Very calm now, no tears. He says he can't just now; that he's in the middle of something, that he'll call me tonight, maybe see me tomorrow.

I say okay, very reasonable, very bright.

I'm over there in ten minutes. If he could see me again, see my face, it would break Miss Box's spell, I know it would, she's not strong enough to hold him. I go up to his door. I bang on it, I keep banging, I can keep this up all night until he answers.

I hear him coming. He opens the door slowly, he knows who's there. "Why have you come over? I told you this was a bad time."

He is seeing me again, but his face doesn't change.

The place is a mess. He's unpacking. Clothes are everywhere. There's a new shirt, blue silk, lying on the bed. She bought it; I hate it.

The place seems different. It used to be home for me, now it isn't anymore. I sit down on his leather chair, not mine. I tell him we need to talk.

He spreads out his hands, like an actor, like someone in a *Godfather* movie. "What do you want from me?"

He smiles a little. "Lori, it's over."

I tell him it isn't over for me.

He gets up and walks around. He's so beautiful, it's the only thing I can think.

Running his hands through his hair. "I'm sorry, Lori, but I've been giving it a lot of thought—we need to end this."

He's been practicing. Driving with her in the car, he's been saying this in his mind.

I tell him, "You're a fucking bastard."

He sighs.

I'm looking at him, this stranger. Ten days ago, he was at my door, crying, he couldn't live without me. What has happened, what has she said, what has she done to him?

"Don't you understand—we're just not good for each other."

I'm taking him to the ER the night he got beat up, I'm giving him my salary so he can buy some clothes, I'm cleaning up his puke all the times he got shit-faced. But now I'm not good for him anymore.

"And she is? She's good for you?"

"Yes," he says.

"You're crazy." I spit it out. "I know you. You'll get bored with her. I give it two weeks. You'll come right back."

"I'm sorry, Lori," he says. "That's not going to happen."

I'm crying. I ask him what I've done, what terrible thing I've done to deserve this.

He turns away. He says, "You want too much from me."

The room starts to fill up with red. First the carpet, then the walls, then the table, the dishes, the pencils by the phone. Finally Troy is all red, too, like he's been dipped in blood.

I want to kill him.

"And she doesn't? Miss Box doesn't want too much?"

He shrugs. "Maybe she does. But the difference is, I want to give it to her."

I start to scream, I'm like something let out of a bottle, running through the apartment, pulling down pictures, turning over tables. Now I'm red, too; joined the club, blood all over my hands. I try to pull everything down around us in a heap on the floor, bury the terrible thing he just said, bury it in piles and piles of broken stuff, so no one will be able to find it again.

Troy isn't moving, he isn't coming after me; he's just standing there, watching. I pull more things down, smash more things, but the noise sounds stupid in his silence.

I stop. I stand still. I look at him. He looks kind. He pities me. "I'm sorry, Lori. But this just isn't what I want anymore. Do yourself a favor and believe me."

His voice, it's killing me; I do believe him.

He brings me over to the door and opens it. He puts his hands on my shoulders. He bends down. He kisses me good-bye on the cheek.

I'm on the inside, still with him, for one second more. Then I'm alone on the outside of his door.

When I was a kid, I thought death was a wall. I used to make it a very big wall. And there's a very big wall now. This is death.

Don't know how I got here, how it all went wrong.

Can't stay. I give up. Never thought that would happen. All this, it didn't count, it was just a past life, we're at the wall now.

Take only a few minutes to pack. It's funny, there's nothing I really want to bring. Drape the scarf over the TV one last time, lay the Prada dress on the bed, put Gene's Oscar on top. Let it all stay and molder, I don't want any of it.

Get in the car. Where am I going? Seattle, maybe, I'll stay with Suzanne. Or maybe not so far. It doesn't matter anyway.

Drive by my mother's street. I should tell her I'm leaving. Slow down, then speed up; I can't do it, I don't want to see her ever again. Watch the building in the rearview mirror—imagine the whole place crumbling into dust. And my mother in her housedress, standing in her living room.

Up Sunset, past all the places I knew, all the lives I lived.

Coming up on the office now. Thinking back to when I first saw it, that ad in *Variety*: "Assistant wanted for Theatrical Agency."

I got up early for the interview, tried on all my clothes, nothing looked right. Took some money from my mother's purse, went to Macy's, bought a little skirt and blouse. Putting on makeup, shaking, I wanted the job so much.

Driving up Sunset, looking for the building. The sign in the lot, PARKING FOR TENANTS ONLY. Promising myself one day I'll be a tenant here. Practicing the bright smile, all the things I would say to get the job. The list of names by the door, the Gene Brown Agency. Taking a breath and pressing the button.

It was going to be the beginning, the big start of everything.

Miss Box isn't here. Pull into her place, PARKING FOR TENANTS ONLY. Go into the office, tidy the desk, check the in-files, the fax from Sweets Productions.

Pack up my desk, all those years, it fits in one bag. Go to Miss Box's office, go through her drawers. Find her headshots, take one.

Write a note, tell her I've had enough, I'm going away.

Standing at the door, looking over this place, one last time.

There's a voice in the hall.

"Excuse me—could I speak to you a moment?"

It's John Bradshaw.

"I understand you've been seeing Miss Brown."

Another voice, it's Troy's.

"Yes, your information is correct." He's amused.

I'm holding my breath.

"I feel—I don't know how to put this—some things concerning you have recently come to my attention. . . . What would it take to . . . lessen your interest in her? I know you want to work in commercials. What if I were to do something?"

I can't breathe. I'm waiting for the answer. I'm hanging on a rope over a bottomless pit.

Troy laughs. "Thanks so much, Mr. Bradshaw. I appreciate your concern, but I'm afraid it's a little too late for anything like that."

"What do you mean?" Bradshaw's voice is rough.

"Well, the thing is," Troy says, "Pandora and I went to Las Vegas this weekend. And"—he's chuckling, he's enjoying himself—"we got a little carried away."

I'm cold, I'm ice, waiting.

"We're married."

I'm staring up at the wall. It's so high, it's way over my head now, I can't see anything above it, no sky, no clouds, just the cold gray stone.

Gary

I hadn't seen Pandora in a long time, not since I'd stormed out of her office back in February. I didn't even let myself think about her much, although occasionally, I admit, I'd catch myself wondering how she was doing. When I was at the supermarket, I'd sometimes sneak a peek at the *Enquirer*, wondering if there were any more pictures of her and John Bradshaw. There never were, though, and I didn't hear any other news.

And then one night at the beginning of June I had a dream, a very erotic one, featuring Pandora and myself by the big dune outside Idyllwild. All morning long, to my annoyance, the dream kept getting more and more vivid inside my head, taking over all decent thoughts. When my mother called that afternoon saying she had news about Pandora, I wasn't surprised.

"I wasn't sure if you'd heard," she told me. "I ran into Meg Brown at Sav-on this morning, and she told me that Pandora's gotten married."

For a second or two, I couldn't speak.

"Who did she marry?" I asked finally. "Do you know if it was an older man—an agent?"

"I don't think so," my mother said. "Apparently, he's a stuntman, very handsome. She brought him home last weekend. Meg said he couldn't have been more charming."

After I hung up the phone, I just sat there for a while, completely poleaxed. I'd always known it was inevitable, Pandora Brown getting married someday; I'd been waiting for the other shoe to drop for years. And now that it had, I couldn't believe it.

At least she hadn't married Bradshaw—I was glad to hear that. I'd always suspected that when it came right down to it, Pandora wouldn't fool herself that far. I didn't know anything about this stuntman, but I hoped that she had married him strictly for love.

I wondered if she was going to call and tell me the news herself, but the days went by and I didn't hear a thing.

Then, about a week later, the phone rang.

"Hi, Gary."

I imagined I could read all kinds of emotions into her voice.

"I hear you're to be congratulated," I told her.

"Yes. I didn't mean to be secretive, but everything happened so fast. We went to Las Vegas for the weekend, we passed by this justice of the peace, and the next thing you know, we're married."

That sounded like something Pandora would do.

"I still can't believe it," she laughed a little nervously. "It was pretty crazy. But I guess I'll get used to it. Anyway, I'd love for you to meet Troy," she chattered on. "He's nuts about cars; that's what he does, race cars in stunts. I don't know about motorcycles, though he'd probably like those, too. I think you'd have a lot of fun riding together."

There was a silence. I waited for her to say something else, something a little more personal. This was the first time we'd spoken since our fight, and I would have liked some sort of apology. But it never came.

"Well, good luck to you," I told her coldly.

"And to you," she answered. "How's Sara, by the way?"

I said Sara was fine, but that I had an appointment to get to.

"See you around, then."

I hung up the phone. So this was it—the inane, uninspired end of my relationship with Pandora Brown. I sat at my desk, feeling so flat I couldn't move.

Later that afternoon I got another call.

"Gary, it's me again."

"Yes?" I said coldly. "What can I do for you?"

There was a pause. "Well, we've been having some problems in the office. Lori quit; I have no idea why. I never even saw her again after Troy and I came back from Las Vegas. She just left a note saying she was leaving, and disappeared."

"What a bummer for you," I told her. I really didn't care what had happened to Lori Max.

"I can't imagine where she is," Pandora said unhappily. "I went to her apartment, but the landlady said she'd left there, too. I called her friend Suzanne, the one I sublet my place from, but she doesn't know anything, either."

"I'm sure she's fine," I said.

"I hope so." She sighed. "I just hope I hear from her soon. Anyway, the office is complete chaos without her. The work just keeps piling up; and then this afternoon all our computers went down."

"Sorry to hear it," I said.

"Nobody can figure out what's wrong. I've got to upload some documents, and I can't even get the scanner to work."

"I suggest you call the company," I told her. "There are plenty of people there who would be happy to help you."

Pandora sighed. "I know. But I'd feel a lot better if *you* came and took a look at it."

"Me? I don't think so. You're married now," I reminded her acidly. "Shouldn't your husband be the one helping out with this little crisis?"

She sounded embarrassed.

"Well, Troy's not very good with practical things."

I let that one go, but I was pretty pissed. I thought of all the times in my life I'd bailed Pandora out, and it seemed a little ridiculous that even now that she was married, even though we hadn't talked for months, I was still expected to be the hero.

"Sorry," I told her. "I'm too busy." And I hung up.

But all afternoon I kept thinking about that call, wondering what was really behind it. Pandora didn't need me to fix her computer; she could have hired anyone to do that. I knew there was something else going on. It finally occurred to me that this might just be her way of getting back in touch with me, of extending the olive branch. It wouldn't surprise me a bit if, now that she was safely married, she wanted to smooth things over with her oldest friend.

And sure enough, I was right. Around three o'clock the phone rang again.

"Look, Gary," Pandora said quickly. "I know we didn't exactly part on the most wonderful terms.

And I know you were right in a lot of things you said. But it's been five months now, and if it's all the same to you, I'd like to have my Best Boy Buddy back."

I gave a sigh. "All right, all right," I told her. "I'll come by this afternoon and take a look at your goddam computer."

Around five, I dropped by the agency. I didn't quite know what to expect. I was afraid it would be awkward, seeing Pandora in her new circumstances, but she came running out of the office and threw her arms around my neck.

"Thanks for coming," she said.

I hugged her back. I had to admit, it was good to see her again.

She was right about the agency—the place was a mess. Phones were ringing, faxes were scattered on the desks, stacks of undelivered headshots were piled by the door. There was a girl working in Lori's old place, someone from the Loyola Film School, but she seemed completely overwhelmed.

I didn't understand it. Things had never been this disorganized before, even when Lori had taken time off. But of course in those days, I reminded myself a little acidly, the agency had been Pandora's number-one priority. Now that she was married, things had obviously changed.

I found myself disliking her husband before I'd even met him.

Pandora led me back to her office and took me over to the computer.

"Now the damned thing's completely frozen—and I can't even turn it off."

I waved her away and told her to let me get on with it.

The problem turned out to be minor. Within a

few minutes, I had the computer up and running—
all it needed now was a new connector cable. I
started toward the front office to tell Pandora the
good news, but when I got to the door, I stopped.

There was a man standing there. I could see only
his profile, but I knew that I recognized him from
somewhere. Then, when he turned his head, I realized where it had been. He was the guy—the
movie-star handsome guy I used to see down on
Santa Monica Boulevard. The one who had been
walking with Lori outside the building back in
February.

But what he was doing there in Pandora's office,
I couldn't begin to imagine.

Pandora was standing by the desk. When I came
into the room, she walked over to the guy and put
both arms around his waist.

"Gary, I'd like you to meet my husband, Troy."

I was so shocked, so absolutely shocked that I
just stood there, staring at them both. I finally
managed to pull myself together. Whoever this
husband of Pandora's was, now wasn't the time to
go into it. I held out my hand and shook Troy's.
His glance brushed over my face—he didn't recognize me.

I gave Pandora the update on the computer.

"That's wonderful," she said. "I'll run over to
Fry's right now and get the cable."

But her husband said he didn't want her going.

"We already have plans for this afternoon,
Beauty—and they don't include baby-sitting a computer."

He said it all lightly, with a big smile. I didn't
much care for the smile, or the "Beauty."

Pandora put her hand on his arm. "Oh, Troy,

I've been waiting all day to get this fixed. If I don't get the cable now, I'll be backed up even more."

He squeezed her shoulders. "Catch up in the morning—you've got to learn not to worry so much. Don't you think this girl worries too much?" he asked me.

I ignored him. "It's all right, Pandora," I told her. "You two go ahead with your plans. I can pick up the cable. I need to run over to Fry's anyway. Just give me a key, and I'll come back and install it. I'll leave the instructions on your desk."

I could see she was embarrassed. "Oh, no, Gary; that's very kind, but you don't have to do that."

Troy pulled her to him. "You didn't ask," he said. "Gary offered. Of his own free will."

It was my turn to get the gleaming movie-star smile.

I'll be honest—I don't think I've ever disliked anyone more.

The next day I decided to drop by the agency again, just to make sure the computer was still up and running. When I came in, Pandora greeted me with another big hug.

"Gary! I was just about to call you. Thanks so much for what you did yesterday—and for going to Fry's. I can't tell you how much Troy and I appreciated it."

I could have done without the Troy part.

The office was, if anything, even more chaotic than it had been the day before.

"When are you going to get another assistant?" I asked her.

"I don't know. I've been interviewing like crazy,

but no one's been right. It's very demoralizing—I hadn't really realized how much I depended on Lori." She sighed. "I wish I had *you* back."

I flushed, not understanding what she meant.

"Working in the office. You were such an incredible help. I was thinking about it yesterday."

"Thanks. I'm flattered."

"In fact," she went on quickly, "is there any way you'd consider working out of here again for a little while?"

I laughed. "No way in the world. I'm a computer hack, not an agent."

"I know, I know," she said. "It's just that you know all the routines and you had such a feel for the work. Things went so smoothly when you were here."

"Sorry," I told her. "I can't."

"Not even for an hour or two a week?" she kept on. "Just until I get an assistant? It would mean so much to have someone I can trust—I'm getting so overwhelmed."

Her eyes were frantic. She had looked the way sometimes when she was a little girl and things got to be too much for her.

It was a ridiculous idea, but this was Pandora, and I couldn't quite turn her down. I surveyed the chaos in the room.

"I'll tell you what. If you really want me to, I guess I could come by occasionally and help out. Just until you get an assistant. But I certainly can't work out of here. And I'm charging you the earth."

"That'll be fine," she said, sounding, for Pandora, almost meek. "That'll be wonderful."

Driving home, I didn't dare let myself wonder why I'd agreed to do it.

I could see that Sara wasn't thrilled when I told

her the news, but she agreed that of course I had to help out an old friend. Sara still tended to be a little sensitive where Pandora was concerned, so I made a big point of telling her all about the new husband and how crazy Pandora seemed to be about him.

Sara smiled. "Well, I'm glad she's found happiness," she said.

But as the weeks went by, I started wondering if that was really the case. Pandora didn't seem happy to me, at least not the way I defined the word. She was nervous and restless, more so than I'd ever seen her, and very scattered. My old protective instincts began acting up, and I started dropping by the office regularly, giving her far more hours than I had planned. And the more I saw of her, the more uneasy I became.

I put it all down to Troy. Nearly every time I came over, there he was, underfoot. He had apparently hurt his shoulder doing some stunt and couldn't work for a while. So he spent all his time at the office, lounging on the sofa, talking on the phone, making a mess, and distracting Pandora. Or he'd talk her into going out with him, to coffee, to lunch, even to a movie, and they'd be gone half the afternoon.

Meanwhile, the agency was suffering. Once or twice, when Pandora was out, I took messages from clients, and I got the distinct impression they weren't any too happy with the way she'd been handling them lately. I told Pandora about the calls, but it didn't make any difference. She still went along with whatever Troy wanted to do.

She was absolutely wild about the guy. You could

see it in everything she did. The way she'd get so excited whenever she heard his voice on the phone. The way she'd rush up and kiss him when he came to the office. The way she'd run around, doing everything she could to make him comfortable. And I hated to see Pandora so completely under this joker's thumb.

I'd hoped that, as time went by and Pandora got a little more used to being married, Troy's influence would start to ease off. But it only seemed to get stronger. Even after his shoulder was better and he started working again, he still kept hanging around the office. And now he was starting to have opinions about the way the agency should be run.

"This whole fucking area's going to pot," I heard him complaining one day. "We should move to Beverly Hills."

I knew how much Pandora loved West Hollywood, and the agency being just where her Uncle Gene had founded it. I also knew what things were like from a business standpoint: the economy was down, and agencies were closing right and left. Not to mention that there was Aunt Marilynn, and the fact that Pandora couldn't make any major decision without her consent. But she didn't say a word about any of that.

"You're absolutely right," she agreed immediately. "One day we'll make the move."

In August Pandora finally found a permanent assistant, an older woman named Cynthia who used to work at the Reece Halsey Agency. I liked Cynthia a lot; she was competent and easygoing, and I was relieved that some of the pressure was finally off Pandora.

Once Cynthia started work, I knew it was my cue to leave, but by that time I'd gotten into the habit of dropping by the agency. I still found myself coming over a few hours every week to customize software and to teach Pandora and Cynthia how to use it.

Troy commented on that sometimes, asking, in a joking way, why I was still hanging around, but I paid no attention.

At the end of September Pandora decided to throw a big cocktail party. I guessed she meant it as a confidence-booster for her clients—or it could have been Troy's idea. He was always complaining that they'd never had any kind of wedding celebration, let alone a honeymoon.

There was a lot of fuss about where the party should be held. Troy wanted to have it in a top restaurant, but the business couldn't stretch to that. Then the plans changed to renting out somewhere less ambitious—a room at the Sportsman's Lodge or the Chateau Marmont. But those plans fell through, too.

At the last minute, something turned up. I was working in the office one day when Pandora called me in.

"We're all set for the party!" she said. "I was just on the phone with Brenda Cooker. She's booking out for two weeks—her husband's taking her to Maui. She's got a beautiful house up in the Hollywood Hills, and I asked her if we could have our party there!"

"You've certainly got your nerve," I commented.

Pandora made a face at me. "I'm going over there this afternoon. Want to come?"

I had a little free time, so after work Cynthia, Pandora, and I went over to Brenda's. The house had a nice layout, a good view, and plenty of space for the hundred-odd guests. We all agreed that it would be perfect for the party.

For the next six weeks Pandora, Cynthia, and I got everything organized for the big night. It wasn't really my responsibility to help, but to tell the truth, I ended up having a lot of fun. We ran around town ordering food, liquor, decorations, and a cake; we chose and sent out invitations, and we hired a combo, a caterer, and three waiters—some out-of-work actors Troy knew.

I offered my services as bartender. Sara and I were invited as guests, of course, but Sara had to go to a conference in San Francisco that weekend, and I figured I'd feel less awkward, alone at the party, if I had a job to do.

Ideally, as the date got closer we would have spent time at Brenda's house, starting to set up, but the plans had changed. Brenda's husband had scheduled a conference that week, and now the two of them weren't due to leave until the morning of the party.

I asked Pandora if we needed to hire someone to clean the house, but she said it wasn't necessary. "Brenda's housekeeper will be there. She'll get everything in order."

The day of the party, I was called out to Ventura to help a client with a crisis. When I finally got back to L.A., around five, I called Pandora to see how everything was going.

"Couldn't be better," she told me. "The caterer's sick with the flu and isn't coming. He's sending his assistant, but she doesn't speak a word of English. No one's picked up the flowers, we never ordered the extra wine, and I haven't had the chance to get to Brenda's yet."

I told her I'd be right over.

Half an hour later Pandora, Cynthia, and I were congregated in Brenda's driveway with our bags of flowers and liquor and decorations.

"Everything will be fine now," Pandora kept chanting, rummaging through Brenda's garage. "Here's the key, just where she said it would be. Here's the code for the alarm"—she started pressing buttons—"and here we are. Just, please God, let the housekeeper have come."

The words died as we stepped inside the front hallway. The place was a complete disaster. We didn't dare look at one another, just set to work. Cynthia ran the vacuum, I did the dishes, and Pandora cleaned the bathrooms and made the beds.

By the time the house was presentable, it was past six-thirty. Pandora began arranging the flowers, and Cynthia got the caterer's assistant started in the kitchen while I set up the bar.

At seven o'clock Pandora hurried in to me. "Cynthia and I need to go home and change now. I just talked to Troy. He'll be over with his friends in five minutes, and they'll help you finish everything up." She came over to me and kissed my cheek. "Thank you for doing this, Best Boy Buddy."

Twenty-five minutes later, when Troy and the waiters finally showed up, I met them at the front door.

"I've got to get over to the liquor store," I said. "You keep an eye on things here—help the caterer with whatever she needs, and get your friends organized."

Troy gave me an ironic little salute.

* * *

When I got back to the house half an hour later, the caterer's wife met me at the door, speaking in agitated Spanish. She pulled me by the arm into the kitchen, and I saw that, in my absence, the waiters hadn't even begun work. The serving dishes weren't out, the wineglasses were still in the boxes, and the food was untouched on the counter.

I heard noises coming from the maid's room and ran in to find Troy and the waiters playing poker.

"Move your asses!" I yelled. "The guests are coming in ten minutes!"

I didn't trust myself to look at Troy. I was scared I'd lay him out flat.

All night long I watched him. I watched the way he flirted with all the young actresses. I watched the way he poured on the charm for the producers. I watched the way he ignored the bit-part players. I could see Pandora looking at him also, but I wasn't able to read what was in her face.

From time to time he'd come up to me, acting like he'd never seen me before in his life, and say, "Bartender, a drink."

After a few hours he was pretty tight. When he asked me for a fourth "Long Island," I told him we were out of tequila.

"There's a bottle right in front of you," he sneered. "Are you blind?"

He kept on with it, teasing me, poking at my chest—the guests were beginning to stare at us both.

I didn't want Pandora embarrassed. I left the bar and found her sitting by the pool with some clients. I told her that her husband needed her and went back inside. I imagined she'd put Troy in a back room somewhere and let him sleep it off—but the next thing I knew, they were both gone.

I couldn't believe Pandora would leave her own party.

Cynthia and I waited it out, paying the musicians and the caterer's assistant and seeing off the final guests. When anyone asked me where Pandora was I told them she'd been taken ill, and needed to go home.

The next morning she called me, full of excuses. But halfway through the speech, I got sick of the whole thing and hung up on her. A few minutes later, the phone rang again.

"Gary, you've got to understand," she said. "I just didn't have a choice."

There was an embarrassed pause. "Forget about it," I said quickly. "Your party was a big success."

"Yes; thanks to you and Cynthia."

I accepted the implied apology.

I was very busy that fall. Work went into overdrive, with all my clients having simultaneous crises. I wasn't able to make it over to the agency very often, but when I did everything seemed to be about the same—Pandora and Cynthia working hard, and Troy brooding in his corner.

One afternoon I saw John Bradshaw getting out of the elevator. He caught sight of me, and hesitated.

"May I speak to you a moment?"

"Sure," I said.

"How is Miss Brown getting on?"

I told him she was doing fine.

He nodded. A few more moments went by. "I know what a friend you've been to her," he said finally.

"I try to be," I told him and asked if something was wrong.

He frowned. "I keep receiving letters. One came this morning. I'm not sure what to do—if any steps should be taken. I don't want to see her unhappy."

"No," I said, though I didn't understand what he was talking about.

"Perhaps it would be kinder just to let things lie," he said. Then, "Does she seem happy to you?"

"Not particularly."

He looked at me sharply. "Perhaps you could wait here a moment."

He walked up the stairs; a few minutes later, he came back down with four or five typed papers in his hands.

"I wonder if you could take a look at these."

I glanced through the pages. They were anonymous letters, rambling and vicious, filled with accusations about Troy.

"I spoke to Miss Brown when I received the first one," he told me. "But that was shortly before her marriage, and she refused to read it."

Of course. That was Pandora all over—burying her head in the sand when she saw something she didn't like the look of. I asked him if I could keep the letters for a day or two. "I'll do some checking, find out if there's any truth in them. Then you can decide what you want to do next."

Bradshaw seemed relieved to give me the letters.

I spent the rest of the afternoon on-line, then made a call to my friend Marc at the Palm Springs sheriff's office.

I didn't get much sleep that night.

As I had suspected, most of the accusations had been nonsense—Troy wasn't a Mafia hit man, nor was he wanted by the FBI as a spy. But some of the information, like the drugs and the jail time, did turn out to be true.

I wondered just how much of all this Pandora knew. It was possible Troy had told her about his past, and that she was so in love with him it didn't make a difference. Maybe it even added to his allure—Pandora had always been one for a little excitement.

But supposing she didn't know. Was it Bradshaw's place, or mine, to tell her? It wasn't as if she were in any danger. At his worst, Troy was a two-bit hustler, not a mass murderer. Did we really have the right to ruin her peace of mind? When Bradshaw had asked me if Pandora seemed happy, I had answered, "Not really," but how could I be sure of that? She loved Troy, that much was certain. And in his own way, I had to admit he probably loved her, too, maybe even enough to have cleaned up his act.

I also doubted that confronting Pandora would do any good. Bradshaw had already shown her one of the letters, and she had refused to look at it. After nearly six months of marriage she was even less likely to consider the charges against Troy.

The next morning I sent the letters back to Bradshaw with an equivocal little note telling him that while there were still a few shadowy areas, the major accusations had turned out to be lies. I added that he could, of course, pursue things further if he chose, but that, in my opinion, it would be best to let the matter drop.

I wasn't sure if I was acting out of cowardice or

kindness, and I didn't press my conscience to find out.

A few days later, however, I started wondering if I'd done the right thing.

My sister's birthday was coming up, and I mentioned it to Pandora.

"Wish her a happy birthday for me," she said. "I always liked Janine." Then she sighed. "I'm so sorry I never got to meet Troy's sister."

I said I wasn't aware that Troy had a sister.

And Pandora told me the whole story of Fanny—about how she had gotten pregnant when she was only sixteen, and had an abortion and died.

"Troy's never really gotten over it," she said. "He carries her picture in his wallet. I look at it sometimes, when he isn't around. She was such a lovely girl."

When Troy came to pick Pandora up that afternoon, I was in the hallway, waiting for him.

"Hello, bartender," he said.

"Listen," I told him. "I've done some checking up. This girl Fanny you told Pandora was your sister . . . well, she wasn't, was she?"

He was silent.

"She was a girl you got pregnant. And then you abandoned her; I know all about it. Her mother tried to sue you because Fanny committed suicide."

He was breathing hard now; I was breathing harder.

"Pandora doesn't know any of this," I told him. "But if you take even one step outside the line, I'm telling her everything."

He gave me a look and walked away.

Pandora

I used to wake early and watch Troy while he slept, his arms folded underneath his head and his dark hair falling on the white pillow. Each time, I felt a fresh little shock of love. During the day, his mouth was tense, but when he slept, it was soft, slightly open. It used to put my teeth on edge with sweetness.

I still find myself remembering those mornings, watching Troy sleep.

In July he hurt his shoulder doing a routine car chase. It wasn't a bad sprain—he was fine in a couple of weeks—but, looking back, I can see that that was when the shift started. Something began to loosen then, to lessen. When he was ready to work again, the work just wasn't there—the luck or the timing had come undone.

It was almost two months before he worked again. During that time he got into the habit of coming into the office and spending his days there. It was difficult getting much done with him around, but I loved it that he wanted to be with me. I would watch him sitting there on Uncle Gene's old sofa, the muscles of his thighs thrusting through his jeans, and it would be hard to look away.

I tried to interest him in the agency work, but the day-to-day routine bored him. He was like a restless child, getting impatient, wanting to leave early for dinner or a movie. And I always went along with it. Troy came first, ahead of the agency.

In August he finally landed a stunt in a John Travolta movie. He prepped for days, talked of nothing else. As I was leaving the office the night before he was to start work, I got a call—the shoot had been postponed.

Troy met me at the door when I got home.

"Early night tonight—the shoot's tomorrow."

I had to tell him that it wasn't. He didn't say anything, but he didn't come to bed for hours. I could hear him in the other room, walking back and forth. I lay awake listening, as I used to listen on Daddy's bad nights.

The lease was up on my apartment, and I wanted us to rent a new one—somewhere that would be Troy's and my first real home together. Troy agreed to go househunting with me, but he said he didn't want to look at any apartments.

"Let's go straight to the top."

So we drove to Malibu and went around three mansions that were for sale.

Troy loved everything about them, the two-story living rooms and the Jacuzzis and the private beaches. I remembered his reaction when we'd gone to Hearst Castle, and how I thought he was kidding when he said he'd like to live there. But he made a similar comment that afternoon.

"I'm not going to be happy until I can live in a place like this."

"But what about what we have now?" I asked. "Doesn't that count?"

He laughed and kissed me, but didn't answer.

October twenty-fifth was my twenty-sixth birthday. It was my first birthday with Troy, and I wanted it to be very special.

"I'll do my best," he grinned.

That morning he woke me up with a breakfast tray filled with croissants and orange juice and coffee. By the side of the tray was a big box, beautifully gift-wrapped. Inside was a nightgown from Neiman Marcus, silk, hand-embroidered, the most exquisite thing I'd ever seen.

Dinner that night was at Ago, complete with champagne and a specially ordered birthday cake.

"How did I do?" Troy asked when we came home. I kissed him for an answer.

"Now get into the nightgown," he told me. "I want to see it on you."

I almost didn't want to wear it, the nightgown was so delicate, but I put it on, and Troy and I made love. I could feel the sleeve rip.

That Friday we went down to Palm Springs for a visit. Daddy was worse than I had seen him in a long time, nauseated and breathless, and Troy kept finding any excuse to leave the house. I had often seen that reaction in people when I worked at the ER, but it was still painful to watch my husband unable to bear being in the same room with my father.

Daddy had a doctor's appointment the following afternoon, and I decided to stay down in Palm Springs an extra day. Troy and I just had the one car, so that afternoon I put him on a plane back to L.A. It was a strange thing—I'd lived right by the Palm Springs airport for most of my life, but this was the first time I'd ever gone in there, actually walked past that chain-link fence.

I watched his plane take off with feelings of guilt and relief.

After dinner, Mama and I set up the projector and ran some old home movies. It made me choke up, seeing a time when Daddy could stand without stooping, a time when he swam and played volleyball, when he was taller than I was.

As I was putting the films away, he also started crying. "Oh, Andy-Pandy," he said, tears like glass on his face. "I wish I could see you settled."

I stared at him. I said, "I am settled, Daddy. I'm married now. Don't you remember Troy?"

He looked at me, a vague expression on his face, and said nothing.

The following weekend Steph came for a visit. I hadn't seen her since I'd gotten married, and I was thrilled that she and Troy were meeting at last. I crammed the kitchen with her favorite junk foods, bought a new set of sheets for the sofa bed, and regaled Troy with all the old stories.

But the weekend never quite took off. Troy was usually so charming, but for some reason he was aloof, almost sullen, with Steph. And I behaved like some manic ringmaster, trying too hard to make things work. I thought how, when I was little, I'd had Gary, my Best Boy Buddy and Steph, my

Glorious Girlfriend, and I tried to invent a similar phrase for Troy. But nothing inspiring came to mind.

"So what do you think?" I asked Steph that first night, as I got her settled on the sofa bed.

"He is without a doubt the handsomest man I've ever met."

"Yes—but beyond that?"

"It's a little hard to get past the looks," was all she said.

And Troy was equally noncommital about Steph.

"She's nice enough," he told me. "But it's hard to believe that a girl like you couldn't do better than a girl like her."

Steph left on Sunday night. As we hugged each other good-bye, there were promises of future visits, to both L.A. and Barstow. I sensed, though, that the visits were never going to happen.

I watched Steph's taxi pull away, tears on my cheeks.

Monday morning, when I got to work, there was a breezy little message waiting on my answering machine.

"Hi, Pandora, this is Ginette MacDougal. I just wanted to tell you, I've decided to join the William Morris Agency. I hope you understand. Thanks for all you've done. Bye."

I had to play the message back four times before I could get myself to believe it. When Gary came in later that morning I rushed at him with the news.

"Can you believe the ingratitude? I only discovered her, that's all! If it weren't for me, she'd still be over at Mel's, taking orders for hamburgers!"

"I don't think she's so ungrateful," Gary said

slowly. "I think she's only looking after herself. And, frankly, I don't blame her. Ever since you got married you've let the agency go to hell."

I told myself that Gary was just in a bad mood, that he'd probably had a fight with his girlfriend, but all day long I couldn't stop thinking about what he'd said.

That night, while Troy and I were lying in bed, watching TV, I kissed his back and lightly touched its little constellation of scars.

"These last five months have been the greatest honeymoon on record," I told him. "And I've loved every instant. But I'm starting to think it's time I started focusing on my work again."

His back became rigid under my hand.

"What's brought this on?"

I told him about Ginette.

Troy frowned. "Don't bother about her," he said. "She's just an ungrateful little bitch."

"But it seems like some sort of wake-up call. I don't want to lose any more clients, and Gary said I was letting the whole agency slide."

Troy jerked away from me at that, and suddenly, we were in the middle of the first real fight we'd ever had.

The anger in his face—I was completely stunned by it.

"You're like a steamroller!" he kept shouting. "It's all about you, only you. You say you care about me, but that's a load of crap. All that matters to you is your precious agency and this power trip you're on!"

I was so stunned I couldn't move. Not care

about him? Not care about *Troy*? All I could think about was that first day I'd watched him do a stunt, and how it changed my whole life.

I started crying and couldn't stop. He came over and grabbed me in his arms. He was shaking, and so was I.

"I'm sorry," he whispered. "I'm so sorry. I didn't mean it. It's just that I get crazy sometimes—I guess I've had too much time to think."

We made up, but that night I didn't sleep. I kept remembering the anger in Troy's face, and I promised myself that nothing like this would ever happen again. I would get him work, as much work as I could, and as soon as possible.

The following morning I called every contact I had and sent Troy's headshot and résumé to every place I could think of. Two days later I got a call back from Sweets Productions, and I left a gleeful message on Troy's cell phone.

"Congratulations," I told him. "You've got a Honda spot. You shoot on Monday."

When I came home from work that evening there were a dozen yellow roses waiting for me.

"You're the best thing that ever happened in my life," Troy whispered, taking me into his arms, "and I never really forget that, not for a moment."

"Good," I whispered back.

He grinned down at me. "And I know just how we're going to celebrate. I'm taking you to The Ivy tonight."

I hesitated. "Are you sure? We've been spending so much money lately—maybe we should go somewhere more casual."

Troy let go of me. "Whatever you want," he said abruptly. "I just thought this commercial was a big deal."

"Of course it is," I told him quickly, and we ended up going to The Ivy.

I remembered the other time I'd been there, with John Bradshaw, and how I'd thought it was the most beautiful restaurant in the world. It seemed sad that now here I was, going with my husband, and all I could think about were the prices.

Troy was gone most of that weekend, working out at the gym, prepping for the commercial. He came home complaining that he had lost all his flexibility, but I could see how excited he was.

Monday morning he left early to go to Woodland Hills for the shoot. I wasn't expecting him home until seven or eight, but when I came back from work, he was sitting on the sofa.

"You're home awfully early," I said. "How did the shoot go?"

"The shoot didn't go," he said carefully. I saw that he was very drunk. "When I got to the set, the stunt coordinator told me I was supposed to jump from a second-story window into a moving car. I told him there'd been a mistake, that I was a stunt *driver*. He said there was nothing they could do— either I did the jump or they called in someone else. They called in someone else."

My mouth was dry. "But I don't understand. I told the producer—he knew—you don't do falls. I don't understand."

Troy just gave me a look. He stood up and pushed past me into the hall. I could hear his footsteps going down the stairs.

* * *

He didn't come home that evening, and I spent two hours driving around West Hollywood looking for him. At midnight I gave up.

At three o'clock he came back to the apartment. He undressed and got into bed. We lay next to each other without speaking for a long time. Finally, I put out a hand and he took it.

"You scared me," I said. "Please don't do that again."

His body was over mine in a moment; he said he was sorry into the silence.

At the beginning of December we got a wonderful break. Troy was hired as a stuntman on a Jake Guylenhaal movie. It meant weeks, perhaps months of work.

I'd never seen him so happy. He was almost euphoric, talking about all the things we could do, all the things we could buy, now that he had this job.

I found I was a little more cautious. My concern was what would happen when the movie was finished. I couldn't stand the thought of Troy going through another depression. It seemed to me that now was the time to start making some long-term plans. Troy had only another six, seven years of stunt work left, and this kind of break didn't come along very often.

One night we went to dinner at the Little Door, and I had my speech all prepared.

"When you're finished with this movie, maybe we should start thinking in terms of recycling your skills. You'd be a marvelous personal trainer, or we could buy part-ownership of a gym—"

Troy reached over and kissed me hard, shutting me up.

"You're just amazing," he said when he finally pulled away. "You can always manage to see the dark side of anything."

That Friday he took me to Las Vegas for the weekend. I was thrilled to be going—the only other time I'd been there was when we'd gotten married, and that had been the most romantic weekend of my life. I hoped we could re-create some of it: dancing at the Bellagio Hotel, seeing a show at Caesar's Palace, maybe even renewing our wedding vows.

But Troy spent the entire weekend gambling. He went down to the craps table on Saturday morning and stayed there for the rest of the day. At first I came down to the lobby and watched him play, but then it got to be too much. I killed time shopping, sitting by the pool, walking around the other hotels. Every time I went back to check on Troy he was still at the table.

When he finally came up to the room at four in the morning, I pretended I was asleep.

Sunday morning he was in a horrible mood— he wouldn't talk at all. When I asked him how much money he had lost, he went storming out of the room.

I think that weekend was the start of it—when all the fighting began. It was the only thing we seemed to do all winter. I hoped that once the movie started things would get better, but they didn't. They just got worse and worse.

All the fights blended, one into the other. Fights

about my parents. Fights about his career. Fights about my nagging. Fights about his drinking. Fights about his coming into the office so much. Fights about his not coming anymore.

I would see him watching me sometimes, with the strangest look on his face. It was as though he saw something in me that didn't used to be there— or was missing something else that had gone.

He started taking walks late at night. I asked if he wanted me to come along, but he said no, he'd only be gone a few minutes. I'd find myself anxious all the time he was away, as if I were afraid he was never coming back. He was always calmer when he came home. But we started making love less and less.

One day, I left work and went to visit him on the set. Nobody knew where he was. I finally tracked him down in one of the trailers, talking with a strange-looking man.

"Who was that?" I asked him afterward.

"Just one of the gaffers."

"He didn't look like a gaffer to me," I said.

That started another fight.

Troy wouldn't go down to Palm Springs for Christmas, so we spent the holiday in L.A. I bought a tree, and Mama sent me a box filled with all my favorite ornaments, even the feather doves.

Christmas Eve I baked cookies and read Troy "The Gift of the Magi." Christmas morning we exchanged gifts—there was another lovely piece of lingerie.

But it was all over so quickly.

* * *

I didn't see much of Troy when the new year started. He was on the set most days, and afterward he went off with the crew to unwind. I knew it was good for him—he needed that companionship—but I missed being with him. When I saw him now, things felt as awkward, as raw, as they had on our first date.

I invented a little game: I'd project myself into the future, to a time when Troy and I had been married for fifteen or twenty years. I imagined us then, a comfortable old couple, affectionate and at ease with each other, with all these misunderstandings, all these distances, far in the past.

When Troy and I did have time together, I planned out fun adventures for the two of us: trips to the boardwalk, shopping sprees, movie dates. Troy went along with all my plans, but I wondered if he was really having a good time.

One Sunday we went to the park on Coldwater. It was full of children, swinging, skateboarding, playing in the stream. I watched one little blond girl who was learning how to walk.

"I'd love to have one just like her."

Troy didn't say anything.

"Not right away, of course. But I'm starting to think about it; aren't you?"

He changed the subject, and I brought it back.

"What's the matter? What did I say? We're married. It's a logical progression."

Troy stood up and slammed a fist into his palm. "Don't you ever think about anything except what you want?"

*   *   *

The next morning Steph called. We hadn't talked in a long time. She asked how things were going, and I started to cry. I ended up letting it all out—the fights with Troy, his staying away all night, his drinking. I felt horribly guilty, talking about it, but it was such a relief.

"Marriage," Steph said thoughtfully. "You may have noticed it's something I've stayed away from. How long have you and Troy been together?"

"Nine months."

"Well, that isn't very long, is it?"

The calm in her voice was reassuring.

"No. It's still part of the infamous first year—*Cosmo* is full of articles about us." But I had the feeling that what was going on with Troy and me wasn't covered by any article in *Cosmopolitan*.

Steph must have thought so, too; she didn't say anything for a moment.

"Have you ever thought about talking to some-one—going to a counselor?"

I had, but it was an idea I hated. It meant failure. "I'll consider it," I told Steph, then changed the subject. "Now, tell me what's going on with you."

Steph had the grace to fill me in on a few problems she was having at work, and she let me get a little self-respect back by solving them for her.

To my surprise, the counselor idea stayed with me. I began to wonder if seeing someone might not be a good idea after all. It needn't be a long-term commitment; maybe a few sessions would be enough. Just something to put Troy and me on a better path.

When he came in from shooting that night, I told him the idea.

Troy stared at me, then shook his head. "I can't

believe you," he said. "I can't believe you'd let some stranger interfere in our business."

And he was out the door again.

Sitting, waiting for him to return home that night, I came to some realizations. No counselor was going to be able to perform a miracle—it was naive to suppose that there was going to be any easy fix for Troy and me. We had barreled into marriage; perhaps it had been foolish, but we had done it. And we could make a success of it; I just had to let go. All my life I'd expected too much of everyone and everything, and now I was expecting too much of Troy. He'd been landed with a new wife, new responsibilities, and here I was, starting in about wanting a baby. No wonder he was overwhelmed.

I closed my eyes and went though my fantasy again, pretending that Troy and I were an old couple, loving and close; this time, however, there were no children.

I told myself I was starting to learn.

I've reached the point now where I begin not wanting to remember any more. Most of the time it stays blocked, but sometimes, especially in dreams, the whole scene comes to me again—the pale face, the smile, the tossed sheets.

Today's a bad day; I'm seeing it all the time. It won't leave me alone.

The ringing of the phone. That was the beginning. The phone call from Mama waking me up.

"Daddy's not doing well. Is there any way you can come to Palm Springs?"

"I'll be there tonight," I told her.

I asked Troy if he would come with me. "I know it

upsets you to be with Daddy, but we could stay at a hotel for the weekend—maybe the Marriott. It would be like a second honeymoon."

He smiled but shook his head. "You go," he said and kissed me.

Daddy was too weak to leave the bed. I spent all weekend sitting beside him, holding his hand while we watched game shows together.

There was a new woman, Kate, working in the house, a trained nurse. I could see how much Mama hated having her there. With Millie, it had been a friend coming to visit; with Kate, it was a constant reminder of how near the end Daddy was.

I kept calling Troy, but he was never in.

On Sunday evening I took a drive around Palm Springs. As I passed by all the familiar places, I found myself wondering what things might have been like if I hadn't left. What if I'd stayed here in the desert, taken the job in real estate—would my life be any better now?

The answer was no. I wouldn't have Troy. The images started coming to me. The way it had been with us at the beginning. Those long hours in bed, his hands, warm and determined. Watching him as he slept, his smile, the curve of his calves, his little jokes. The way he looked at me. The way he'd cried when he showed me Fanny's picture.

That was Troy. That was what I loved and wanted. And suddenly I was so lonely for him that I couldn't bear it.

I turned the car around, went back to the house, and told Mama and Daddy that I needed to get back home.

I got to L.A. just before midnight. When I pulled

up to the apartment building, it was very dark. It took me a while to find my key. I've gone over that, so many times—if I had been more patient, if I had had to knock, if Troy had had to let me in, it might all have been different. But I found the key and came in quietly. I wanted to surprise him.

I went into the bedroom. He was lying in bed. His eyes were closed, his mouth was relaxed, the way I loved to see it. My eyes wouldn't leave him. For a long time they refused even to interpret the shape lying beside him, the pale blond blur. But at last she moved and I had to look.

"Troy," she said.

His eyes opened; his mouth drew closed.

I don't remember much about those next weeks. I went back to Palm Springs. I think I slept most of the time. The pale face, the tossed sheets, never left my head, asleep or awake. They were all I had left in my life.

Mama, Daddy, Steph, they said it was better to know the truth, but they were wrong. I had been very happy not knowing.

At first Troy tried to call. I didn't let myself pick up the phone. He left messages; he said it hadn't meant anything, that he loved me, that I was the only one he'd ever loved. Finally one night I picked up the phone. I said, "I want you gone, off the edge of the universe."

I tried to get up the momentum to leave Palm Springs. Cynthia said not to hurry back, that everything was under control at the office. She told me that Gary was coming in nearly every day to help out. I wanted to thank him, but I didn't have the energy to call.

* * *

I went into Daddy's room one day when the screaming in my head was very bad.

"Do you think this will ever get better?"

"I don't know, Pandora," he said.

His eyes were filled with despair. I could see I was killing him, me and all my selfish misery.

I called Cynthia and told her I was coming back to L.A. that night. "Just please go to the apartment. The landlady will give you a key. Make sure he's not there."

Cynthia called back and said he was gone.

I went back to L.A., back to the apartment. I couldn't get over how sweet and normal it looked. It seemed impossible that anything bad could have happened there. I went into the bedroom and looked at the bed—it was perfectly made up now, the scalloped edges of the pillows fluffed. No traces were left at all.

I closed the door and went back to the living room. I slept on the couch.

The next morning I went into the office. Cynthia was wonderful, calm. We talked about business. Gary wasn't there—that was a relief, in a way, though I'd wanted to thank him for all that he'd done.

I worked straight through the day. I cut checks, sent out headshots, took meetings, made calls. I was grateful for how automatic all the work had become. I finished around six o'clock. As I was leaving the office there was a knock on my door. It was John Bradshaw.

"I heard you were coming back today," he said. "I've been waiting to find a moment to speak to you."

He was very kind. He didn't mention anything

about Troy—he just said he hoped I would stay on in town and keep up the agency.

"And if you want my help in any way, I'm right upstairs."

"Thank you," I said. "I'll remember that."

He lit right up. I thought, how awful, how strange—that after all that had happened, I could still make him light up.

I came back to the apartment. I went into the bedroom, into Troy's closet, and sat on the floor. Even without his clothes there, it still had his scent.

I closed my eyes and breathed it in.

Gary

Cynthia called and told me the news. I can't say I was surprised. Troy had never struck me as the kind of man who would be faithful for long.

"Where's Pandora?" I asked.

"Down in Palm Springs."

That made sense. What Pandora needed at the moment was to be around people who loved her, who thought she could do no wrong.

I considered calling her but decided not to. She knew I'd never liked Troy. Anything I said now would sound hypocritical.

But I did what I could for her. I went over to the agency as often as I could and helped Cynthia out. I made calls and delivered headshots. I even went through the breakdowns and started sending out photos. I have to say, I think I began developing a flair for the job—a few of my people actually got called back for auditions.

Cynthia spoke with Pandora on the phone several times a day, but I never heard from her, other than the message she left on my office machine, thanking me for all I'd done.

But when she came back to town, I stopped

going over. I thought that, under the circumstances, that was the wisest thing to do.

Sara and I had been having some issues lately, and my working at the agency seemed to be a sore spot with her. I knew that Sara had always been a little sensitive about Pandora, but in this case I honestly couldn't see what the problem was.

"Pandora's not even in town. I haven't seen her in weeks."

"Which makes it worse. You doing all this unpaid work without her even being there. It just shows the power she still has over you."

I laughed and told her I would have done the same for any good friend.

"Really?" she asked. "Putting your own work on hold for week after week? You'd do the same for any good friend?"

So I ended up promising Sara that when Pandora returned from Palm Springs, I would stop dropping by the office.

I kept the promise, but it didn't really solve anything. The truth was, though I hadn't wanted to admit it, Sara and I had been drifting into trouble for quite some time.

I knew the reason, and it was my fault. We had been going together over a year now, and at this point Sara was waiting for some sort of commitment from me. A commitment she had every right to expect.

But I just hadn't been able to give it. Not that I didn't think about it, or even plan it. I'd never had a better relationship with a woman, and I knew we had every chance of being happy together. But every time I was on the verge of buying the ring, or proposing over a romantic dinner, something stopped me. I knew that Sara was getting impatient. I knew that if I didn't make a move soon, I might lose her; but something in me—cowardice? self-sabotage?—kept saying to give things a little more time.

One afternoon in May, when I was picking Sara up from work, I was surprised to see John Bradshaw in the lobby of her travel agency. I hung back, thinking the sight of me might embarrass him, but he came over straightaway.

We chatted a little; I thought he looked well. And he seemed at ease—certainly much more so than the last time we'd talked.

"Are you here to plan a trip?" I asked.

"Yes. I'm taking my daughter to Maui for her birthday."

"What a great present."

"I think she'll enjoy it."

There was a pause. "Have you seen anything of Pandora?" I asked.

"Oh, yes," he said. "I drop by the agency nearly every day." I could tell from his face, the moment I mentioned her name—the guy still loved her.

"How's she doing?"

"Very well. Surprisingly well, actually. Even with this economy the agency's had a good quarter. She comes to me for advice from time to time," he added. "That's very gratifying."

I said, trying not to let an edge get into my voice, that I was sure it was.

Then he brought up the subject of the anonymous letters, saying how right they'd turned out to be. I asked if there had been any news of Troy.

"I don't believe so. Or at least Miss Brown's never mentioned having heard from him."

Then he smiled at me, rather stiffly.

"Pandora has told me about all the assistance you gave her while she was . . . recuperating . . . in Palm Springs. It must have been at considerable inconvenience."

I said something about that being what old friends were for.

Bradshaw nodded. "I've been considering installing some new computer equipment in my office," he went on. "I'd like to have your business card."

I guessed this was meant to be a gesture of thanks because I had helped Pandora out. The fact that he was making it bothered me, though. It seemed unnecessarily proprietary.

The travel agent came up then with brochures on Maui, and we said good-bye.

When I got home I found a message from my mother on the answering machine. Frank Brown, Pandora's father, had passed away in his sleep the night before.

I sat there at my desk, all the old memories buzzing around me. Drinking lemonade together on the porch. The red leather recliner with the fraying arms. His fleece-lined slippers. His robe. And all those games of Parcheesi. I was just about to call Pandora when the phone rang.

"Hi, Gary," she said.

"I already heard," I told her quickly. "You don't have to say it."

But she kept repeating the words, "Daddy died. Daddy died," as if that would make her finally believe in it.

We didn't stay on the phone long. She said that

there was going to be a memorial service for him on Saturday and that it would mean a lot to her if Mom and I would come. I promised that we'd be there.

I called Sara that night and told her that I was going down to Palm Springs for Frank Brown's memorial. She asked if I wanted her to come with me, and I realized I didn't. Those memories had nothing to do with her—they belonged with Pandora, her mother, and me. Having Sara there, trying to keep her from feeling left out, knowing she'd be weighing every little word I said to Pandora, was more than I felt like handling.

"Thanks," I said, "I appreciate it. But I think I should go alone."

I drove down to Palm Springs Friday night, and at ten o'clock on Saturday morning Mom and I made our way down Vella Road to Weifels and Son Memorial. I was pleased to see that the parking lot was filled.

Pandora and her mother were standing out in front of the chapel. Mrs. Brown was wearing a dress of bright, fiery red—I found it a courageous gesture. And Pandora looked almost like her old self; there was no Hollywood hairstyle, no makeup. She kissed me on the cheek and said how much she appreciated my being there.

"Didn't Sara come?" she asked, looking around. I found that ironic.

It was a good service—if these things can ever be called good. The minister spoke about Frank Brown, saying what a sweet-natured man he was, how optimistic and uncomplaining. And then four or five people—neighbors, friends from Barstow—

got up and reminisced. Mr. Brown was always so quiet, never putting himself forward; it was gratifying to hear how well thought of he was. Certainly it must have been a comfort to Pandora and her mother.

I sat in the pew behind them. Pandora was shaking all over. Finally I couldn't stand it anymore. I reached forward and put my hands on her shoulders, and kept them there until the shaking stopped.

After the memorial we went back to the Browns' house. It was filled with more people than I imagined it had ever held before. Pandora was hectic, running around, welcoming the guests, passing around drinks and food.

After an hour or so I noticed her eyes didn't seem to be focusing anymore.

"Are you all right?" I asked.

"Not really." She reached for my hand. "Come with me," she said, "I have something to give you."

We started down the corridor toward her father's little den.

She paused for a moment by the door.

"I keep thinking I'll find him sitting in his chair."

She took something from a little leather box on the bookcase and handed it to me. It was Frank Brown's favorite tie clip, the one that looked like a ship's steering wheel.

"I'll keep it for the rest of my life," I told her.

Pandora put her arms around me, and we both began to cry.

I cried for a lot of reasons—for Frank Brown, for Pandora, for me; for bad choices made, for days that were gone, and for what could never be ransomed back.

I held her closer. "Pandora," I whispered.

My hands gripped her waist; my lips started to tilt down toward hers.

And then the indecency hit me: her father had been dead three days, and here I was trying to kiss her. I pulled away and patted her shoulder. I didn't look down into her face. I also didn't dare think about Sara.

I went back to the party and told Mom I was ready to leave. I drove home in a rage at everything and everyone—at Frank Brown for dying, at Pandora for almost letting me kiss her, at myself for not having done it.

When I got back to L.A. that afternoon I found a message on my answering machine: "Gary, it's Sara. I'd appreciate it if you'd come by as soon as you get into town."

I guessed from the tone of her voice what she was going to say, and I was correct. She told me that she'd been thinking things over, and that she wanted to end our relationship. "Although I love you very much."

"I love you, too," I told her quickly.

She smiled and shook her head. "No, you don't," she said. "Not really. It's always been Pandora."

As I drove back to my apartment, my mind was filled with plans for getting Sara back. I would send her a hundred roses; I would go back to her apartment; I would propose then and there on my knees. But I knew I wouldn't do any of it.

I wondered what was stopping me.

It didn't take me long to figure out that Sara was right in everything she had said.

The moment I realized the truth, it became my only truth. For months, I'd done my best to push down the very thought of Pandora; and now it was all there was. Pandora. Pandora Brown. How could I ever have thought that I was free of her?

Her image never left me now. I found myself remembering things I hadn't thought about in years—a game of miniature golf we'd played back in high school, a straw purse she'd carried when she was twelve. I could summon up the most trivial things she'd said, and the way she'd looked as she said them. I would dream about making love to her, and wake to the memory of her scent all over my body.

But I did nothing, made no move to see her. What would have been the point? She was still married; still, I suspected, in love with Troy. And even if she were free, the two of us had already had our chance—several chances. We had never been able to get it right before; it was naive to hope that some sudden miracle would turn us into the winning combination now.

So I kept away. As it happened, work brought me into Pandora's neighborhood quite a lot that summer—I was even in her building several times, doing some jobs for John Bradshaw. But whenever I went down the hall, the door of the Gene Brown Agency was closed, and I never knocked.

One afternoon late in August I ran into Sara outside Il Sole. She looked wonderful, with her hair cut in a pixie style. Beside her was a man, tall, graying, well-dressed. She introduced him as Jim.

That night, she called me. "It was good seeing you today—I'd been meaning to get back in touch."

"So what's with this Jim?" I asked protectively.

Sara laughed at my tone. "I met him at a wine-tasting party. He's in entertainment law."

"Is it anything serious?"

"I certainly hope so."

I wished her the best.

"And how's Pandora?" she asked me.

"I haven't seen her," I said.

She gave a little laugh. "Don't worry—you will."

I didn't sleep that night. Sara's laugh kept cycling through my head, and I lay awake, wanting Pandora with a violent, feverish ache.

In the morning, I made up my mind. I had to see Pandora, had to tell her how I felt. It no longer mattered if I made a fool of myself—I couldn't hold out any longer.

Later that day I received an engraved invitation in the mail. It was from John Bradshaw, inviting me to a black-tie party at the Beverly Ramin Hotel, to celebrate the twenty-fifth anniversary of his agency.

I called his office and accepted. I was sure Pandora would be there.

It was raining slightly the night of the party—a drizzle that settled over everything, including my rented tux, like damp dust. I arrived at the Beverly Ramin half an hour early and walked around the lobby feeling very out of place. Everything was much too elegant for my taste: the uniformed doormen, the string quartet, the huge crystal chandeliers.

Finally it was time to go up to the ballroom. I didn't feel like riding in an elevator with ten other guys in tuxedos, so I walked up the stairs.

I wondered if Pandora was already there, if I

would have to wait long for her, or if, in spite of my hopes, she wasn't coming at all.

She was there at the door, wearing a blue-green dress that shimmered as she moved. She looked like a mermaid, the way she had at that long-ago homecoming dance—and she was more beautiful than I had ever seen her in my life.

"Gary!" she cried. She ran over and hugged me. "I'm so glad to see you. You were the first person on my guest list."

That took a moment to register. "You and Bradshaw are giving this party together?"

"Oh, no," she said lightly. "John just wanted my input on a few things."

But I thought of how he had thanked me at the travel agent's for helping her out, and the way he looked whenever I so much as mentioned her name—and I felt uneasy.

I started watching the two of them closely. I was relieved to see that Pandora behaved just like a regular guest—she didn't pose with Bradshaw for any photographs, and she didn't stay by his side. But for him, I could tell it was a completely different story. No matter what he was doing, no matter who he was with, his eyes kept coming back to Pandora.

His expression, as he watched her, was intense, gratified—but at the same time he seemed almost startled, as if she were some rare blue-green dragonfly he couldn't quite believe had settled on his shoulder.

I also saw the way he kept track of everyone she talked to. The moment their conversation was over and Pandora had moved away, he went over and talked to the guest himself—as if being with that person would somehow bring him nearer to her.

It was pathetic to see, but I couldn't keep myself from watching. I wished I hadn't come.

I told myself that as long as I was there I might as well try to make some contacts, but I wasn't in the mood. I hadn't come for business, I had come for Pandora, and I didn't have the courage to approach her. I went to get a glass of champagne, telling myself that once I'd finished it I'd leave.

A woman in her fifties was standing in front of the bar. She wore a bright gold dress and a face full of makeup.

She tapped me on the arm. "Are you one of Johnnie's?"

I said I did computer work for Mr. Bradshaw and asked her if she was an actress. The question insulted her. She started reeling off the name of movie after movie she'd been in. I kept having to say that I was sorry, but that I hadn't seen any of them.

She turned her back on me finally and asked for another drink.

I was putting down my glass of champagne, ready to leave, when a sudden shift came over the room. There was no sound, no movement, but it was as definite as if some signal had been given.

I looked up—and there was Troy, standing in the doorway.

He looked just as he had all those months ago, those nights on Santa Monica Boulevard, with a black leather jacket and gold chains around his neck. He wasn't moving, but all eyes were on him. Even the waiters were motionless now. Every-thing had stopped. We were all looking at the doorway, staring at Troy.

He was smiling, easily, almost insolently. He glanced around the room until he found the person he was looking for.

"Pandora," he said.

She was standing over by a side table. Her face was patchy, yellow-white.

"Troy," she whispered.

Then someone pushed past her. It was John Bradshaw—I was shocked by how fast he had moved.

He put a hand on either side of the doorway.

"You're not wanted here," he said.

Troy laughed. It was a lazy laugh, arrogant, the kind that goes right under your skin. Bradshaw said something else in a low voice, and I heard Troy answer, "That's right, old man."

Bradshaw turned and strode back to the ballroom. He picked something up from one of the tables—I couldn't see what—and went back to Troy. No one moved; no one tried to stop him. I saw that he had picked up a knife.

"Please be good enough to leave."

When Troy saw the knife, he laughed again. He reached out his long arms, and began to pluck at the jacket of Bradshaw's tuxedo.

"What are you going to do, old man?"

Bradshaw began to swing the knife. Troy dodged the wavering arcs easily.

"Is that it?" he jeered. "Is that it for me?"

Bradshaw kept on slashing the air. Finally, with a disdainful grab, Troy twisted the knife from his hand. It skittered the length of the marble hallway, an embarrassing toy.

"Pandora, let's go," Troy said.

With a cry, John Bradshaw lunged at him.

I hadn't been able to move, but now I started forward. By the time I reached the door, the two of them were by the stairs, swaying beside the wrought-iron railing. Bradshaw's hands were on Troy's shoulders; he took a step back and threw his whole weight forward. For a second Troy was thrown off balance. A look of sheer surprise came over his face—and then he fell down the stairs.

He didn't cry out; he didn't make a sound. He seemed to fall almost in slow motion, rolling, spinning, until he reached the bottom of the staircase. There he lay still, his head against the marble cornice.

I don't know when his neck broke.

Everything was silent. The guests were knotted by the door of the ballroom. Bradshaw was alone at the top of the stairs.

I went over and stood beside him. Below, on the ground floor, all the elegance had evaporated. People were shouting, rushing over the marble floor, pointing upward. A crowd was gathering around Troy.

Pandora came up behind me. She stared over the railing. Her mouth was moving, but her voice was so low that at first I couldn't hear what she was saying.

"The thing was . . . the thing was . . . he didn't know how to fall."

I touched Bradshaw's arm. I led him back inside the ballroom, to a chair beside the buffet table. I sat down beside him—no one came near us. Pandora was watching us from the door, but for once John Bradshaw seemed unaware that she was even there.

We sat in silence until the police came.

A Lieutenant Stevens wrote down my name and number, saying he would be needing a statement from me at a future date.

I stayed with Bradshaw until they took him away.

Pandora

I couldn't sleep again last night. The weather has been so strange: breathless and gray. Two reporters were there, waiting for me when I came out of the office. They followed me to the car, running behind me, saying Troy's name, John's. I have nothing to tell them, but they keep on coming.

I saw Emmett this afternoon. I run into him on the street sometimes. He always looks away from me, walks off in the other direction. I never try to talk to him. I don't know what to say.

I try to concentrate on work. I spent all of yesterday cleaning the office. I've found a lot of Uncle Gene's things—old pilot scripts, headshots, demo tapes. I'm not sure what to do with them. This morning, Cynthia asked me if I was planning on giving up the agency. I said I didn't know.

They've started renovating John's old offices. It's very noisy. It's driving Cynthia crazy, but I don't mind all the drilling and hammering; it keeps me from thinking.

I imagine it so often, taking the turnoff and going down to the prison, but I don't do it. I despise myself for being such a coward. Cynthia has gone to visit. She says John's doing fine. It was so wrong, his not getting bail. But she says his lawyer is wonderful; he's sure to get him off.

I don't look at newspapers. I try to stay away from newsstands and from supermarkets.

Today I took some of Uncle Gene's things and brought them over to Aunt Marilynn's.

The house was the same. I went into the den. I sat down in Uncle Gene's leather chair and closed my eyes. I imagined what he would say to me if he were sitting in that room. I think he would tell me that I've ruined everything.

I explained to Aunt Marilynn I had been cleaning the office and had found some things she might want. She didn't look at them, didn't even open the box. She said, "If you hadn't taken over the agency, none of this would have happened." She asked me if I was going to give it up. I said I didn't know. But every time I say that, it sounds more like a yes.

Steph is here, visiting. I've had a good time with her. We've done fun things, girly things. She hasn't asked what my plans are; she hasn't mentioned the agency, or Troy or John. She ignores the reporters, pretends they're not even there.

She went home today. She left her hair clip behind. Seeing it makes me miss her, but I'm glad to be alone again. It's too tiring, being with someone else.

* * *

I went down to Palm Springs this weekend. Mama's doing well; she spends a lot of time working on the garden. We don't ever talk about what happened. Today we planted some honey mesquite and white sage. It smells wonderful. I sit in the garden and close my eyes and breathe it in.

She asked if I've heard from Gary; I said I hadn't. She told me, "Now that all this is over, maybe you two can get married." It broke my heart to hear her. She was like a child, wanting a happy ending.

I had the dream about Troy again. We were in the empty room, sitting on the packing boxes. The cold wind was blowing through the white curtains. I wanted to speak to him, but I couldn't remember any words. I could only smile, but his head was turned and he didn't see me.

The work upstairs is finished; John's office is a photography studio now. I went to see it today. It was strange to be there again.

A young woman showed me around. The office is beautiful, done in bleached woods. There are blown-up pictures on all the walls: weddings, couples kissing. They've reconfigured everything. It was hard to tell that this was once John Bradshaw's agency.

The girl asked me if I had been there before, if I had ever seen it in the old days. I said that I had.

I drove by the cemetery. I think about stopping, but I don't do it. Instead I conjure Troy up in my mind—the way he looked the first day I met him, the feel of his hand, the softness of his mouth when he slept. It's like a burst of fireworks. They fade out finally, though I try to hold them as long as I can.

I went to the prison today. I didn't let myself think about it, I just got off at Cesar Chavez and drove to Vignes. I parked in the structure and walked across to the jail. The doors in front could have been any doors, the doors to an office building, the doors to a mall. I walked up to the counter. A guard asked me who I had come to see.

"I'm here to see John Bradshaw."

"And what is your relationship?"

I thought of Amanda, and the time we had coffee at Le Clafoutis.

"I'm his daughter."

I was given a pass, and I walked down the hall. A second guard was standing by a closed door. He pushed a button; the door slid open, slowly, silently, and I walked through into a holding chamber. Another door opened, and a third guard checked my pass.

I went down the hallway and came to a large room. There was a thick glass window with a stool in front of it.

I was prepared to wait a long time—Cynthia said she had waited forty minutes—but I was only there fifteen.

He came in at last. I'd been afraid he would be handcuffed, but he wasn't. He was wearing a bright orange jumpsuit, but he still looked dignified, even in the prison clothes. He made them look like pajamas, elegant pajamas.

"Thank you for coming by," he said. He didn't tell me I should have come by a long time before.

I said I heard he had a wonderful attorney. He

said yes, everything was going well. They had entered a plea of involuntary manslaughter; with any luck, he would be there only a month or two longer.

"I hope so."

I didn't want to ask what he would do when he got out. I didn't want to tell him I had seen the photography studio where his office had once been.

He said, "I'm so sorry, Pandora."

I thought of Troy. That's something I try to keep from doing. Seeing Troy lying on his back, twisted up on that marble floor. His head against the banister.

He told me how pretty I was looking. He said it as lightly as if he were taking me to a party, as if he had just opened the door and there I was in an evening gown. "So very pretty."

I could have stayed longer, but I left after ten minutes. When I stood up to go, he asked if I would come again.

The guard appeared and led him away.

I am scared to take a step, I am scared to do anything. I am disaster to everyone I come near.

I think about quitting, that's what I think about mostly, giving the agency back to Marilynn, giving up the keys, closing the door. The relief of going back to Palm Springs. But then I remember Uncle Gene. I've let everyone else down; I need at least to keep faith with Uncle Gene.

Someone knocked at the door. I didn't want to open it. There are so many people I don't want to see. But the knocking kept on.

It was Lori.

I couldn't believe she was there. I reached to hug her; she was stiff in my arms.

"Where have you been?" I cried. "I've tried and tried to find you. Why didn't you tell me where you were?"

Her eyes were opaque as green olives.

"You've run it all into the ground," she said. "I always knew you would."

It was what the voice in my head said to me every day. I pulled away from her. She smelled rank, as if she were living on the street.

"What's happened to you?"

"I think about you all the time," she said. "Everything you did. All the people whose lives you ruined." She smiled at me. "I came to tell you something you didn't know. Gene used to fuck me—right there on that rug, right on that desk over there."

I said she was lying, but I knew she wasn't.

"You're so much like him," she told me. "You're so pathetic."

She turned and left.

I stared at the door. I tried to summon Uncle Gene, my bright, shining Uncle Gene, but he no longer came. All I got was this poor old man fucking his assistant there on the shag rug.

I thought I'd lost as many as I could lose: Uncle Gene, Troy, Daddy, John Bradshaw. And now I'd lost Uncle Gene all over again.

I drive around, wanting the images I see, the sounds I hear, to fill me up. I watch people walking, all of them with lives. I'm a pendulum that has stopped. Stay—go home—stay—go home. The words make up the four corners of my universe, and I am motionless, helpless, suspended in the middle. I'm waiting for a wind, a sign, anything— to show me the direction I should go.

When I come home the phone rings.

"Have you heard the news?" my mother asks.

"No."

"I saw Gary's mother at the card shop this morning. One of his clients is going national. They want him to move to New York City and head the office."

I can't stop crying. I want to call him up and tell him not to go. But I won't—I won't be that selfish.

I can't ask him to stay. I know what it would mean if he did, and I won't do that to either of us. It would never work out; it never has before. I'm just fooling myself if I think it would now. It's just that the last few months have been so horrible—I want to crawl away from everything. And Gary has always been a safe place to crawl—the safest place I know. That's all it is; that's the only reason I'm crying.

But I keep thinking of those moments. Those memories. All those years. His kindness, his loyalty. His letters, I've saved them all. The way he looks at me, the way he's always loved me even when I've been horrible to him, even when I haven't deserved it at all, even when it was the last thing in the world he wanted to do. My Best Boy Buddy.

I called his number. It rang and rang. I got scared he was gone, that he'd left for New York already, without saying good-bye to me. But finally he picked up the phone.

"May I come over?" I asked him.

* * *

He had already started packing. The place looked abandoned already. On his dresser was a photo of him and his dad.

He stood there without moving. He was wearing a T-shirt; the neck of it was dark with sweat.

I said, "I hear you've moving to New York."

He nodded.

"You could have told me."

He shrugged. "I didn't think you'd care one way or the other."

"I know it's none of my business, but are you sure you want to go to New York?"

There were only a few feet between us, but he took a step toward me. I could see the muscles moving on his arm. I didn't look up at his face.

"And what do you think I should do instead?"

"Go back to Palm Springs."

I made myself look up then. He was smiling down at me. It was a slow smile, slight but intense. Troy had sometimes looked like that.

"So you're telling me to stay?"

"Yes, I guess I am."

"Well, Pandora," he said, "there's only one way I'm going to do that."

His voice was shaking. I knew what his next words would be. There was no help for it.

He put his hands on my shoulders. The warmth of them came through my blouse.

My mind took off—it started to fly away. It flew all around. Suddenly I could see everything, everything that had happened these last two years, unfolding like a little storybook: Troy, Lori, Daddy, John Bradshaw, Gary, and me. I could see us all, doing our little dances, trying so hard to make our little lives work. We looked so small and fragile, so precious and so completely unimportant.

I thought of Pandora's box, that box that had haunted me all my life. She had let out all the troubles of the world, she had ruined everything, and now she thought the box was empty. But, so the story goes, it wasn't—not quite. At the bottom lay one more winged spirit. Hope.

I found myself staring up at Gary's face. It struck me that the ratio was perfect, absolutely perfect—from his nose to his chin, from his forehead to his eyes. Odd I'd never noticed it before.